THE WOMAN *WITH* THE STONE KNIFE

DALE NEAL

THE
WOMAN
WITH
THE STONE
KNIFE

HISTRIA
FICTION

Histria Fiction

Las Vegas ◊ Chicago ◊ Palm Beach

Published in the United States of America by
Histria Books
7181 N. Hualapai Way, Ste. 130-86
Las Vegas, NV 89166 USA
HistriaBooks.com

Histria Fiction is an imprint of Histria Books. Titles published under the imprints of Histria Books are distributed worldwide.

Library of Congress Control Number: 2024931070

ISBN 978-1-59211-466-5 (softbound)
ISBN 978-1-59211-475-7 (eBook)

For Cynthia,
Merlin, and Opie

Chapter 1

London, 1786

Richard, do you lie awake in the smoky warmth of the winter house in our old town, listening to the wind rattling the dry canebrake, to the river running forever in the Overhills? Do you ever call for me, for your mother? I know I am likely a ghost to you. My voice you barely know, yet I hope you see me in dreams, the flicker of my face in the home fire.

Over these twenty winters we've been separated by an ocean and wars, I can scarcely retrace the paths that brought me here to London, all the ambushes of fate that stranded me so far from you and my homeland. I followed my husband, your father, but I lost him in this cold, wet city. I left you behind, but I can only hope I've not lost you forever. I left my life in the mountains, but I have always carried you in my mind, just as I once bore you on my shoulders, your hands tugging at my hair. I was once a new mother in my best buckskin, dancing my baby boy around the high flames, stomping the arbor grounds. You held and shook the rattle, the pebbles inside the tortoise shell, laughing beneath the shining stars and the bright moon.

You lost your mother at such an early age, so did I.

I've often dreamed of my mother's face, at least her warm presence, a hovering shade against the hot sun. Closing my eyes now in London, I can hear the ancient rustle of wind through green leaves of corn, squash, and beans in the fields of our town, Tomotley. My mother is close by. She has cradled me against the roots of a walnut tree while she and the other women tended the rising corn. Sun blinking through the leaves overhead. The women are talking softly in the breeze. The gargle of my own tongue as I tried to master the soft language of the People around me. I slap the ground and laugh.

A scream. She comes running, raising her hoe overhead. A strike on the ground beside me. Blood sprays warm against my skin.

She scoops me in her arms, turns her heel against the writhing snake that had slid so close to my foot. My mother saved my young life and cursed herself, slaying the rattlesnake that had crawled out of the sun and into the shade, close to my basket.

Clan protects clan, blood calls for blood, one life for another, my grandmother, Cat Walker, later told me. My mother had not said the right formula for forgiveness after slaying a snake. The snakes were allied with the deer and the ginseng. The death of that sidewinder, a cold-blooded mother who had just hatched a hundred young, made the harvest of the deer harder that fall, while the ginseng that made good medicine hid its leaves in the hollows of the hills.

Come summer, we traveled to the high passes. We walked among the blackberry bushes, heard rattlers sing on the warm rocks whenever we tread too close to their dens. A rattle in the air froze us on the trail, but no one ever saw the singing snake. My mother cried out, collapsed, had to be carried down the mountain.

My grandmother, Cat Walker, gathered the proper herbs and roots, according to the ancient formulas, but the snake clan took their revenge. The plants that were their allies would not cooperate in healing. A powerful poison coursed through my mother's blood. My mother grew pale and feverish, until she turned her head to the wattled wall of the winter house.

"We pulled you from her breast lest you suckle the poison as well. She died from abandoning you as much as the bite." My grandmother shook her head.

My mother had marked herself and our family for the vengeance of vipers. Blood responsibility has always been the law of our people. When anyone in the clan is murdered, other members are obliged to strike the offender.

Guilt spreads as well as blood. Cat Walker would never say it plain to my face, but I grew up knowing I was responsible for my mother's death. Leaving you behind, I still blame myself.

***

So many names I have been called by various men who loved me for my heart and hated me for my skin, but I would tell you my first and real name is Skitty.

Most names that the mothers give their babes come from the animals, the Pigeon that was roosting in the thatch roof when my uncle Woyi came out, or the

Frog that splashed in the creek where the mother washed her babe. Other girls had names that came from the world, Running Deer or Little Bird or Buffalo Girl.

Skitty. A word that really meant nothing like the animal names that the little girls of Tomotley were known by. It was more like a sound an animal would make, a scampering, a skittishness, like a squirrel chasing her mate, spiraling around the trunk of the hickory.

Where my mother had come up with my name, no one could say. And my mother wasn't there to tell me.

These days, I sign myself by my baptized name. Helena Ostenaco Timberlake, honoring my given Christian name, and those of my Cherokee father, Ostenaco and your father, Lt. Henry Timberlake.

As a girl, I had not often seen my father. Ostenaco stayed busy with wars against the Mohawk and later the English, earning his most powerful name — The Mankiller. But when the mighty warrior was home, he was agidoda, my father. He let me tug at the silver rings dangling from his earlobes, rub his head's stiff scalplock that had so narrowly escaped sharp Shawano knives and now the swords of the white men or yoneg, coming into our world.

One summer evening after we had eaten by the fire, my father took my hand and led me down to the river. We sat, and I leaned against his strong knees and watched the wire-legged creatures dancing over the current. Without a thought or meaning to, I picked up a pebble, long rounded by the rushing water, and tossed it at a poor water spider.

"Careful, you'll put out the fire."

"What fire?"

"You don't know the story?" Ostenaco laughed. "See the water spider, that dot of red? How, girl, do you think it got there?"

In the beginning, before the Real People, there was no fire. The world had to wait until the Thunder that lived on the highest cloud fell one day with a mighty crash. The lightning left a dead sycamore burning on an island amid the ama eqwohi, the Great Water. All the animals stood at the water's edge and watched the glow on the horizon.

In those old days, all the beasts, birds, fish, insects, and plants could talk freely. Who would go and fetch the fire?

With a flap of his strong wings, Raven cried he would go. He flew high over the waters and alighted in the sycamore, but the fire burning in the hollow seared his feathers black, and the smoke made his once sweet voice into a hoarse croak.

From the darkening woods came the call of the screech owl.

"Guess who went next?"

"The owl?"

My father nodded. "Bright girl. But not the little owl. This was the Great Horned Owl that flies at night. He flew over, but ashes blew into his face and gave him the white rings you see on his face. The birds said it was a bad business, but the snake clan said they would try. One of them wiggled into the water and held his head high above the waves, whipping his tail to swim to the island. When he got to the tree, he found a hole and crawled inside, but the ashes were so hot, he nearly caught fire, and wiggled free, the racer scorched as you see him to this day."

Dejected, the birds and snakes and four-legged beasts shivered on the shore because the world was cold. All had excuses for why they couldn't go, though no one would say the real reason was they were afraid. But a small voice piped up outside the circle. The animals turned and saw the little Water Spider. "Not the one who looks like a mosquito, but the one with black downy hair and red stripes on her belly," my father added.

She reared up on four of her hind legs and darted across the water, she is so light. The animals waited until the night was coming, and the dusk like now, my father said, and slowly they could see a spark come across the water, darting this way and that, just as a water spider does. And when she danced onto the shore, they saw that the spider had spun her silk into a bowl on her back where she carried the ember, burning a red spot.

"Mark, girl, that spot, that tale," Ostenaco told me. "Remember to tell it to your child someday."

***

The coal stacked in my grate crumbles. I rise from my armchair to poke more red life into these black lumps. The English dig these soft rocks from the northern earth and cart them to Londontown, fuel for the black fog that smudges the sun and settles on the fouled river.

Fire was sacred, and the waters were blest back home. Time was in Tomotley I was a little girl sitting cross-legged before a warm fire, drying my hair after walking out of the river. Each dawn, I used to dunk my head dutifully seven times in the cold currents, praying the right words to walk in balance in this shifting world.

I miss wood fires and cold, clean water. I miss my father, the feel of his hand held only in my memory. I told my father I would go to London to bring back fire, life to the Real People like the water spider in the story Ostenaco told. How long did it take her to swim back over the sea?

Was she gone twenty years?

I followed my heart, and my husband to this alien island. Now I find myself a widow in cotton petticoats and woolen mourning gown, the lace cap tied tight beneath my chin, minding a stingy fire in the grate of a Cheapside flat in London. My stripped quill hesitates in my hand, the foolscap blank in my lap where I once dandled thee.

Richard, if we are to meet again in this life, you will likely want answers, not a long-winded story. You would want to know about your father, how I followed him, how I lost him. You wonder why your mother remained so long in this cold wet island, this place that is not my home.

How best to begin?

Your father wrote his version of our story:

"My circumstances, however, are not so much in the decline, that when I satisfy my creditors, I must retire to the Cherokee, or some hospitable country, where unobserved I and my wife may breathe upon the little that yet remains."

The Memoirs of Lieut. Henry Timberlake,

(who accompanied the Three Cherokee Indians to England in the Year 1762)

CONTAINING

Whatever he observed remarkable or worthy of public Notice, during his Travels to and from that Nation: wherein the Country, Government, Genius, and Customs of the Inhabitants are accurately described.

Dear Richard, you never met your father, and that pains me, my son.

You had the look of his eyes even as a baby, and your name, Richard, he picked for you when I told him I was with child. Richard means brave ruler among the English, and I believe you will live up to that name someday.

Your father was Lieut. Henry Timberlake.

Henry was a brave man who wrote his memoirs before his death. It took me years, learning to decipher his words scratched by goose quill and ink of oak gall, what Henry had scratched and scrawled in Wood Street Compter, London's worst debtor prison. I can see your father trying to part the bars set in the high window with his pen, the vane furiously flying over the foolscap, the yellowed pages by his guttering candle and his spastic coughs. Trying to settle his debts and buy his freedom again with his words. Henry had rubbed his brainpans, trying to recall and record all that he had seen and smelled and tasted and survived during his time in our towns. He was among the first yoneg, or white man, to see us, the Tsalagi or Real People, and where we raised our crops and children, hunted for deer, played the ball game.

In turn, Timberlake escorted our delegation, led by my father, Ostenaco the Great Mankiller, my uncle, Woyi, and the Chota chief, Cunne Shote, from our shores to England in the year 1762. The so-called Savage Chieftains drew the curious and the gawkers, wherever they passed in their plumes and war paint, jingling with silver gorgets and bracelets. Rumors of their presence among the pallid hordes of Englishmen sparked riots in Vauxhall and Covent Garden. In his book, Timberlake tallied his troubles, what was owed, how he spent his whole fortune.

Not once, but twice, Timberlake would sail to England, taking the plight of the Real People before the throne, pleading for peace, and an end to war, what little good it did. He proved less celebrity on a second voyage, the one on which I accompanied him. Only a little of that did he cover in his book, this cherished, dog-eared copy I keep in my lap, to serve as the writing desk for the paper I am filling with my own pen. I will consult and copy some passages for you.

Someday I swear I will bring you his book and tell you my story as well.

The English are now so nigh and encroached daily so far upon them, that they not only feel the bad effects of it in their hunting grounds which were spoiled, but they had all the reason in the world to apprehend being swallowed up, by so potent neighbors, or driven from the country, inhabited by their fathers, in which they were born, and brought up in fine their native soil from which all men have a particular tenderness and affection. The Indians cannot from the woods of America see the true state of Europe: random reports are all they have to judge by, and that often comes from persons too interested to give a just account.

Timberlake

Henry was the first man I would fall in love with, but he was not the first white man I had ever met.

The one called M'Cormick had made his way to the mountains from down in Charleston. In his buckskins and moccasins and his fur cap, he could have passed for Tsalagi except for his horribly hairy mouth. Later, when he had learned more of our tongue, M'Cormick explained his origins. "I've heard my grandpap hailed from a place called Ulster, he was a Scotsman through and through." He waved a long way across the woods in the direction of the rising sun and the long waters of the ocean. "Me, I washed up on the wharves of Charles Towne and struck west for my fortune."

M'Cormick aimed to his living among us. He built his trading post from tall poplars. Tall trees that had taken our people seasons to fell with stone axes girdling their trunks he could fell with a morning's work with the bite of his broadax.

As children, we would file through the woods to the clearing he was making, to watch what this strange smelling man might do. He roared strange oaths when he cut his hand, but he never thought to dunk himself in the water as a healing agent. He seemed afraid of water. M'Cormick announced his presence by his funk, a peculiar blend of sweat, what he last ate, blood and stool, and various greases and oils from deer hide and bearskin. You would wrinkle your nose, and he was there before you could say Siyo or hello. He often scratched at the bush that hid his mouth. You could swear small animals were burrowed next to his jowls, stashing the crumbs from his last meal.

For all his hairiness and poor hygiene, he kept marvels inside his storehouse. He pulled out his wares into the sunlight. Satin and grosgrain ribbons to weave through a warrior's scalp lock or a braid in a vain girl's mane. Bright hammered gorgets and coins, bits of glitter and metal, mirrors, magical polished surfaces that showed your smile, your own face, better than your reflection in the water.

Trading these goods for the deerskins that hunters brought him, he piled up a herd of hides inside, up to the rafters, and each fall, led his mountain ponies across the Twenty-Four Mountain Trail, down to Charles Towne for trade. He would return by next full moon with new treasures, blankets, beads, silver ornaments and spoons, cloth and guns, tributes from the English to keep us from siding with the French.

In their ongoing war, the English begged us to send our fiercest warriors. They promised to protect our fields, our women, and children while our men were away on the war path. They sent a garrison of red-coated soldiers who felled trees by the river and pitched a palisade, Fort Loudon, commanded by Capt. Demere.

Demere was the first man I had ever seen who watched the world with eyes colored blue. Yes, my husband, Henry Timberlake, would boast blue eyes, but his were warm as a summer sky. Demere had ice in his eyes that made you shiver. And his thin lip would curl as he studied us, high from the platform behind his stockade of sharpened trees.

The English were not very neighborly. They would not play stickball with us nor share their food. When our crops were not good and the women went to the gates of the fort with their baskets, thinking it was time to trade, Demere drove them off. A haughty man, he held his nose in the air, like a dog or a wolf sniffing for its next supper. "Let them eat the grasses of the field. The meat is for my men only."

Our Bony Moon when food grows scarce comes at winter's end, in the month the English call February. I grew as skinny as my name, Skitty. Other girls I had played with grew sick and frail. The deer were fewer that our hunters could find, kill, and bring home. I could see our men talking darkly among themselves.

Cat Walker was furious. "You call yourself warriors? You must stand your ground. Defend. Attack," she badgered the balky men. "Mothers who cannot feed themselves enough to bring milk deserve blood for every baby that has starved this season."

***

Your deeds dictate what you will be called.

True to her name, Cat Walker was never one to back down from a foe.

My grandmother had been not much older than myself when she won the name that would follow her through this life. Walking through the woods from the spring, balancing a fired earthen pot, now filled to the brim with sweet spring water atop her empty head, so cocky, so sure of herself, she would close her eyes and walk all the way home without spilling a drop.

Then a low growl halted her in her silly tracks. She slowly pivoted under the weight of the water sloshing inside the vase.

A great cat leapt down from a granite boulder onto the trail, twitching its tail, baring its teeth. Fear slithered down her spine, while a trickle of water sloshed out of the vase and rolled down her forehead into her left eye. She blinked hard, but she didn't cry or make a sound other than the sharp intake of her own breath.

Here was the choice that little girl had to make: not to scream or run, but to slowly take one step backwards, still facing her foe. The panther advanced on its huge, padded paws, enjoying this game.

Girl takes a step, cat takes one. A misstep or hesitation and the cat would make its great leap. Slowly, step by step, they danced this way, face to face, breathing hard, both of them, gasping for the next minute of life when a blink of the eye meant death.

She walked backward over the mountain, down the trail toward town. She reached the edge of the cornfield. The panther saw its chance and leaped, but caught not a little girl in its claws, but a shafted arrow in its screaming throat. Her father drew his hickory bow again, let fly the second arrow through the heart of the beast. Only then did the little girl sit down. The vase of water shattered on the ground, and she began to weep, cutting her hands and stabbing the wet shards into the sacred dirt.

Afterwards, they called the settlement Panthertown. And she was known as Cat Walker.

My mother had faced down a rattlesnake, my grandmother, a panther. I knew I would never be as brave. I knew I would never grow up to be a woman like Cat Walker, let alone my departed mother. The beancakes I made never had the right texture, falling apart before you unwrapped the wet leaves. The fires I built were too smoky or burned out too quickly. The deer or turkey I cooked was charred on the outside and raw within. When I went to weave a sash, my fingers were clumsy and tied themselves in knots more than the fibers.

Cat Walker kept after me to remember the names of the herbs in spring that we gathered, the shape of their leaves, how their shoots divided, high and low, more than I would ever master. I despaired of knowing all I would need to survive. I would surely poison my children with the wrong plants, I would break the taboo and bring punishment to my people. I would fall off the right path. It would be all my fault.

***

One morning, I went out and squatted and let out a yellow stream that wet the dirt, there was only a little blood, but the red spots were startling.

"Your life as a woman has begun, girl." Cat Walker frowned deeper than usual. She took me to the watch tower in the fields, told me to wait until the blood had stopped spotting. Then I could come home.

Climbing up the wooden stand, I crouched with cramps in my stomach. I sat cross-legged on the platform, alone out there where the war parties, Senecas or Choctaw, might creep in, hand over your screaming mouth, stealing you as a slave or new wife in the ongoing blood feud between our tribes.

Our women had planted the Three Sisters in the rich field. The corn grew like tall children waving lazy tassels under the summer sun beating down on my head, while the beans wrapped their vines around the cornstalks, and the squash rolled underfoot. I guarded the ripening crops against the scavenging birds or the marauding raccoons, shouting away any feathered or furred thieves come to steal the sweet ears, pods, and gourds.

I lay back and watched the blue sky overhead, and I felt myself going blue, the sure sign of going West, into the darkness where the sun died every day.

I thought of the monsters in the mountains that preyed on mortal men. Cat Walker and the elders told of great leeches that lurk in some rivers, or giant Yellowjackets that buzz down to carry off small children. Or Judaculla the giant who leaped down from the mountaintop and left his claw marks in the rock in the valley. There was Spearfinger, the woman with a coat made of stone, who would serve up your liver on her sharp fingertip. How I had shivered by the winter fires, listening to those stories while the elders smiled at my childish fears.

But the most feared was the Uk'tena, a great horned snake that lived in the darkest pools in the deepest coves of the highest mountains. With a swipe of its tail, the monster could send a flood of water waist-high through the town, knocking aside the slight summer houses and washing out the wattle from even the heaviest winter house.

I also suspected these were stories that old people tell to scare the young. There were real monsters in the world that worried my elders.

What worried me was that I would never be like Cat Walker, content to follow the old-fashioned ways, wear only dull buckskin, never anything bright like the stroud cloth and the grosgrain ribbons from Charleston or Williamsburg. The Real People didn't know everything, there was another world, they said, across the waters I had never seen.

I wanted another world — I'm ashamed to admit it, but I thought those thoughts. I wanted to see what lay beyond the Overhills.

***

The Overhill settlement is by the two chiefs divided into two factions, between whom there is often great animosity, and the two leaders are sure to oppose one another in every measure taken. Attakullakulla has done but little in war to recommend him but has often signalized himself by his policy and negotiations at home. Ostenaco has a tolerable share of both, but policy and art are the greatest steps to power.

Timberlake

That spring, we paddled downriver to the sacred capital of Chota. Climbing the great mound, the clans from all the Overhills filed into the seven-sided council house, four hundred men and women. The sweet smoke from the sacred fire enveloped us all.

We sat and listened to Ostenaco and Attakullakulla make their arguments for war or peace.

Slight of stature, barely coming up to the shoulders of most males, At-takullakulla wasn't even Tsalagi by birth. Some said he was of the Little People, those unseen sprites who have been known to snatch naughty children in the far woods. He was a baby when they brought him to town from a northern raid, still bathed with his mother's blood. But he took to our ways, our tongue, short of stature, but quick with his tongue.

His name meant "Leaning Wood," but he had never been much for sticks in ball play, fast outpaced by taller men, nor had he ventured out on the summer raids and returned to town, singing of his victory, with still wet scalps tied to his belt, the blood of his foes running down his bare thighs. The English knew him as the Little Carpenter, a clever man who was able to build coalitions and consensus, by his very words. He could talk circles around bigger men, stronger warriors in the council, until the clans were all nodding their heads and agreeing.

"For such a little man, he talks too big," Ostenaco scoffed.

While Ostenaco argued for a show of force to keep our honor, Attakullakulla would shave his words carefully, whittle his words down, caution against rashness.

"The nation remembers sending me as emissary to the English King."

As a youth, Attakullakulla had gone to London, talked firsthand to their king. He came home and cautioned that the English were not like other tribes or nations, the counsel he repeated.

"We have sworn our friendship, and we, the People, are nothing if we do not keep our oath. And we benefit," Attakullakulla insisted. "We send deer skins which we have aplenty, and we are rewarded with guns and axes, pots for our women to cook in, fine ribbons, and shiny things that adorn our daughters."

"A man's honor is not for sale," Ostenaco interrupted. "The English talk only of land and who owns it. This is our homeland. How many deer hides would you take for your family, for the earth that feeds you?"

"Listen, listen. The English are a strange folk and not to be dissuaded. They have seen our mountains, and they are like the tide of the sea. They will wash us away."

"We are men as well, but the mountains are on our side, they are a defense against the invaders. We have fought off intruders, Shawano and Catawba and Seneca. We can vanquish the whites as well."

"Do not underestimate these foes," Attakullakulla raised his voice. "They are not like the tribes we know and have bested. They will scalp our men, rape our women, dash out the brains of our babes, cut down the corn, burn the townhouse. They will kick our world aside with their high boots. In their preening pride, they aim to pull down the mountains and snuff out the sun once they build a ladder to reach the sky."

"More stories, tales that old women tell by the fires to scare their children," Ostenaco raised his voice. "We are not children. We are AniYvwiya. The People who are not afraid."

It came time to decide. Each man who would go to war and each woman who would bloody the captives had their say. In the right hand, a red bead for Ostenaco and war. Palmed in the left, white for Attakullakulla and peace. An earthen pot went around the council, and each man and woman dropped their beads inside.

A wizened conjure man carried the vessel and raised it over his gray head, let fall the beads onto a tanned buckskin. It looked like drops of blood falling, over-flowing as the Real People raised a war cry, Cat Walker trilling her pleasure the loudest.

The reader will not be a little surprised to find the story of the Amazons not so great a fable as we imagined, many of the Indian women being as famous in war, as powerful in council. War-women who can no longer go to war, but have distinguished themselves in their younger days, have the title of Beloved. This is the only title females can enjoy, but it abundantly recompences them, by the power they acquire, which is so great, that they can by the wave of a swan's wing, deliver a wretch condemned by the council, and already tied to the stake.

Timberlake

The nation's six hundred warriors laid siege to Fort Loudon and slaughtered all within, taking the blood revenge, eye for eye, life for a life, scalp for scalp. But they saved Demere, that insolent man, for a last vengeful dance.

They took him to the west bank of the river. We went to water each morning, turning to face the eastern light. But the far bank was saved for ceremonies of blood and sending souls off into the western darklands.

I stood behind the angry women with their flaying knives, but I could not watch what they did to that man. A gorge of nausea rose in my gut, and I turned away.

When his terrible dance ended and the screams finally stopped, I looked again. The man's mouth was stuffed full of the grass that he had said was meant for our children's hungry mouths.

Cat Walker walked away, wiping her knife clean. She was grim faced, taking no joy in her duty, the necessity of the man's slow and terrible end. Blood calls for blood to correct the balance of the world, but Cat Walker could answer that call, better than I ever could.

***

Ostenaco the Mankiller took his six hundred warriors in their best paint to meet the English army sent to destroy us, pacify us, punish us like terrible children. At Old Estatoe Fields, he set ambushes along the ridges. They watched and waited as Scottish Highlanders in their kilts marched with drum and bagpipes, their bayonets flashing in the sun. Our warriors waited in silence, and then at the war cry of the Mankiller, the arrows flew like rain, the shots rang out, and the kilted men fell, and the river turned dark with their blood.

Back in Tomotley, women danced in glee with bloody hanks of hair, trophies from the battlefield. Cat Walker wore a bloody Scot's kilt as she danced around the fire to celebrate our victory, wailing and keening and clicking her tongue.

"It is over," Ostenaco boasted. "The Real People are victorious. We have defeated our foes and vanquished their armies."

Attakullalulla did not join the celebration. "Wait, just wait. It is not over. It will never be over with these people."

***

True to the White Chief's words, the English returned in force the following spring. Once again, Ostenaco led the men of the nation. Once more, they lay in wait along the ridges overlooking the trail at old Estatoe. But this time, the Scots in their kilts didn't give warning blowing their bagpipes. They didn't march in formation in the open, but filed through the woods, following their newly enlisted scouts, Choctow and Chickasaw who had seen their towns raided by our young men, their kin killed in the back and forth of the game that is war. Men who knew how to fight in the mountains.

Arrows nocked and flew. The muskets fired, and smoke filled the summer woods. My father fell back with his warriors into the higher hills. The kilted men and their native scouts swept up the valley into Nikwasee, guarded by one elder too feeble to run. He sat cross-legged on the trail, waiting. As the soldiers surrounded him with their bayonets drawn, he calmly sang his death song. They helped him along, caving in his skull with a musket butt. They torched the summer houses and the corn cribs, razed it all. They ran their horses through the corn and galloped up the sacred mound and into the council house, where they took turns pissing on the sacred fire until it was extinguished.

The smoke of the razed Middle Towns rose over our mountains. Out of those passes, gaunt-eyed women and listless children staggered into the Overhills towns, the only survivors. They were the ones who ran fastest while their unfortunate sisters had fallen behind. Babies squalled beside their mothers with saber-slit throats. No one left to bury them.

Ostenaco sued for peace. His last warriors decked out in cane breastplates and magic paints, the red of war and black of death smeared on their faces, they paddled their canoes from our side of the river. The British, in clumsy barges, came from their new ground, and they met in the Long Island in the middle of the river.

Ostenaco took a great war hatchet and split the earth at his feet with a mighty shout. Then kicked the dirt over the blade that had cleaved more than a few white skulls.

"No more. Enough," he said. He buried the war into the past, the way that the dead are laid to rest under rocks. One by one, his men piled a river rock on the grave for the hatchet. Peace comes when the war is dead, and the ground drinks blood.

But after the ceremony, my father had one more condition. He could not return home without a trophy of his own.

All things being settled to the satisfaction of the Indians, the chief told Col. Stephen he had one more favor to beg of them, which was to send an officer back to their country as that would convince the nation of the sincerity of the English. The Colonel was embarrassed at the demand: he saw the necessity of some officer's going there yet could not command any on so dangerous a duty. I relieved him from this dilemma, by offering my services, my active disposition, or if I may venture to say, a love of my country, would not permit its losing too great an advantage, for want of resolution to become hostage to a people, who tho' savage and unacquainted with the laws of war or nations, seemed now tolerably sincere. The Colonel seemed more apprehensive of the danger than I was myself, scarce giving any encouragement to a man whom he imagined going to make himself a sacrifice."

Timberlake

M'Cormick the trader relayed the demands of Ostenaco to the commanding officer of the British forces, Col. Stephens. His face turning red beneath his bushy beard as he heard the Tsalagi and tried to turn the words to English. "One more thing. They need one of your men, a high one."

Col. Stephens hesitated. "What do you mean?"

"A hostage, plain and simple," came M'Cormick's answer.

"How about you?"

"I'm a trader, not a warrior, so I don't count to the Cherokee. They want an officer."

"I can't in good conscience consign one of my men to them. Not after what those women did to Demere," Stephens protested.

Richard, mark this turn in our story when your father stepped forward.

"I'll go," Henry volunteered.

Chapter 2

Tomotley, 1762

Ostenaco sped home to the Overhills.

We paced the riverbanks, watching until the moon waxed and waned, waiting for Timberlake, who had oddly decided to take a canoe rather than accompany my father by horseback. Along with Timberlake, a Sgt. Thomas Sumter had volunteered his duty and his honor to accompany the expedition. M'Cormick reluctantly stayed as guide to bring them safely down the river to Tomotley.

After a fortnight, we began to wonder if the three men had lost their lives to the Shawano or drowned in the river. What kind of fools would take a canoe in winter rather than travel by horse?

Finally, Ostenaco dispatched a scouting party. They finally found Timberlake, M'Cormick, and Sumter, shivering by a fire, having abandoned their dugout lodged between two huge boulders in the river. "They were as wet as muskrats when we found them," said my uncle, Woyi. "But they looked happy to see us."

Word came by one runner that the party, both scouts and the rescued, was nearing the town. My father, the Mankiller, the War Chief of the Nation, painted his face black and red, the host preparing to welcome his guests.

About 100 yards from the town house, we were received by a body of between 300-400 Indians, ten or twelve of which were entirely naked, except for a piece of cloth about their middle, and painted all over in a hideous manner; six of them with eagles tails in their hands, which they shook and flourished as they advanced, danced in a very uncommon figure, singing in concert with drums of their own make, and those of the late unfortunate Captain Demere, with several other instruments, uncouth beyond description. The headman of the town led the procession, painted blood-red, except his face, which was half-black, holding an old rusty broadsword in his right hand, and an eagle's tail in his left. Singling himself out from the rest, the headman cut two or three capers, as a signal to the other eagle-tails, who instantly followed his example. This violent exercise, accompanied by the band of musick, and a loud yell from the mob, lasted about a minute, when the headman waving the sword over my head, struck it into the ground, about two inches from my left foot.

Timberlake

"What took you so long?" I pulled M'Cormick aside, who stank even more than usual after his misadventures.

"Good God." The trader shuddered. "Everything that could go wrong, did. We're lucky the bears didn't eat us alive."

For two weeks, they had crept down river, lost one rifle in the river, broke another's firing pin, finally rigged the weapon to shoot again, shot a bear before they starved to death, and nearly scared themselves silly, by their fires at night, beset by howling beasts in the wilderness.

"That little Johnny-upstart acted like he was the admiral of our little voyage, bossing us all about," M'Cormick complained about Timberlake's leadership. "Idiot. He couldn't even swim."

Sumter was even more blunt with his superior when they were found. "I would tell you to go to hell, ensign, but you already led us down to the door."

***

The first I saw of then Ensign Henry Timberlake, later to be promoted to lieuten-ant for his bravery if not his common sense, he took my breath away. It was the same shiver as I felt going to water in my morning ritual, dunking my head in the freezing cleansing currents.

If asked to paint my true love in words, what would I say? Henry was a fine figure of a man, dashing in his red waistcoat and his white stockings, muddied even as they were and reeking of his own fearful sweat. Stripped of those clothes, I could get the true scent of him.

Middling of stature, fair of skin, with a rose in his cheek, and eyes blue as the sky, his hair like the sun-light sedge of a field. Almost slight compared to the boys I knew in Tomotley.

Why did my fancy fall on Henry and not Sumter? They were both brave, white, and soldiers. Both came to Tomotley, both went to London with my father. Sumter came back to us. Henry never would.

But Sumter did not make me thirsty as Henry did, the first time I laid eyes upon him.

Sumter: a neck barbecued by sun and wind, ginger-haired and freckled, like a red pox had afflicted his skin. His face would flush with blood when he grew angry or excited. The sergeant was a stocky, short but feisty man who came up only to my father's shoulder, a little taller than Attakullakulla. His was the temperament of a bantam rooster who won't back down from a fair fight, nor a dirty brawl.

That spring, when I was sixteen, the sergeant wandered our town at will, watching our games and how the men gambled while the women did the field work and minded the houses. And he would stop and look and spit.

I've never seen a man so fond of spitting, once straight into the fire, until a warrior offered to split his head open with a club, and it was explained carefully by M'Cormick to the South Carolinian that fire is sacred, and it was blasphemy to spit into it.

Sumter tried his hand at our game of chunkey. The men would roll a polished stone fast along the packed dirt where we had danced just last night. The pair of contestants would run behind, hurling their short spears at the rolling rock. The winner, of course, was the one whose throw came closest to the stone. Wagers were made with hunting shirts vs. good trader's blades. After a few rolls of chunkey, a few sharp-eyed men had more than a few knives to their good name, while the slow and weak of eye had no shirt to cover their nakedness.

The sergeant had heard that our people were fleeter, faster, stronger than a good white boy, which set his temper on edge. "Goldarn it, you red boys ain't worth a lick. Let me show what a Carolina woodhick can do."

He shed his coat, rolled the sleeves of his linsey shirt, spit on his hands.

Woyi rolled the disc. Sumter took off running and flung his javelin, which sailed wide. "Goldurn it!" He ran harder, diving after the rolling stone. "Stay, you stony bastard."

Cradling the heavy disc against his muddied and sweaty shirt, he rose, panting and staggering under its weight. "What do I win? Hey, lass, give me a kiss. I won."

Sumter was a monstrous little man, proud of his spittle, his piss, his shit, and certainly his come, which he had spread around a few of Tomotley's most comely lasses, but not me, never me.

Henry, meanwhile, went about the houses and fields, carefully writing down all that he saw, scratching out his strange marks on curled parchments.

We all kept our eye on our guests, Cat Walker, especially. Her dark eyes narrowed, her thumb already feeling the edge of her hide scraper, anticipating how she could flay their flesh, braiding long bloody ribbons from their arms, the men lashed to the stake while the fire was already licking up their legs. She dreamed of their yoneg screams, I could tell.

But she was an old woman, and those were the old bloody ways. They were guests of the nation now. I was determined to demonstrate our hospitality.

I was not a little pleased likewise with their ball-plays (in which they shew great dexterity) especially when the women played, who pulled one another about, to the no small amusement of a European spectator.

Timberlake

Henry, our honored guest, our negotiated hostage with the English army, laughed and huzzahed our favorite sport — the stickball game that we only jokingly called "Little War."

There were prettier girls in Tomotley, slimmer of waist, fairer of face, with better hair or darker eyes, but I was the Mankiller's Daughter, and I was not afraid. I pulled the hair and scratched the faces of more than a few of my rivals when we played. We shed our long skirts, and painted our breasts red with paint, to protect us from the summer sun. We ran screaming up and down. I would smack Corn Tassel Girl's shins and make my rival cry, stealing the ball from her stick. I hauled up the field, headed toward the trees, the mountains in the distance, the shouts of my clan in my ears, my hair flowing as I ran faster than the rest, almost escaped, until face down I fell, tripped by a sneaky stick. The ball and battle flowed the other direction, curse her, Rabbit Girl.

But the sport grew even fiercer when big men took the field.

Grassy field flattened by teams of twenty and thirty men already raked with blood. The conjure-man used a comb of rattlesnake fangs to score their skin as he recited the sacred words, calling for favor, for success on the field, against failure and disgrace.

Blood and bruises, broken limbs and noses, gouged eyes, all is fair on the field as you race up and down the grass, chasing the rawhide ball with your netted stick, scooping it up and carrying it in your fist as you race toward the goal at the far tree line, the shouts of your kinsmen calling your name.

We once rooted for one player, a man from the Wolf clan, who must have weighed seven stone, but for a big man he could move like a landslide, rolling over his opponents as he trudged laughing toward the goal, carrying two players on his broad back. His name was Walking Mountain, and he was a mighty player until he was felled at the battle of Old Estatoe with a bullet that grooved his thick skull.

He did not die, but staggered home as our warriors came back from the lost war. He laughed like a child and sat at the water's edge, with no more understanding that the rocks he threw into the water hour after hour, then was led like a child to his bed at dark. Walking Mountain did not play the ball game after that.

I was almost every night at some dance, or diversion; the war dance, however, gave me the greatest satisfaction, as in that I had an opportunity of learning their methods of war, and a history of their warlike actions, many of which were amusing and instructive ... they are likewise very dexterous in pantomime dancing, several of which I have seen performed that were very diverting.

Timberlake

Timberlake and Sumter sat by Ostenaco's side on a great buffalo hide, its blunt horned head glistening in the firelight. They were guests of honor, but even then,

Henry kept scratching at his parchment with the flicking quill, making his strange marks.

I brought him platters of our roast corn and bear meat and venison, bean bread I had made myself. I smiled and lowered my look.

"This is your helper tonight, Skitty, my daughter," Ostenaco said.

Sumter snorted and elbowed Timberlake. "Did he say 'Skinny'? Girl weighs a few too many stones to merit that name, but she's plump in all the right places." Sumter laughed and made that leering face that men sport around the lasses they would love to bed, but never bed for love.

To my relief, Henry ignored his sergeant. I made sure the ensign had the choice pieces of meat and the best bean bread.

Around the fire, my People danced the dances of the animals. First to fly into the circle, the men swoop around the fire with capes made of the great feathers plucked from the wings of Eagles, taken by only the most magic of hunters and the right formulas. A hunter must first take a deer and lay its carcass out on the crags and wait for the bird to come for its dinner, setting aside the vultures and buzzards. He must blame the Spaniards, deflecting vengeance away from our People.

The Beaver Dance is less serious. A man tried to grab the pelt that was pulled across the ground by a string while the women laughed. In the Ant dance, we went about waving our fingers at our heads like the antennae of the black and red insects, busy building their colonies, dragging back bits of leaf.

Then came time for the Bears. Timberlake smiled at the sight of the men pawing the air over the women's heads, their hands on their partner's bare shoulders. The men and women came out into the great circle and began to dance when they heard the song. He-he. Ani Tsaguhi Ani Tsaguhi. I want to lay them low on the ground.

These were the words a hunter prayed going into the mountains, the no-good places where the droves of bears made their dens. Bears were distant cousins of the Real People. There was once a Bear Clan among us, Cat Walker once told me, and its people had sacrificed themselves for the greater good.

There came a great famine when no game could be found in the woods, nor corn planted in the fields for lack of rain. The clan had abstained from food for seven days and went away from their houses. The hair grew long and shaggy on their bodies. Their fingers raked the trunks of trees, sharpening and strengthening what had been puny human nails into fierce claws. They departed forever, saying, "We are going where there is always plenty to eat. Hereafter we shall be called yanu, and when you yourselves are hungry, come into the woods and call us by name and we shall come to give you our own flesh. You need not be afraid to kill us, for we shall live forever."

Next the booger dances. Timberlake laughed at the figures parading in carved masks, with hanging locks of hair. When I was a girl seated around the fire with woods bending in on us, they came out of the darkness, those hideous faces, and I made myself sit still, when my heart would run away, out of fear. Oh, I could see my uncle's limp leg, and recognize my father's thin arm, but they were the Other now, spirits dancing in and out of the shadows, lunging toward the children like myself.

The dancers thrust their hips, the women laughing at the smallness of the penises they pretended with little squashes. Here were whole tribes of men who would never pleasure the women, coaxing them to have strong babies.

And after the masked dancers had left the circle to great laughs and clapping of hands, Cat Walker stepped out in her best blanket, signaling the women's turn to dance. And I joined in, the flames warming my left hand as we circled the glowing fire.

Draped in our shawls edged with tinkling cowrie shells traded with the vanished Yemassee on the coast, holding our heads high, hair plaited and shiny with bear grease, our faces bright before the full moon, the warm fire glow. Rattles of tortoise shell and pebbles tied below our knees, we lifted them high, stomped the ground as the singers called out:

Ha ha age hyi.

There's a good woman living here.

See her shake those rattle shells.

I'm going to take that pretty woman home with me, home to my town.

The old men would sing in their high-pitched taunt voices, beating the water drum in a great circle, as the girls made the rounds, raising high their pretty knees, stomping hard bare shapely feet. And one by one, the bashful boys came to join us, forming another line. And we moved together and apart, held hands, and swayed our hips, mimicking how boys and girls meet and court, and what they do in the dark of the moon, the pleasure they can take.

On the next swing around the fire, I took Henry by the hand and round the fire he went. He followed my motions, even though he did not know the words to the song. I wanted to believe he knew my intention.

***

It came time for Timberlake to taste of the visions.

Cat Walker set a fired-clay cauldron on the coals of the sacred fire of the town-house. The women had brought gourds full of springwater, which she poured into the pot. She opened her medicine bundle of roots and dried leaves and threw them into the bubbling pot.

We had wandered the mountainside, gathering only on the eastern slopes where the sun touched the best plant. In the patches of snake plantain or bloodroot or ginseng, I would wonder which was the most powerful, but she stopped me. "Wait," she said, and we would stand there in the bird-singing woods, the crows cawing overhead, until one of the leaves would wave a welcome to us. She would sing under her breath the spell, and only then would she let me go dig the right plant.

There were secret plants I didn't know that went into the Black Drink brewing on the fire.

Cat Walker took up the wing of the swan, white and long, shot on the river cane so many seasons before by my father. She waved it seven times over the pot. Soon, all who would drink would be able to fly and glide like the birds who float on the river and ride high against the moon. Finally, she put in the yaupon holly leaves, the plant that had been carried up from the ocean dunes carefully tended in the wintertime.

We dipped the conch shell that came as well from the salt waters, and I served our guests, their faces shining by the light of the fire. Henry looked down into the black liquid sloshing so slightly against the pearl of the shell, and he made his yoneg face.

"Drink it. You'll see," I said though I don't believe he understood a word that I said.

"Much obliged." He slurped down the potion.

And I passed on to Sumter, who licked his dry lips.

It was a sacred drink suitable only for the bravest of warriors. Anyone untested would likely die from what they would see when the drink took hold of their minds. The drink didn't take long to work its power.

"Oh my," Henry said and held his head between his knees. He retched and spat out a fine, thin thread of bile.

"Oh, good God," Sumter groaned.

The Black Drink swirls in your belly and makes you throw up, but then the retches reach into your brain. Vomiting opens you up to the void, and a White Light suddenly strikes your eyes. Men say you see past all shadows, into the pulsing sunlight cloaked behind the darkest night, past the fur and hide of this rough world into the light that holds us. We are held in the swaying bed of this world, hung from the four ropes bound to the corners of all reality.

But I did not drink from Cat Walker's cauldron that night. I had seen my desire. I would watch Henry as he held his head between his hands, and I waited my chance.

There is no kind of rites or ceremonies at marriage, courtship, and all being, as I have already observed, concluded in half an hour, without any other celebration, and is as little binding as ceremonious; for though many last until death, especially when there are children, it is common for a person to change three or four times a year. Notwithstanding this, the Indian women gave lately a proof of fidelity, not to be equaled by politer ladies, bound by all the sacred ties of marriage.

Timberlake

Man and woman, swains and maids, what every girl dreams of.

Cat Walker had warned me against playing now too rough with the Wolf Boys, or to go deep in the woods. My breasts were filling out, my desires were coming upon me. Boys who once bothered me now caught my eye in strange ways as they walked past our house. And I could be heard to sigh.

Tutsahyesi — he will marry you, what every girl dreams to hear, holds the breath in her trembling throat, until it sighs out sharp as a trader's knife. Ever since we were girls, even too young to wear dresses, dancing our cornhusk dolls through the combed dirt before the summer house, we stole the bashful glances at the boys we would marry, little savages yelling and shooting the darts from their cane blowguns, spitting the eyes of birds on the branch or the frog by the river's edge. That sharpness traveling into our hearts, waiting for the breasts to grow to bring the boys' return look, the full rich teats where our babes would suckle under our faint smiles.

Later that night, after the dances and the couples had repaired to their beds for a little pleasure, I reintroduced myself without a word, slipping out of my doeskin, letting it fall about my ankles and slipping beneath the bear hide where he slumbered. Henry and his manliness awoke soon enough under my grasp.

"Bear killer." I ran my fingers through the plucky hairs of his chest. M'Cormick had told me of how Timberlake had saved their own hides from the marauding bears that had stalked their camps along the winter river, when they were close to starving, he felled the great beast with a single shot from their musket.

Snuggled that first time with my father's blessing, together beneath the flayed hide of the bruin Henry had slain and brought to town. I smelled of him under the bear hide, the strange, honeyed smell, different, I could breathe in his thin pelt on his pale chest between his nipples.

"Who are you again, girl?"

My fine Virginian studied me with those blue eyes, warm as the summer sky. His words were just sounds that I would memorize until later when I knew their meaning. I had only a little of the English tongue from M'Cormick, and Henry had a smattering of Tsalagi. But that night, we made ourselves known to each other.

"Skitty. It means me." And I stopped his soft mouth with my tongue.

Later, when the moon peered through the smoke hole of our hut and the light fell on my beloved's sleeping face, white as bone, I said the right prayers to fix Henry's love forever.

Your spittle, I take it, I eat it.

Your body, I take it, I eat it.

Your flesh, I take it, I eat it.

Your heart, I take it, I eat it.

Listen. This woman's body has come to rest at the edge of your body.

I spat into the palm of my hand and rubbed his breast beneath the bear hide. He was mine now. I whispered the words to fix him forever.

***

I may have said the proper formulas and gathered the plants that would make a man love me, but I didn't weave the spell to make him stay.

Once I watched my uncle, Woyi, make a thong tree to mark the right fork to take the trail home. He found a sapling and bent the supple trunk, tying it with sinew to a stake. In time, the tree would grow out from the bend before righting itself straight toward the sun. A signal to all who would follow, long after we had fallen by the wayside and rock cairns covered our bones. The traveler would know the way to Tomotley long after we were dead.

Stories are like signal trees, bent to point the directions of the four corners of our world, aligned with the powers that run through our lands. Still, I wondered if we could read the signal trees, to find our way home, what would stop our enemies from following in our footsteps?

***

Came the spring and the first warm days after the cold winter nights, Timberlake was ready to take his leave of us. There were war parties again, and the truce had been broken by rogues and other tribes. The whites were restless on the borders of our mountains, and Henry was ready to go home, back to Virginia.

Ostenaco and his warriors planned to accompany our guests safely back to Williamsburg and continue our talk of a lasting peace between our peoples.

I fretted that Henry would leave me and not return.

In the end, I should have worried about my father's ambition. He wanted to bypass Attakullakulla, the little man with the quick tongue, who was always a step ahead since he had made that journey to see the Yoneg King. So long as the little White Chief could say, "I remember when in London, I saw this when I was in London, this is how they do it in London," as long as Attakullakulla lorded it over us with London, Ostenaco was like a poor mockingbird that everyone ignored.

My father had brought Timberlake to our People as part of the treaty. It was time to return the white hostages to Williamsburg for a new ransom. He had hoped to simply return with more guns and horses, pots and pretties for the women, reassurances of hunting grounds.

But Ostenaco would be haunted by a picture, a life-sized painting made after the likeness of King George III, hung in the great hall at Williamsburg. He had to meet the man in the painting and so he talked Timberlake, his new son-in-law, my only lover, into making the long voyage to visit the King of England.

Chapter 3

"All because of a picture?" I had to ask Ostenaco after his long journey that took all summer, fall and into the winter. "You went all that way because of a face on a wall?"

My father peered through his new wired mask that held a pair of polished crystals before his aging eyes, giving him a second sight. He had returned from London with a sack of these clever contraptions, called spectacles. Our elders could suddenly see what had been blurred before their noses, the eyes of youth restored by English ingenuity.

"Attakullakulla was right." The chastened Mankiller blinked behind his new glassy eyes. "They are a canny tribe, full of magic beyond our conjure men or medicine women. They are so cunning, they can paint a ghost of a man on a wall, so real that you feel it can speak, that the eyes see through you."

While in Williamsburg, my father had spied the man on the wall, looking down on him. A slender man in yellow silk tunic, draped in white ermine, his legs slender in white hose, delicate ankles turned just so.

Ostenaco went over to touch the rough paints on the canvas, trace the grain left by the horsehair brush.

"Timberlake, who is this?"

Henry bowed toward the likeness. "His Majesty, George, king of England and Scotland and Wales, defender of the faith. He is our king."

Ostenaco stepped back and stroked his chin, sizing up this man painted on the wall. His likeness looked off into a future, over the head of any subject bowing toward the royal portrait. This king my father wanted to see, face-to-face, man-to-man. He decided then and there to travel to London, and he would talk Timberlake into escorting him.

Ostenaco sent home his one hundred warriors. He took only the chief Cunne Shote and my uncle, Woyi. Just as Timberlake had schemed to scout out the weakness of our nation, Ostenaco wanted to see firsthand the defenses of the English and how many men were in their army.

***

After his return, my father recounted all that he had seen in the yonegs' home island, telling story night after night as the snows drifted against the fields and rattled the dead stalks of the corn in the fields. We huddled in the winter house under warm furs around the fire, shivering with delight, reliving the summer that Ostenaco had spent with Henry and the English.

But first Ostenaco faced the ocean, a body of water that I had heard of, only in stories of how a spider had crossed it with the fire on her back. My father sailed the sea for a whole moon before he reached the island of the English on the far side of our swaying world. The crossing proved arduous, and many of the crew took to their quarters with a fever. More than a few men expired on the passage and were sewn into canvas shrouds and tossed overboard.

At last, Timberlake gestured to that first glimpse of land after weeks of nothing to be seen but water.

"Portsmouth."

While in the boat that took us to shore, Ostenaco, painted in a very frightful manner, sung a solemn dirge with a very loud voice to return God thanks for his safe arrival. The loudness and uncouthness of his singing, and the oddity of his person, drew a vast crowd of boats, filled with spectators and the landing place was so thronged that it was almost impossible to get to the inn, where we took post for London.

Timberlake

Anchoring in the harbor, Timberlake, Ostenaco, and his two chiefs were ferried by dory through the flotilla of warships, barques, and cargo craft, a floating forest of masts with furled sails, their flags and pennants snapping in the stiff salt breeze. They approached the busy ports of arrivals where cranes lifted nets filled with hogsheads, even a poor beast or two, cows and horses winched up with their legs dangling and set on dry land once more.

Through this parade of goods and possession, the world's riches flowing into the mouth of this harbor, down the greedy throat of England itself, Ostenaco stood proudly, planting his moccasin in the prow of his craft. His voice rose like a stream cascading through the mountains, the roar of waters that washed over the great councils, his words that moved men to great deeds in war, or women to weep in admiration for our People's storied ways.

He began to sing, the first time that the island of England had heard speech by Real People, the sound of Tsalagi in their pale white ears. Ostenaco sang, not of war, but of peace and thankfulness, coming alive across the endless water, into our former enemies who we would learn now how to live with in peace. My father sang the old words and raised his hands to the heavens, and the longshoremen on the piers and docks, and the sailors climbing in the hawsers of the masts, all began to point and shout with amazement, listening for the first time to our words.

The chiefs came down the plank and into the cobbled streets set with rounded stones, and the crowds pressed around them, staring and pointing and shouting their unknown tongues. Ostenaco and Cunne Shote and Woyi tread the streets of Portsmouth in fine moccasins and beribboned loincloths and stripped leggings, silver gorgets shining on proud chests, and the paint of war and peace and death drawn on their faces, winged birds and lightning storms, the emblems of the mountains on their skin.

Later in London, even larger crowds gawked after the chiefs. They plied Ostenaco with beer and ale, sherry and port, gin, and rum "I am not sure that we were once given a draught of clean water, sweet as the Tanassee in our whole tour of the English realm." Ostenaco shook his head.

The uncommon appearance of the Cherokee began to draw after them great crowds of people of all ranks, and they were forever teasing me to take them to some public diversion The favorite was Sadler-Wells, the activity of the performers and the machinery of the pantomime agreeing with their notions of diversion. They were also pleased with Vauxhall, tho' it was always against my inclination that I accompanied them there, on account of the ungovernable curiosity of the

people who often intruded on them and induced them to drink more than suffi-
cient.

I cannot indeed cite sobriety as their characteristic.

Timberlake

"It was like drinking the Black Drink, but worse," my father said that winter,
still shaking his head as if reliving the dull ache he awoke with after an evening of
English revels.

Squired about London, treated by Timberlake to sundry amusements, celebrated daily in the gazettes and pamphlets, the chiefs were the talk of the capital.
But Ostenaco had his goal in mind.

He had vowed to cross the main to seek an audience with this Highness, this
Quality, this Royal Being who slew giant serpents and presided over a mighty empire wrapping itself about the world like a snake swallowing a bird's egg. One
mighty leader to another, one nation visiting with another.

At last, the three Cherokee chiefs were admitted into Buckingham Palace and
escorted by ruffled footmen into the throne room. The king had fine legs in his
silk hose, the same he wore in the painting that had possessed Ostenaco. The
mighty monarch wore no crown that day but kept scratching beneath his curled
wig. George tapped his ringed fingers against the carved armrest of the throne,
studied my father and his chiefs, whispered something to the courier who nodded
and scurried off.

Ostenaco had practiced his speech all the way over the ocean, and for the
months they were in England, but he had to trust Timberlake to translate his
words.

He recounted it to us in the winter house many times.

"Some time ago, my nation was in darkness, but that darkness is now cleared
up. My people were in great distress, but that is ended. There will be no more bad
talks in my nation, but all will be good talks. If any Cherokee shall kill an Englishman, that Cherokee shall be put to death.

Our women are bearing children to increase our Nation, and I will order those
who are growing up to avoid making war with the English. If any of our headmen

retain resentment against the English for their relations who have been killed, and if any of them speak a bad word concerning it, I shall deal with them as I see cause. No more disturbances will be heard in my Nation. I speak not with two tongues, and I am ashamed of those who do. I shall tell all my people all that I have seen in England."

"What did the king say in return?" I asked.

Ostenaco frowned, the firelight glinting on the glass covering his eyes. "I'm not sure the king got everything Timberlake said in passing on my speech."

After all was said, and nothing was left to be done, King George the dragon-slayer, applauded. "Very nicely said, yes, indeed."

The court applauded in turn, politely.

The scurrying courier came forward and presented Ostenaco and his chiefs with beribboned medallions, bearing George's fine profile embossed in the silver metal.

Cunne Shote marched right up to the throne and squeezed the king to his breast, vowing eternal friendship.

The court tittered in shock. The king was untouchable by his subjects, of which we were now counted.

"He smelled like a woman," Cunne Shote said. "Never smelled a man so sweet. And soft to the touch, but without breasts."

Chapter 4

Tomotley, 1762

During the long summer while Ostenaco and Timberlake were sashaying about London, back home in the Overhills, I felt my body change, watched my belly swell. Cat Walker did not chide me as I bore my child, an addition to the clan, even if the sire was suspect.

But my lover had gone missing, and my heart ached after him, wondering what it was like on that distant island. I found myself idling about M'Cormick's trading post, eager to hear that strange tongue that Henry had spoken.

"Why are you bothering me, girl?" M'Cormick was trying to count the tanned hides, a heavy load for his mule grazing in the clearing. He had brought the stubborn creature from his last foray to Charleston, its back loaded with bolts of stroud and a clinking of iron pots and new skillets. One woman had already found a ready use for hers as a war club, braining a man unlucky enough to get into the strong spirits.

"How do the English say love?" I asked the trader. "What is the yoneg word for sky, for water, for heart?"

"Quit pestering me, girl. Do I look like a damned dictionary?"

"What is dictionary?"

"There is a bright feller over in England, name of Johnson, making one of all the English words and what they would mean. Go ask him."

I laughed nervously. "I'd have to go to England then."

M'Cormick let fall the deer hide his fingers were fumbling through, his lips quit moving, and he shook his head in disgust. "Now you made me lose my count."

"Just teach me the right words to say."

I had watched Henry wander through town. Forever sitting down with his papers, or whittling at the nib of his dip pen, or grinding out more oak gall for his ink, always making his strange marks. Writing, he called it.

I wished I could leave my mind, my heart on a page, a message for the future.

Our ancestors had used rock rather than paper to make their marks. They had sat for moons by soft rock, chiseling their exploits and the legends of the monsters they had seen for generations to come, even if no one could tell their meaning anymore. In a great rock lying in a field, I had seen such markings. I had traced my fingers in the grooves worn by rain where legend said the giant Judaculla had leapt off the great mountain and landed here.

But that was the story told to scare children. I knew old people not that different from me, not monsters, had carved these marks long ago.

"What do the marks mean? What were they trying to say?" I asked Cat Walker in all innocence.

"Who knows? Pay attention to what's growing in front of you." She yanked another root from the field for her medicine bundle.

***

One day, Cat Walker led me past the corn down the trail to the Far Creek. We did not veer from the path to pick berries, root for mushrooms, or unearth roots or pluck leaves for medicines. My grandmother hurried along. I followed her crooked back, the braids of her proud hair showing gray now behind her haughty shoulders. "Agilisi? Agilisi? Wait for me."

But on she marched without a word or a glance over her shoulder. She was taking me to the water, for my own good, a healing formula for a soul who had sidestepped her way from D'uyukduh, the True Path.

I knew my grandmother disapproved of me and my dress. She zealously guarded the old ways lest we be lost in the fancy glitter of the gewgaws of M'Cormick's trading post, bright beads, shiny metal bracelets, gorgets, scarlet and sky-blue ribbons that bedecked your hair.

We were a league now from town, far from prying eyes and tattling tongues. "Off with those yoneg rags!" she barked, and I obeyed, slipping the dress from my shoulders, letting it puddle around my feet.

"All them gewgaws too, girl!"

Off came my best wire bracelets, my heavy earrings, even the strand of cut glass that hung from my bowed neck.

Cat Walker nodded toward the deep cold pool. I stepped from the bank into the flowing water, my toes finding purchase on a mossy round rock. I waded, up to my knees, my thighs, a sharp intake of breath as the water reached my full belly now carrying Timberlake's child.

My grandmother began chanting the old words to induce spells, songs to cast off spirits. Our People were known for potions and poultices, teas and tonics that would win lover's attention, promise plentiful crops of corn, and healthy babies to be born.

I dunked underneath. My ears were plugged with water and the drumming of my own heartbeat. My head emerged, I slung my wet mane back, gasping for warm air. Each time, dunking deeper, and finding the breath harder to bring into my lungs with the freezing water. Seven times, bowing underwater to the north, south, east, and west, to all that was above and everything below and the seventh place of this center, this now, the wheel that moved the world and the Real People.

Forgive me, Timberlake, I told myself. Not the prayer or supplication I expected, but the words that came to mind at that moment, what filled my heart and came in a whisper on the rushing water.

Forgive me.

Cat Walker stood on the banks of this pool, said by some to be a spawning ground for the Uk'tena. As I stood naked in the water, she unwrapped a buckskin bundle.

I saw she held a long crystal with a blood-red streak down its center. She held it overhead between her pointer finger and her thumb until it caught the sun and began to shine a rainbow across the water.

U'lunsuti, the crystal diadem pried from the severed head of an Uk'tena. I had only heard stories from Woyi and my father about the monster and the prophecy stone it wore in its viper's crown. Supposedly such a stone emitted a terrible light that paralyzed anyone who came across the path of the great horned and winged serpent slithering through dark woods.

Cat Walker had never mentioned this powerful medicine or how she, an old woman in Tomotley, had come to possess such a crystal.

Squinting into the magic stone, she cried, "I see seven strangers, seven blessings or seven curses will be your choice in the path you take from today. Of these sacred seven, One you will love to the end of your path. One will save you from yourself, and One you will save. One will make you rich and One will make you poor. One will stand in your way and One you must slay. With that circle of seven men the path is completed."

A cloud came over us, the light failed in the stone. An old woman on the banks of a black pool, and a naked girl with the cold currents against her belly and the child she carried.

"Come up out of the water, girl, and get dressed."

At last, shivering, but cleansed, made right with the world, I stepped dripping from the water. Cat Walker wrapped the strange clear stone again in the buckskin.

"Where did you get that? Is that really an U'lunsuti stone? Did you really see an Uk'tena? Who are these seven men? Did you see their faces? Is Timberlake in their number?

She shushed me. "So many questions. You will find your answers soon enough. You're on the right path now."

***

The journey to London and back had changed our chiefs.

If Ostenaco could not help but talk about all he'd seen and the wonders of the yoneg, Woyi seemed more silent than ever, and worried. One day, my uncle went up into the hills with a new steel-forged ax he had brought from Williamsburg. I could hear the ringing across the mountain passes, a strange sound.

He came back down, and I asked him what had happened.

"I chopped down the signal trees. We don't want them to find us."

But what of Timberlake? He had not come home with my father. How would he find me again, and see his baby?

Woyi shrugged. "Go ask the banty rooster."

Only Sumter had made the journey back to Tomotley returning with my father, Cunne Shote, and Woyi.

Sumter, who came up to my shoulder, always pushing his red nose and his whiskey breath into your face, to make his point, until I dropped my womanly gaze and stepped aside. I could stick my knife into his gut and fillet him like a fish from the river he had swum and nearly drowned in. Sumter was back, why not Timberlake, why not my child's father?

Sumter said the lieutenant had stayed behind in England to clear up debts before he set sail for Williamsburg. He showed me a paper with the fancy marks I remember that Henry could make with his quill.

"Timberlake sent me this letter. Says here he's married a fine filly in England and brought her to Virginia to make a new life. He aims to be a gentleman-farmer, collect his soldier pension, raise tobacco. He's a gentle man all right, too tender to return to your wilderness, I reckon."

And something fell inside me, like a rock loosed from the side of a mountain careening down through trees and brush, wiping out the trail home. It was you, Richard, kicking your little legs inside my womb.

Chapter 5

As soon as a child is born, which is generally without help, it is dipped into cold water and washed, which is repeated every morning for two years afterward, by which the children acquire such strength that no rickety or deformed are found among them. When the woman recovers, which is at latest in three days, she carries it to the river to wash it; but though three days is the longest time of their illness, a great number of them are not so many hours, nay, I have known a woman delivered at the side of a river, wash her child, and come home with it in one hand, a gourd full of water in the other.

    Timberlake

Henry knew only what he had been told, and women never share all their woes with menfolk. What happens in the huts where the women spend their time each moon and by the river where they bring forth the nation's offspring seems like magic to men.

Only Ostenaco came back with the miraculous treasures of the yoneg and many tales of what he had seen first-hand in that distant and cold, wet island. He brought a new name for you, my son, a strange name that would meet with Timberlake's approval.

I named you after a yoneg king who conquered a Holy Land far to the East. He was Lion-hearted. My hope for you when you grew up, and so Richard, that strange mouthful, is what we called you. No worse than Skitty, I suppose. But Cat Walker soon translated the yoneg name into a more suitable Tsalagi-sounding name — Ukwena'i.

I nursed you by the fire and told all that I knew of how brave he was. Perhaps I lied or embellished or wished or dreamed what I wanted. That we would live in happiness, that winter would never come, nor famine, nor the river rise in a white rabid froth, that the rain would never lash us, that we would always live in Tomotley, that Henry would return.

What M'Cormick taught me by day, I would try to put in your mouth at night, whispering the words of the father you would never meet.

You heard both English and Tsalagi from the start, and your mouth burbled out. Mama, I heard you call out as I carried you home in the gathering dusk. I stopped and held you at arm's length, your legs and arms already kicking, ready to run. "Mama." You reached for me. "Mama?"

"Agitsihi," I said. "Mama?"

Mama is Agitsihi. I felt the strange sound like a stone or taste on my tongue. It was the same, and the world grew wider for me in that moment.

You are an orphan by the laws of England, having lost your father, abandoned by your mother. But I know how Our People are, that my father has adopted you and Cat Walker, as old as an agilisi as she is, good only to guard the cornfields from the ravens and the enemy scouts, she watches over you in my long absence.

So long as the clan cares for all the children, for all the old people, for those who can't hunt for game, nor till the fields, nor pick the forests full of greens, sweet berries, fragrant roots and the soft mushrooms, you will eat your fill, grow tall and strong, run fast and far.

I told you that when I nursed you by the home fire.

I tell myself that, sitting by this sad English fire, writing these words.

***

After chopping down the signal trees, Woyi walked by the river, his shoulders hunched, his hands clasped behind his back as if he had been bound by some unseen foe. Woyi had always faithfully followed my father, Ostenaco the Man-killer, but now he had seen a people who could call themselves the Nationkillers. They were like the great flocks of pigeon that took an hour to cross the spring sky, their droppings turning the forest floor to snow. They were white, and they had sent a black cloud before them.

They had felled and burned the last forests, leaving open heaths and moors and waterlands, all around their mother town of London, which was said to be the largest town of any tribe in this world that everyone knew hung from four ropes tied to the four directions. They are jostling that world, making it swing; someone said they were slowly cutting away at one of the ropes that held our existence, ready to spill us all into the black Underworld. They devoured all game, they dammed their rivers and made infernal machines that moved of their own accord.

They brought guns that made noise like thunderclaps in summer storms. In olden days, Real People had been content with bow and blowgun, but now weapons could bore a bloody hole in a man at the length of the ball field, twice the flight of any arrow.

The tide was cresting, and Woyi saw that the mountains that guarded us were not high enough to stop what was washing over the whole world.

The English king had promised my father an end to war. The sovereign looked forward to the day when the fruits of civilization would benefit his red children and we would live in peace, with plowed fields and dumb cows munching grass, waiting to be milked or slaughtered, when venison and bear hams would be a distant dream. We would be like the yoneg, dressed in tight garters and stockings, hoisted into the corsets, women worshipped by suitors with money. We would be his trusted subjects, and he would be our beloved Father.

He should have told that to his yoneg subjects along the coast, who kept moving toward our mountains, pressing at our lands, despite the sacred oaths sworn.

Chapter 6

Overhills, 1764

"First Attakullakulla, then Ostenaco. Our head men returned from audiences with the king with all these promises. The British headman loved us like his children, they said. We were faithful subjects and his friends. He called himself the Great Father. But we are not children to be patted on the head."

Chutatah was complaining in the Chota Council House again. He stamped his foot on the ground, very close to the sacred fire itself. All the clans gathered muttered. Ostenaco and Attakullakulla looked at each other but held their tongues.

"The king said such and such, but his subjects didn't seem to honor his word. The whites have crossed the river where they said they would never come, felled trees they claimed were sacred to the Tsalagi, until the sun never rose again, would they honor their word, and by the next season, there were dead trees and their slow cows shitting on pastures, and the smoke of their fires running wild through the forests, and fewer game for us, and less hides to trade with these same whites."

The headman of Citico, Chutatah, was too used to ordering people around and speaking in council until the day was nearly done. You could see the tendons in his neck working, grinding the broken teeth in his back jaw, like meat caught there.

The muttering grew louder. Many wondered if Chutatah was not simply drunk.

Since Ostenaco returned from England, he had banned all strong drink from town, forbade any of the men to come in with those spirits on their breath. He sent men to chop in the barrels of rum that M'Cormick kept in his cabin, despite the red-faced, red-bearded Scot's protests. He hated to see his liquid trade drain away into the ground.

Chutatah's men of Citico still traded for the spirits, the drink that stole all reasoning and made your words slosh in your mouth until you fell down, dead asleep until the following day when you went down to the river holding your aching head between your hands, praying the pain would go.

But no, Chutatah was stone cold sober. He drank only spring water cupped from his own hand, not given us by any race of men across the ocean. But he was intoxicated by his own anger.

He gave a war cry that would curdle the coldest blood. "Kill them all, any one of them caught wandering in our woods, stealing our game, stealing food out of our children's mouths. They are a blight on the land, smite them all before they slay us."

The People shook their heads and muttered darkly when they heard Chutatah talk of annihilation rather than retribution. It wasn't right. Wrong in fact, the swinging bed of the world would be upended. Might as well sever all four directions and then no one would know which way to walk, let alone hunt. The sun could forget how to rise over the mountain and cross our river to head toward night. The law said only a life for life, blood for blood, not wholesale slaughter.

Chutatah rightly observed that the yoneg observed no sacred law. If they saw one of our hunters in the woods taking a deer, they would shoot him and scalp him. His bloody hair could be traded for twenty-five pounds in Charleston, or Williamsburg. The man's kinsmen may come back the next season and cut off a yoneg's scalp, burn the cabin, bring back a few screaming children. But there was no equal balance of bloodshed.

An army would sweep into the nearest Cherokee town, burn everything, kill whoever couldn't run fast enough into the woods, ride them down with horses, and trample a few children under sharp hooves. They cut off the heads of a hundred women and warriors and even our children that they stuck on the sharpened posts outside their forts, a warning to us what savages they are.

"Talk is better than war," Attakullakulla said, and Ostenaco nodded.

Both had been to London, seen how powerful the English armies were, how many ships would come with their soldiers and horses to our shores, to march into our mountains. They had reasoned with the king and gave their word we would live in peace.

"Surely their king would want to know his sacred word was no more than a pile of droppings or a stream stomped to mud by their slow shitting beasts," Chutatah said.

Attakullakulla and Ostenaco had had their turn, Chutatah said. Twice was enough to be lied to. A third visit, said Chutatah, was now necessary. He was going to Williamsburg and on to England. "I will speak my peace before this king, let it be war or not. What say ye?"

Ostenaco and Attakullakulla looked at each other, the peace chief and the war chief, but both blanched at all that they had seen.

At last, Attakullakulla said, "But you do not speak the king's tongue."

"I will go find our friend Timberlake." Chutatah was a stubborn soul, not to be dissuaded. "He has been a guest of our nation. He will help us again."

"But Timberlake did not speak our tongue that well. You do not know him."

"I will talk to him."

Everyone turned to me, standing at the Council's edge.

"I am not afraid. I know what they say." My heart fluttered as I forced the words out.

Women are meant to be bashful, to cast their eyes down, keep their voices low, but I had enough of M'Cormick's tutoring, and I had tasted Henry's own tongue in my mouth. I wanted to believe that we understood each other in love and in reason. I would read him. He would read me.

Together, we would be reunited.

Together, we could save the Real People.

And I wanted to see the world beyond our mountains, see people other than Cat Walker and everyone I knew in Tomotley, I wanted to see the ocean. I wanted to walk the wondrous streets of London, paved with river stone, and surrounded by giant houses. I wanted all that, and then in the end, I would bring Henry home to be with his son, with his wife. We would live in peace.

I swore then and there before our whole nation. "I will go to Williamsburg."

***

I bid my father farewell at the town's edge. Two summers before, he had set out and crossed the great waters. I could only imagine the wonders of London he had described. Now I would follow in his path, see what he had seen.

"Skitty, dutiful daughter, my child." He lay his warm hands on my shoulders, his strong arms not holding me tight to him, but straight out, holding me at a remove. "Do what is right always. Be true to yourself and your husband, but to your nation as well. We are with you forever."

I turned my back with you, my baby son at my breast, but Cat Walker came forward and caught my arm. She lifted you from the swing I had fashioned. "You can't carry a child all the way to the coast. You'll slow down the men. Mother or warrior. One path at a time. It is your choosing. The boy or the man, you cannot have both."

Chutatah, along with the giant Walking Mountain, waited at the corn's edge about to take the trail into the trees. The smoke curled from our homes by the river. I felt the bed of the earth, the great web shifting, my balance at risk with the weight in my arms and in my heart.

Cat Walker pressed into my hand a gift and closed my fingers around it. I felt a sting and then opened my palm. Her flaying knife, the flint napped by her own father years before, the sharp stone that she had scraped hides from both deer and men. Sharp enough, the beads of blood were springing against the lines of my palm.

"You may find use for that where you go. Remember, Richard will be here when you get home," Cat Walker promised me.

She set you, Richard, on the ground, holding your small hand. You were unsteady on your bare feet, swaying against her steadying grip. You had just learned my name. Agitsihi, you called after me. But I hurried down the trail along the river, my eyes too full of tears to see.

Richard, I had meant to be gone only a season. Little did I know where my journey would take me, how far away, nor how long. I had not meant to abandon you. I meant to save you.

I surrendered you without a word, but until I die, I will always see that last look on your face, your arms waving after me, the shock, but you did not cry.

He will be home when you get here. Richard is home.

I've held her words in my heart through a fortnight of years in this cold island.

Chapter 7

Williamsburg, 1764

We made the long walk to Williamsburg. The moon waxed full as a wild plum and waned thin as a fingernail in the time it took us to journey from the Overhills to the coast. Traveling through the woods along the beaten path, down from the high ridges, into the lesser hills and then flatter plains, following in the footsteps of traders and hoof prints of pack horses piled with deer hides destined for England. Passing ox-drawn wagons traveling uphill bearing trade beads and blankets, hatchets, pots, pans, trinkets, and of course guns and powder, implements of the modern world. The rawhide and sinews and wood of the Overhills no match for the metals that the yoneg fashioned out of fire, melting what they scraped from earth into marvelous tools.

Closer to the coast, we crossed where ancient towns of other tribes once stood, now covered with rows of new plants or herds of beeves, pens of sows. What was once Tuscarora and Powhattan hunting grounds, the yoneg now called the land "Virginia," after an ancient spinster queen. The world was changing shape under their plows, their fires, and the mountains dissolved at our backs, the land flattened out and the sun grew hotter, the air sticky.

I served as interpreter, intermediary, mouthpiece translating the words of the farmers and merchants we encountered. Or at least, I pretended to know their meaning. I had enough from Henry and M'Cormick to catch the sounds of "food" and "east" as they motioned toward their mouths or pointed to the horizon. But no interpretation was needed to follow the shift in a man's eyes or his hand itching on the trigger of the lowered gun to know we were not welcome on this stolen land.

The trail led straight to the wharves of Williamsburg where the ships unloaded. Finding Timberlake himself was trickier. An old man waved us toward the fields north of the town out into the country. We took a rutted road along a slow black creek, swarms of mosquito and clouds of deerfly testing our skin, then turned south by a great pin oak until we found the fields of golden tobacco. An unpainted plank house with a porch, a few outbuildings, nothing made of brick here, no flash of glass or crystal that finer homes in town boasted.

We could see a man in his shirt sleeves, the white linsey stained under his arms and clinging to his damp shoulder blades. A brown slouch hat shaded his sweating face. Mud caked on his knee-high boots, he chopped a broken hoe through the weeds, alone in his plot of tobacco.

He froze in his field. We must have been a sight, a band of feathered and painted Tsalagi, ghosts out of the journey that had cost poor Timberlake his inheritance. It came back in a flash. The friendship dance by the great fire, lying beneath the bear hide he had brought in the canoe, catching my eye when I served him a bowl of honeycomb, licking my fingers as a sign. The masked boogers dancing out of the darkness, the wild drumming. He thought it was all behind him, and here we step out of the woods, savaging his civilized life again.

"Henry, who's there?" A faint voice, a wraith moving in the shade of the porch, a white hand reaching up to the post to steady herself.

My first glimpse of my rival, the other wife, the white one that Sumter had warned me of. She watched from the shade while I stood upright in the sun. We took our measure, while Henry looked back and forth, panicked, and caught in between. He finally bolted for the shaded porch and escorted his English bride back inside.

***

We slept in the field and when the rains fell, we sometimes came on the porch, but no farther. Not invited over the threshold. We ate what we had brought, the last of the parched corn, and drank water from the rain barrel, waiting for Timberlake's answer.

We took council in the shade of the woods.

Would Timberlake take us over the main? Would Chutatah have the chance to speak his peace to the yoneg king?

Chutatah had no English to speak of. His offering of oratory, all the proud words he had practiced in efforts to best Attakullakulla and Ostenaco, to finally sway George, I had whittled his words down to a serviceable English. "We want what we have. Take no more from us. We mean you no harm. Mean us none, we beg."

"Can you talk him into it?" the headman wanted to know.

I sat with my arms wrapped tight about my knees, staring into the small fire. I did not say. I did not know.

***

I helped Henry in the field.

"Women's work, that," Chutatah said, his men lounging in the shade, smoking rolls of Henry's bright leaf.

But Henry had no woman helping him.

She was a thin, frail creature who held the key to money, to paying off his outstanding debts if not warming his bed at night. A poor import from that northern clime, always with a bonnet outdoors to keep her white skin from tanning in the sun, she kept mainly indoors, inside that pinewood box like she was a gift to this place.

I drew my knife from my belt and went into the rows. I bent and cut the stalks, the heavy, sticky leaves gumming my arms. The sacred plant grew wild in the woods, to be prayed over, its warm body held in the hollow of your mouth, warming your throat before you blew its ghost back into the world.

The English had taken the wild plant and tamed it to their purposes, planting long straight rows of the sticky brown leaf. They cured it by the barrel and shipped back to their island, Virginia burley, to be smoked for a few coppers in the coffeehouses along the Strand. This was whiteman's weed, a bastard plant. Nothing sacred about this tobacco, its sweet smoke hung in the air, meaning nothing.

But cutting it was a chore. The sun riding hot on your back, and your tongue drying in the cave of your mouth no matter how hard you swallowed. The blood starting to run in scratches in your fingers. Insects screamed in the distant trees, and if you stood too quick, you felt dizzy and nearly fainted.

By the end of the afternoon, we had cut the whole field, Henry and me, and we straightened our bent backs, the bones cracking.

We walked his fields towards the slow creek, keeping a coy distance from the other, but our paths destined to cross at the trees ahead. We had all day ahead, wading through the high weeds, the buzzing insects leaping before us. I ran ahead and laughed. He smiled and walked toward me, but I retreated, smiling as well.

"This is all mine, you know, all you can see down to the water."

"You own the sky as well?" I laughed. "The clouds trespass on your property?"

"Everything you can see."

I closed my eyes. "So, if you close your eyes, it all goes away and you're poor?"

"I have papers to prove it."

"Can you hold it in your two hands?" I threw a fistful of torn grass in his face. "If I walk across your field, am I yours as well?"

I walked backwards through the field, retreating before his slow advance. The tall grasses brushed the palms of my hands, and the heels of my bare feet. A strange light in his eyes and a gathering smile.

"Skitty," he said softly, the first time he had used my name since our arrival.

We weren't smiling now, but still walking. We moved out of the sun and into the shade, beneath a grove by the creek, the splash of water breaking over a rock somewhere. I led him on, or he stalked me, like Cat Walker with her namesake panther walking so slowly back to town, keeping eye contact with the squinting golden eyes that measured your fear, your pounding heartbeat, as you resisted the instinct to break and run, when the beast would be on your back in a space between heartbeats, the sharp teeth in your neck. To run is to die.

I backed myself against a tree, my hands flat against the rough bark, a sycamore waving branches overhead, and let Henry, my husband, come to me. His stubbled face rough against mine, his breath warm on my skin, his teeth nipping at my lips. I closed my eyes, felt myself sinking, sliding down to the roots, drawing my man like a blanket over me, clawing at the back of his shirt until I could trace the ribs of his fine chest.

I had thought he had forgotten me, what he remembered from his short stay at Tomotley. It was if he had never left. We would never be parted now.

I heard the beating of his heart, my head on his chest as he stared at the Virginia sky. The house hazy in the distance, the clouds piling higher than the tallest pines.

His hand brushing through my tangled hair. I listened to the words deep inside him. I still did not have all his words, but I understood the meaning, the meanness of his fortune.

"I had to surrender the shirt off my back to meet the bailiff's demands. Left me a thin coat that I pulled close by the lapels to cover my naked chest. Crossing London Bridge on a dark night, with only my hand covering my forehead, having lost my hat and my last periwig, no sword in my scabbard, only a stick I had stuffed there, hoping no gentleman would look in my direction, look down on my pitiful affairs. A clodhopper from the colonies, just flapping boots, no buckle shoes, on the cobblestones."

He was growing hot to my touch now, the anger rising from his core.

"Tell Chutatah he has the wrong man. I don't have the time now to go sailing off to England again, nor the money. Virginia is where I've made my stand, where I've invested. Eleanor and I mean to start a family, once she's feeling more herself."

Henry had planted his seed in Virginia, clodhopping around the black mud of his fields. But by the looks of my skinny rival, whatever seed he planted each night was falling into a most unforgiving and dry dirt. That white girl, like trying to grow a garden in a snowfall, so white, but so cold, you could tell. When he had the rich fields of me to himself in the Overhills, my bounty opens to him. He had proved himself a plowman before, hoisting himself into my loins, as I manhandled him, my legs around his waist, our sweat and other juices mingling as we bucked against the cold nights in the Overhills.

"If you won't go back for Chutatah, for me, then go for your son," I said.

Henry had a quizzical look, his white brow knitted.

"Your heir, your flesh and blood. You already have a family in the Overhills. You are a father. Do you owe no allegiance to your own son?"

Richard, you should have that strange look in your father's eyes, the same color as yours, his eyes that have never seen your face. You are strong and handsome; I explain to your father. You are a smart boy and quick. Not as big as the others in the town, but you will hold your own. I could see the intelligence in your face, how closely you track the squirrels leaping in the sycamore, the birds dipping across the sky, marveling at it all, rolling the sounds in your gurgling mouth, happy to take in this world.

Henry was dumbfounded, his jaw gone slack, his eyes wide.

"How old? When?"

His mind running through the months, our ballgames and dances, those nights snuggled in the Overhills, then his ill-fated voyage, the close escape from the creditors in London. Men are not good with the months that women know in their blood, but he fumbled through the calculations, "Oh," and then a more knowing or resigned, "Oh." A swell of pride, the cockiness of a man's powerful cock, the seed sprung, then the quick fear, another mouth to feed, a claim on his estate, reduced as it was. How will this son see me? The sire always measured by his prodigy.

"He has your name among the clan. Timberlake. Tlugui Udali, in the People's tongue."

"Does he have a Christian name?"

"Richard," I said. "Ostenaco came home and said that Richard was the name of a king with a bravery as powerful as a lion."

"Richard," he weighed the name in his mouth. "A boy," he said slowly to himself, working a bit of grass between his teeth, pleased with the prospect. "Fancy that."

He stared across the buzzing distance of Virginia, of his small plot of land into the east, and the distant island burned in his mind. He chewed his long stalk of grass and spit the pulped stem from his lips. "Let me talk to Trueheart."

He stood, hoisting his trousers, and stalked off.

**

Henry had no money to finance the trip, but fell in with Mr. Trueheart, his neighbor and a landowner of more means and more acreage. Trueheart had been in the country now for a decade and made a tidy profit from the tobacco that his Negroes were able to cultivate, which he in turn would sell to fragrantly cloud the coffeehouses and cafes of London and Paris.

But the country had taken its toll on a man forever trying to live up to his surname. He had the fevers of summer, coughing up spots of blood into a rag he forever held to his pale lips. Truelove wanted to return to the mother country, wear his tweeds and slicker in the nurturing rains of Cardiff, out of the steamy summers of Virginia, away from the infernal clouds of mosquitos and night vapor that drifted from the fever swamps.

I watched them trudge the lane between Henry's plain house and Mr. True-heart's larger abode. Henry waving his hands, waving, ofttimes walking backwards to hold his audience's attention, while the shorter, stouter Trueheart kept his meas-ured stride, his head slowly nodding, his hands clasped behind his back as he dodged the mud puddles.

It was a negotiation. Barrels of Virginia bright brought one price, but Indians might fetch more interest. London had gone agog before over savage chieftains parading down their muddy lanes, stalking their heralded halls, meeting with His Majesty.

Trueheart would take a fast clipper while Eleanor and our delegation would follow in a slower lumbering brig. If the winds were in our favor, he would make Plymouth before us, sell the tobacco for Timberlake, and finance our clear road to London and an audience with the king, avoiding the discomforts and confusion of the expedition only two years ago.

The men stopped in the lane and clasped their right hands, a sign, a pact. Little did I know that the white men shook hands all the time, gave their words of honor, and then promptly cheated and took their advantage.

                                    ***

Back in the sycamore's shade, Chutatah squatted by the small fire, puffing on a red-embered roll of bright leaf he'd plucked from the field. He blew a ring of smoke.

"He'll go," I said.

"Good." The Citico headman slapped his thighs as he rose, ready now for the voyage.

Good, indeed. I was hopeful. I would be with Henry.

Chutatah kicked his moccasin at the brown flank of Walking Mountain, doz-ing in the crook of the sycamore. "Come on, Big Man, time to move. We have a king to see."

***

Listen, Richard, I had not meant to leave you behind for so long, but I was but a girl, little knowing how high this great world swings, how far this suspended bed of earth can tip off balance. Foolishly, I had sworn that, bound again with Henry, we would never be separated. Together, we would go tour London as the Real People's emissaries, see the king, then return to the Overhills with a new pledge of peace.

I had dreamed of Henry and me living in a timbered house by the rivercane, growing corn and children, your own brothers and sisters. You would walk from the woods, handsome hunter, my son with the buck over your broad shoulder. I would make you corn stews and bean cakes and serve you honeycomb.

Much did I dream, but little did I know. The spider once swam so far to steal the sacred fire. How long would it take to cross an ocean? And what lay ahead on those foreign shores?

Chapter 8

We were sailing for England on the morrow. That last evening, I walked the fields of Virginia, running my hands over the soft heads of the tall grass. Henry stood at the field's edge in the dusk.

"You're still coming, aren't you?" he asked.

"Do you want me to come?"

He was thinking, but I must not rush him. Perhaps he saw you, Richard, in his mind's eye, considered how he must figure you into our future.

"It will be dangerous, but I never wish to be parted from you, dear heart," he pledged, raising his hand in the sultry Virginia air. I took the rough palm of his hand and kissed it and held it to my bosom. He softly squeezed my small breast. I thought my heart would burst.

He left me in the field and went to make his final preparations.

I felt that warm place where his palm had been. I went over his words in my mind, reading into his face, his eyes, what he would say if he spoke better Tsalagi.

I stood not far from the tree where Henry had pinned me, and we had renewed our lovemaking. Something stirred in the sedge.

I stooped and watched the grasses wave, then thrust my hand quicker than what I caught: A snake writhing. The way she fought and tried to bite, I knew she was female. I held her behind the head and cradled the long body, soft to the touch, scales gleaming in the light. Her coils whipped and wrapped about my forearm, but I slipped Sister Snake into my gathering bag amid the field greens I'd picked. Walking to our camp, I could feel her slender muscles thrusting against my hip.

The Great King would need a gift from this world. Henry said serpents were a rarity in that kingdom. Some holy man who crossed himself with the sign of the Christ had exiled the venomous reptiles from their rocky shores. Long ago, another

saint named George like the king had slain a dragon, cousin of Uk'tena and grandfather of all snakes. The creature had gone about feasting on men, as a field snake
on a nest of mice.

On the wharf, as the ship slowly rose and fell with the coming tide, ready to be
loaded with Truelove and Timberlake's best Virginia bright, I found a hogshead
with a knothole. I opened my gathering bag and let the little snake find her escape
inside, the soft scales slowly sliding into the nest of warm leaf.

I aimed to bring a baby Uk'tena with me over the waters, summoning the
monster's crystal to shine light on my deeds, wherever my path took me in England.

***

But other passengers were coming who I had not counted on.

Eleanor arrived on the wharf the next morning, a dark cloak and hood shading
her pale face against the pleasant Virginia sun. I supposed she would make a scene
of heartfelt farewell to the man she claimed as husband. Then I saw her ordering
the sailors and crew to take care with the trunks and satchels being stored onboard.

"She's going, too?" I stormed at Henry.

"She's homesick. She wants to see her mother."

Eleanor and I glared at each other as cargo was loaded, neither one of us wanting to be the first nor the last to board the ship, wondering who Timberlake would
escort on his strong arm. Turns out neither. Henry was too busy making sure the
hogsheads of bright leaf were stored in due order. Eleanor raised her skirts to watch
her pointed shoes mount the slick planks. I hopped aboard in my deerskin boots.

Walking Mountain set one of his moccasins on the gangplank and tested the
boards with his weight. The board bounced and groaned and nearly cracked. He
shook his head.

"Come aboard," the captain cried. "The tides are calling us." The Revenge,
Trueheart's clipper, was growing smaller already, the white sails like clouds on the
salted horizon.

But Chutatah and our delegation hesitated. In Tomotley, it takes two seasons
to fell a girdled poplar tree, then fires to burn and hollow out the inside, scraping

out the ash with a stone ax and later trade bought steel, before a man can set foot inside, sit down, and float the river to the next town. The Mountain had ridden in stout dugout canoes, but never a ship so large. This was the largest contraption manmade other than the National Councilhouse at Chota that he had witnessed in his Tsalagi life. This was magic he did not trust.

"We have not time for this. We must go. Now," the captain commanded.

Chutatah and the rest crept up the gangplank, but Walking Mountain refused. I had never seen him go into the winter house, preferring the open of the summer shelter, even in winter's worst, wrapping himself in a buffalo hide, turning into a mound of white. "No holes, no dens, no graves." He feared closed darkness, even in a warm house.

I went down and led the big man up by the hand. He swayed uneasily on his large feet. But then when we went to the hold and the steps leading down, he shook his head once more and would not budge. He was scared to go below decks.

"The yoneg will think you're weak, scared like a little girl," I hissed and pulled, but he balked, all seven stone of him.

"Tla yonah, tla yoneg." He shook his addled pate.

"What's he saying?" Henry asked.

"He believes there are bears down there."

"Scared of the dark, is he?" the captain cried, motioning his crew forward. "My boys will make him go down."

"Leave him be." Henry raised his hand, understanding firsthand how even the biggest man may fear bruins.

The Mountain turned and fled down the gangway, the planks bending with each heavy step of his moccasins, thumping across the wharf and into the canebrake at the river's mouth.

The canebrake kept waving from his passage, like a great beast cutting through the thick stalks. Then the cane was not just waving but walking across the wharf, cane coming board. The long stalks collapsed on the deck. The Mountain was underneath a sheaf gathered in his mighty arms. He began to build an arbor, lashing together reeds into a roof at the foremast to shade him from sun and keep him dry from storm.

"I can't have this disorder on my deck," the captain complained. "Is the savage to stay above decks the whole way to Bristol?"

"Who's paying the passage?" Henry demanded.

The cranky seadog quit his barking, retreating to his wheel with dark looks thrown our way.

***

The sun was setting, burning into the horizon over the land. I stood watching Virginia recede in the distance. Ahead, nothing but endless water. Beneath his makeshift shelter, Walking Mountain kept watch, muttering formulas in Tsalagi against monsters, storms, and Death.

Henry assured us that this craft was not easily capsized if the sailors stayed sober, God willing, and no great storm overtook them, if … and then his voice trailed off. Henry was a soldier and not a sailor, having once under his command that terrible canoe and his two-week river cruise down the rapids, nearly drowning himself, Sumter, and M'Cormick on the way to Tomotley.

We were but cargo and a bother to the crew who muttered darkly about women aboard their ship they talk of as female. The sailors eyed me, trying to decide if I was the fairer sex of what they only knew of as a savage race. Half the crew were sodomites, catamites below the decks, coming up hoisting their trousers, taking their quick pleasures on the hogshead of tobacco. Fond of females, but dirty-faced cabin boys would do in a pinch. As a precaution, beneath the folds of my trade blanket, my thumb tested the keen edge of the flaying knife Cat Walker gave me.

***

The only exercise was to walk about the decks, leaning into the wind and spray heading toward the prow, then leaning against the squall that shoved you aft. The deck that moved not just side to side, but up and down, pitch and yaw, but you could pace the ship bow to stern once you found your balance.

I went the same direction that we dance around the fire, keeping my left hand and my heart toward the flames. The yoneg are different in their natural direction, following their right hand, like the sweep of the clocks they keep and obey.

I passed by Lieut. and Mrs. Timberlake. Eleanor pulled Henry's arm harder when we passed, and poor man, he dared not turn his head in my direction. We resolved not to speak to the other, let alone acknowledge that Other's existence. Eleanor no longer existed, that white wraith in my mind. We had swept each other clear out, like a pile of ash or bones or dirt, with a new broom. Begone, you blight on my tidy affairs.

At the bottom of the steps, I went to the corner where we were allowed to make our damp camp. Huddled in blankets, Chututah puffed at his pipe, softly singing the formulas that would keep us healthy. At least the sweet smoke kept away the fetid airs, the smell of vomit and shit and piss.

Henry retired to the fore, behind a curtain hung to hide his Eleanor, his dainty wife.

If I listened, I could hear what she said, what she whispered, and sometimes shouted over the wind and waves. What were you thinking with that red slut, that savage bitch? Why did you bring her along?

I winced in my mind's eye to see her naked, stripped of her fine gowns and her necklaces and her prim, proper look. She had been with my Henry for two winters and she gave no sign of children. I could see them in my mind's eye, two white sticks, like herons trying to mate over a river, their cold eyes, and sharp beaks, their necks intertwined. They were white and cold where Henry and I were all ash and black. We had sweat in the dark of the winter house, that first time my fingers found his manly parts, coaxed him under the bearskin while snowflakes fell through the smoke hole and kissed my upturned face.

We have been apart, and I have missed his touch, his warm length against mine. I have missed him inside me, completing me, stirring with our juices the possibility of a new child.

I could have told Eleanor a thing or two, how to grab and hold a man's attention is no great curiosity for a woman of any race or people. From what I've seen, we are all the same between our legs and in our hearts.

If the world is suspended like a swinging bed, then a small ship tossed on the water is a topsy-turvy world to itself. With the sea swings of the boat, I couldn't help imagining Henry and myself setting out each night on our warm journey, rocking and swaying and sweating together in the joys, the cries that carry forward.

***

Even with winds and currents favorable, progress was slow, the voyage interminable. Trueheart was leagues ahead in the Revenge, while we lumbered along in the ill-named Raven. We certainly weren't flying along. Days on end, we climbed and fell down the great waves. Rain lashed anyone who dared go above decks. Only the Mountain braved the elements.

In the bowels of the ship came creaks and thumps. Great fish bumped into our great dugout. Chutatah muttered that there are creatures beyond our ken. The Giant Leach that lives in the Valley Towns, a monster as big as the river itself that once swallowed a canoe and two men whole and dragged them under the waters.

"Those are stories you tell children," I said brusquely.

"Hah, girl. We don't know what monsters we meet ahead," the old man shook his head.

The Mountain may have been right to fear the darkness below decks. The small serpent I had smuggled into the bright leaf was coiled somewhere unseen, but soon the ague and fevers began to claim our crew and passengers.

"Must be a Ravenmocker among us," Chutatah said. "And we have no spells to resist."

These witches were said to take the shape of an elderly crone, eyes marbled and unseeing, teeth long lost, hair gray. But at night, they will shed their wrinkled masks and fly overhead. They caw like ravens as they dive on dark wings. Invisible, they wrestle the sick warrior, the troubled wife to the ground, snatch the breath and stop the beating of the heart. They are gone with the strange last rattle of breath rising out of the open mouth, the eyes clouding over. The family finds the victim at daylight, begin to wail their loss, and beat their breasts.

At first, I feared that Eleanor was a Ravenmocker, striding the decks with her black tweeds, glaring balefully in my direction. I kept saying formulas to ward off her evil eye and her curses that I could feel heaped on my head.

We passed one other on deck, and her face was green. A rush to the railing and her head disappeared. I could hear a delicate retching. The hood of her cloak over her head, she resurfaced and turned toward me, her fingers wiping her lips.

What Henry saw in this woman I'll never know, other than her whiteness, cold as the moon through the winter trees. Eleanor was the only daughter of Peter Bineal, a draper in St. Martins. Henry had shaken the pater's hand, arranging for Eleanor's hand in matrimony, but mainly hopeful that more money would come with their compact.

Precious little in the way of blessing, miserly too with the dowry, the furniture and a few gold coins the disapproving father sent with the couple to Virginia, but the father's last will and testament stated she could only collect her inheritance in person.

In your sleep, dreams shifted uneasily and there was the scampering.

We were not alone in our appetites on board, by the nibbled corners of dried biscuits and gnawed globes of the small apples. Mice and likely larger vermin had made the passage with us. Something had started to gnaw on the rawhide stitches of my moccasin. I had to mend it best I could, finding twines in the hold, unraveling a few threads, and rolling them between my palms to twist into a serviceable cordage.

I tried to find the hogshead of tobacco with the corn snake again, the one I had marked with my design, a double chevron, but I could not discover where the slaves had packed it, casks stacked as ballast in the darkness, the remainder of Timberlake's tobacco and treasure.

***

Tobacco was not the only trade on those seas.

One day, we saw a lumbering craft making slow headway against the currents, hung low in the water. Grim-faced men stand on the decks but do not return our waved greetings, our halloes across the brine. Over the wind, you could almost hear cries that came from below decks.

"Slavers." The captain spat over the rail.

He had sailed a slave ship once as a mate, and once was enough to turn the stomach of any Christian: How they opened the hatches and the first direct daylight spotlighting white eyes raised and blinking, dozens, perhaps a hundred souls. "Like looking into the pit of hell." He grimaced.

Once ashore, they would hoist the chains, pulling them out of the hold like so much fish, and what was wasted or dead, they dumped overboard. The rest would file away, falling to their weak knees in the surf. Their new owners had camps on the islands, to fatten them up from the hard crossing. Human goods marched in rattling chains to auction at the Charles Towne market.

Those faces had once been ours.

Among the war titles that men aimed for in the Overhills were Mankiller, Raven, and Slavecatcher. While the white traders vied for more deerskin and buffalo hide and beaver pelt, they wanted live flesh as well. For a living captive, bound in rawhide, a woman or a child, they would pay more than a flayed skin.

Men eager to buy guns and horses would set off on raids north and south, hunting the Seneca and the Chickasaw. Raiding parties filed out of the woods with loud whoops. Captives lashed by their necks to long poles on which we slung other bounty, blankets and other hides, dead at least, to be traded for what the Real People lacked back home.

But the captives would not stay put. Sold to white settlers aiming to cut down whole forests and plant new plantations, the Indians would melt into the woods. They had no aptitude for hard work, stubborn as the mules, offspring of horses and asses, not even flinching at the lash of a whip on their bare red backs.

This new land demanded new labor. The trade for red slaves went by the wayside.

The yoneg sent for Africa to bring black bodies, thousands of strong backs to be broken and flayed with their bullwhips. When those bodies fell, when the black skin melted into mud, showing only white bones, those white teeth, the masters would send for more black bodies, more strong backs to build their cities, work their plantations, increase their wealth.

Sullen women, too, their souls broken, manned the kitchens and cookfires, tended the wash and gardens, changed diapers of babies, and truth be told, serviced their masters in the evenings when lust saw fit, while their men marched into the hot fields, their bent shoulders licked by the lash of the overseers' constant whips. They broke their backs day after hot day, year after year.

What to do with the Red Man in the woods who would not work to the yoneg's satisfaction? When cornered, they would not cower. Indians bite. Thus, they were vermin to be cleared like the land itself.

Dead Indians, Live Negroes, Rich Yoneg.

***

One day, the clouds scudding along, the deck heaving beneath my deerskin boots, a wild-eyed Henry grabbed my wrist. It was the first time he had touched me since our voyage began.

"It's Eleanor. She's not eating."

I pulled away, folded my arms across my breasts. "She's your wife."

"Help her if you can," Henry entreated me.

The ship's surgeon was climbing from the hold, like a blinking woodchuck from his burrow into the bright sun. "We've tried all we know. She's in the Lord's hands." The doctor shook his head over a pewter dish covered with a linen. I stopped his hand and lifted the bloody cloth. The fat leeches swam in a fine red froth, even they were seasick and vomiting their dinner.

I went down the shadowed stairs.

"Siyo," I whispered. "It's me," I said. My eyes were slow to adjust to the dimness.

She was little more than a raft of bones collapsed in the corner, more ghost than flesh and blood.

"You!" she hissed and tried to get away but was too weak.

They had let too much of her blood. She wasn't strong enough to surrender any of that life coursing inside. She needed all the spit and piss, shit and blood, phlegm, and humors to keep from becoming a dried husk.

I checked between her legs, even as she tried to kick me away. She had not cleaned herself and she smelled bad, sweat and piss, but none of a woman's expected blood.

"When came your last time?"

She grabbed my wrist, and her grip was shockingly strong like the death grip of a drowning man who won't let you go, seeking to pull you beneath the water. "You can't tell a soul, especially him."

"He doesn't know?"

"No. And he mustn't. We're too far along, me and the child and the ship now."

So, the seasickness had not been just due to rough waves, but the quickening within her.

My hand in the space between us, the new distance, the drops of water running from the nursing rag in my hand, tracing the curve of my wrist. I daubed her hot forehead, but she turned her face from me and toward the bulwark. She suddenly seemed prettier, a fierce light in her once milky eyes.

"I believe with all my heart it will be a boy in due time. And he will be English, not Virginian, by Christ. I swore God I could not bear a child in that godforsaken place. His firstborn must make England, grow up good and proper, safe at least."

She had determined this, willed it. Now at last I understood Eleanor and what Henry hadn't seen in her. Mrs. Timberlake would be a terror and the undoing of any husband who stood in her way when she stamped her small foot and ordered an avenue of her desires to magically appear.

She had sworn me to secrecy like a sister, instead of the rivals we were.

I wished I had packed a larger medicine bag. I had only a handful of the more useful plants, feverfew, sassafras root, gravel root, yellow root, to take care of most complaints and discomforts. For more serious sickness, I would have needed seven different plants and the right words to complement their powers.

While I tended with my women's medicine to Eleanor below decks, the Mountain was melting away from the relentless sun and salt spray over the bow. The temporary wickiup, the brush shelter he had lashed from rivercane was leaking badly. The storms had turned the shelter into little more than a skeleton. The Mountain shivered continually.

I brought him broth and crumbled biscuits, at least what the white worms and mold had not eaten below. There was no meat, no corn cakes. I fed him the white drink, which may or may not have been a mistake. I squatted beside him, beneath the dripping leaves of the cane, our last vestige of Virginia, against the heave of the great canoe, like riding through rapids, and the sea never stopped slapping white froth against our bows.

"You are the greatest ballplayer to take the field of Little War. I remember the game when you ran through ten Tanasse men, carrying the ball high in your stick. You thundered down the field, raising dust, like a buffalo charging through a herd of doe. No one could stop you. A man named Wolf ran at you, but you swept him aside with the crack of your stick. The one named Big Bear stood in your way and yelled his war cry, and you lowered your hard head and butted him down. Your bare foot smashed his face into the bloody dirt and still you ran for the goal. The nation cheering your name. Listen, we saw you win that day for Tomotley's great glory."

"Hunh." The Mountain slumped and drips of water fell from his nose.

The brain-addled warrior shook his dented head where the bullet at Echotoe had carved an ugly tattoo, a white worm burrowing through his temple. They say he came back to life on killing field with a Shawano sawing off half his scalp. The Mountain shook, roaring out of Death's swirling darkness, and sent his would-be murderer into the dark lands, twisting the man's small head askew on his shoulders until the neck snapped.

At night as the waves rocked us and kept us from any gentle sleep, you could hear the Mountain chanting above decks, a death song, at war with the elements.

By day, we sometimes caught sight of the great backs of beasts breaking the waves, flowing spumes into the salted air. Flocks of birds followed us, alighting from ship to ship and sometimes they lit in the rigging overhead, until the angry sailors came out, shouting and climbing like crazed squirrels in the netting. A marine aimed a musket, and we had a few scrawny pigeons that night to eat.

One by one, the crew grew smaller, more wraiths shivering in the corners of the hold, hooded in their thin blankets, the lights of their eyes grown milky. Each week, more white shrouds were sewn and borne above decks to the rail, delivered to the endless waves with a prayer and a small splash.

Landfall was still a fortnight away, the sailors said. We saw more white birds now, flocks wheeling and screeching above our masts. A good sign, or at least the sailors believed, their eyes scanning toward the East beyond the rising sun, to where they would land. Civilization, they called it, England, Home.

I kept watch for columns of smoke, the belching of a great fire on a distant isle, what I imagined my father had seen, riding in the prow of the ship, squinting his eyes.

It had been weeks since I've gone to water, cleansed myself in a cold river. Here we were in a waste of water, salted and useless and cold enough to sweep away any luckless soul overboard.

***

"We would take a barque named Raven, no good omen there," Eleanor complained.

"Raven is smart," I said.

"The raven is untrustworthy. When Noah released the black bird, he never returned with any sign of land. Only a white dove, the second I believe, according to scripture."

I should have told her that Ravens are tricksters, liable to fly upside down, laughing as they go. Better the buzzard that beat out the shape of the drying mountains with his wings.

So, Noah sent out white birds, Eleanor said. Doves, first one, then another, until the dove flew back with a sprig of olive tree.

Eleanor sat up for a spell, able to take broth from my spoon, crumbles of stale biscuit. I could swear there was color beyond the pallor, almost a blush of spring in her wintry visage.

We argued over the creation of the world. I told the stories that my father and grandmother gave me by the fire.

"The world is a great bed suspended by swinging ropes from the four directions swinging to and fro, making men seek a better balance."

"Suspended over a lake of fire. The wicked will fall off into their everlasting perdition."

"No, if you follow the right path, men and women keep the world righted, not awry."

"Devilish superstition. Bless your heathen heart, you've never heard the Word of the Lord."

Eleanor tried to tell me how the English God created the first people, that the woman had been taken as a rib from the man naked on the ground as he slept. That's only a story, not mine. I would say that Harry was a bone that had been broken and taken from me, like my arm, or my own eyes. I was bereft.

In Eleanor's telling, woman had betrayed the man giving him a forbidden fruit, and the Spirit banished them from the Garden into a harsh world of briars and thickets, which sounded to me like a story only a man, and never a mother, would tell as the truth.

"I've heard a different tale," I said. "Listen, this is what my grandmother told me when I was a girl."

The Spirit made the first man, Kanati the hunter, who grew quickly bored and started to kill too many of the deer. So, the Spirit caused him to sleep one day and planted a seed in his dream and out of his chest grew a tall plant. When he awoke, he could see a fair maiden seated at the plant waving overhead. He helped her down. She was Selu and she took the seeds of the plant that was corn.

"You think they lived happily ever after?" Eleanor laughed bitterly.

"No, they fought as only men and women do, the war between us when we aren't making love. The woman ran off one day, and the man gave chase, but could not catch her. The man prayed to the Spirit for help, and so the Spirit stopped the forward flight of the woman by sowing the wild heart-shaped strawberries in her path. The man at last caught his wife, her mouth red and her teeth sweet with the berry."

"Ha, a story for children and weak-minded women!"

Eleanor would have none of it, preferring her tales of destruction, how humans needed to be wiped off the earth, sent down below to roast in fires of her own imagination. She was stubborn and dour in spirit. Perhaps sensing her own weakness, she desired to see others cut down to size, bloodied, broken. Her tongue flicking over the dry lips as if she could taste blood and not her own in the salted air.

Cat Walker's story made better sense. Man and woman must work together. Food is a rare gift, and the path is difficult, but this world provides.

***

With no one to walk with, his white wife growing paler below decks, Henry paced the decks like a ghost. We passed each other in our rounds, and then he came and took my arm silently.

We made our rounds, the light falling at our backs and then at our faces as we retraced our usual path on the small deck. Arm in arm, he was uncertain of resuming our conversation from the Overhills. He cloaked me against the spray or the faint rain, me feeling the muscle in his upper arm. He was getting skinnier himself.

The seadog assigned the night watch at the foredeck had his head folded on his arms, and we were alone with the stars. We stopped against the mast and turned to each other, let the waves and the ship's rocking speed our own coming together. My cries were carried off with the slap of the waves against the bulwarks. I could lick the taste from his lips, his cheek, the soft whorl of his ear. He was flesh to me then.

"Oh God, what if she dies? What will I do?"

I stop his complaints with my own mouth pressed tight against his.

***

A week before we made land, we buried the Mountain at sea.

He had been nodding sadly, sitting under his arbor for days, and one night his faint song was no more. Chutatah crouched and looked beneath the limp leaves. He stood and began to wail out a death song for his friend.

The crew refused to touch the body, terrified of some contagion. They poked at our Mountain with long boat hooks and pulled a canvas over him, then stitched the edges into a tight cocoon. The men could not lift him, so they rigged a rope and a pulley from the spar of the mast. It took five sailors to hoist the load into the air and swing it over the rail. The captain sawed at the rope with a dull knife until the last hemp snapped and Walking Mountain, the best Ballplayer of Citico, fell into the waters with a great splash.

"Listen. Where the black war clubs shall be moving about like ball sticks in the game, there his soul shall be. Instantly shall his soul be going about in peace,"

Chutatah sang the old chant for the best ball players before they took the bloody field.

One by one, I carried the rocks that were ballast and dropped them over the railing. A Tsalagi warrior was deserving of a proper burial, his passing on the trail marked with a cairn of rocks. I would leave a trail on the seabed, the cobbles from Williamsburg, floating down in the Atlantic where Walking Mountain lay in a white shroud.

***

Eleanor nearly made it home. We had only a few conversations where she had her senses about her. She was shrinking fast, her flesh falling into the caves of her skull, sunken into her shroud. Fever had overtaken our vessel. A dark cloud seemed to follow us, and each day out brought fewer souls up on deck to take the light. Down below, more had sunk into the corners of the hold, shivering denizens.

Before the ague took her, when I could still follow her words, she had clutched my wrist, halting my hand daubing her forehead with a damp rag.

"You win."

"Hush, girl, hush," I said, repeating the words she kept singing to herself in her fever.

"No, no. You win."

"This is no game, girl."

"Take good care of Henry. He's such a fool, you know."

"Hush, now, don't talk foolishness."

"No, you listen. You know it's true. Don't let him lie to himself." Her weak hands clawing at my wrist, frantic but not enough to hang on.

Her last breath came with a shudder and a long last rattle, and then did not return. The light slowly drained from her eyes, leaving only a last dead glint. I pressed her eyelids shut with my wetted thumb, blessing her passage. I took the last clean water and washed her limbs. She was thin as a girl with only a little flesh in her hips, and her small breasts with the pink nipples. I covered her nakedness, wrapped her in the white sheets, the last linen she had brought.

I took the wooden slop pail from beneath her pallet, its bloody issue. I could divine the semblance of what might have been, but only started to knit together, the life lost before it fully arrived, not quite made for this world. What pulls at any woman's heart, what I would never forget seeing, I dashed it overboard.

I was singing to myself, not a victory chant or a lamentation, but the lullaby that Eleanor had whispered to me. "Hush little babe, don't you cry."

Chapter 9

Bristol, England, 1764

Ostenaco had sung his great war chant coming into the harbor at Portsmouth, but when we came ashore at Bristol, Henry was not singing. He was sobbing, his nose running, tears he kept wiping from his angry face. His wife was laced in a shroud at our feet, as the oars splashed us in.

Eleanor had her wish not to be buried in the sea, in the water that had drowned the human race in scripture, that Word of the Lord she so feared. She was laid to her rest in a church graveyard, hallowed earth, dry land. Henry signed the proper papers at the local parish hall, paid the gravediggers, and then commissioned a small stone to be engraved. He planned to return to her grave when our delegation to London had been accomplished before returning to Virginia, then I hoped on home to the Overhills.

Henry was short one wife now, and their child was lost. I tried to reassure him that at least in the Overhills, he would see you, Richard, our son.

***

We found Mr. Trueheart's ship anchored already, waiting our arrival for the past fortnight. The Revenge had caught the brunt of those storms we had merely skirted. Their mast had splintered, the hold had taken on water, and that they had escaped with their lives the sailors swore was a miracle. The vessel had limped into Bristol and the barrels of Virginia Bright that Henry and Trueheart had banked on were found to have taken on water, most of the golden leaf wilted and ruined by the salt water.

Mr. Trueheart had seen his own son take ill and perish. The body had gone to rest in the waves and the poor man had only his lad's few effects, a woolsey cap, a lace handkerchief embroidered with his initials, a buckeye nut the boy had carried in his pocket for luck.

"I'm so sorry for your loss." Timberlake held his hat in his hands and stretched its brim as he sought to comfort his partner.

"You've lost a wife. I've lost a son. We've lost half our cargo," Truelove said. "We cannot afford to lose any more, Mr. Timberlake."

He would have said more but began a coughing jag and waved away our useless condolences.

We made the slow journey inland, the carriages creaking up the muddy thoroughfare toward the capital city. Trueheart emptied his silk purses, signing accounts, bills of lathing, the slow financing that drains a self-made man's small fortune. The rheumy-eyed and haggard Trueheart took to his bed in cheap rooms he'd leased for us in Long's Court, Leicester Fields.

***

I helped Henry forget Eleanor those long evenings, cuddled together. We lay in the small bed, my heart beating against his, skin to skin, limbs entwined. I had dreamed of his pelt against my skin for two winters now, and at last I was warm, slick with sweat and the juices, slaps and signs and moans and the little cry he gave out at the last.

"Brave bear killer." I traced his fine pelt on his bare chest.

"I hate bears," Henry said.

I had to laugh, recalling his misadventures with beasts in his canoe trip down river to Tomotley. "Bears are just people with claws. You have to say the right words when you kill a deer, lest you will be visited with rheumatisms. Bears are the clan who used to be people, but liked the wild so long, the hair covered their bodies, and their teeth and claws grew long."

"The devils."

"It's a good story. We'll tell little Richard, when we get home, and his little brothers and sisters to follow."

"But we have to get clear of this City, these snooty people, damned England," Henry said, staring at a water stain on our dim ceiling, below the sloped leaking roof, the hovering miasma of fouled clouds. Somewhere overhead, the stars that shone on the Overhills were winking at us, the spirits of my ancestors.

***

In the mornings that blared through the fogged windows and the cracked glass of the panes of our upstairs flat, Henry made his ablutions in a dented tin bowl. I sat in the bed and watched. He decked himself out in his uniform, the vest and breeches, the great red coat with the buttons and sashes and braids of regimental lieutenant of the Virginia 2nd. For good medicine, I tucked into the slit of his breast pocket an eagle feather, a reminder of his home with the Real People.

He was ready to call upon Lord Halifax and the Board of Trade, who oversaw the coin that flowed into the City.

We waited in the tight quarters for word of Henry's success.

Chutatah and his men squatted on their haunches, playing mumbly-peg with their knives, chopping up the floor until the landlady came in and cried at the damage done, and threatened to toss us out.

They played for the bright beads and medals with the likeness of the White King on their face, trinkets they would wear on their necks to catch this feeble English sun. Chutatah and Standing Deer and Stalking Turkey grunting and grabbing as the blade stuck in the floorboards. A Tsalagi man would gamble away his best gun, or even his wife. Who could run the fastest, swim the farthest, reach the goal with the stickball first, who could hit a tree with a bullet or an arrow. Life is short, the odds are long. Why not gamble the great gift? Never be afraid to bet all or lose all. Life is that generous.

I watched other sport out the begrimed glass of these lodgings, all of England it seemed, parading down our lane. Children with their dirty red cheeks begging coins from passersby, judging their wealth by the cut of their coats, the ribbons of their bonnets. Scowling women sweeping by the urchins, gentlemen swinging their canes at the urchins, but I saw a small one reach a quick hand into a pocket and grab a coin as the man cursed the orphanage of this open street. "Back, back you impious imps." Soldiers on horses, bailiffs with their cudgels, men in black coats and dour faces, lawyers likely or their priests. No one smiles lest they be beset by beggars, guarding their own thoughts in their scowling faces. Louts staggering out from taverns, tipsy on their feet, weaving first one way and then bouncing off the bricks of the walls, or women leaning there, calling out to the gentlemen, raising a skirt to show the turn of their fat ankles, as if that would be the measure of what pleasures to be had if they opened their legs wide to a paying customer. I saw supposed gentlemen counting out coin in their trembling palm or folding a particular note, an assignation for later, the supposed ladies folding the loot into their bosoms.

Watching from above, through a dirty glass, I saw everyone and everything in our street. Seeing them, I imagined I could smell the yoneg tang. Evidently, no one in London ever went to water, or scarcely bothered to scrub the soot from their greasy hair, tucked beneath hats and bonnets, caps and scratchy wigs, the odors of themselves disguised with perfumes and scents, but always the underlying trace of fear and sweat and poverty from under their arms and between their legs. They were human like us but lived like brutes in these close quarters.

Then I saw my husband, my handsome Henry, turn the corner, his hat pulled down over his haggard face, a great rent in the shoulder of his regimental coat. Defeated, a man in retreat, he stopped only when a rain of shit fell in his path from a chamber pot tossed out a top window across the way. "Hey," he cried upward, and the woman there laughed and made a rude gesture. I caught her eye, and I would have pecked it out if I could have flown across the way like a bird.

Up the stairs, his face flushed, he could scarcely catch his breath. "The perfidy, the outrage, they treat me like a clod. Throw me out into the street, they put their hands on an army officer."

"Troubles, Timberlake?" Chutatah cupped his half-ear, pretending to listen.

"There are reports of Chutatah down at Vauxhall, dancing and singing for the mob in motley feathers and warpaint."

"I have not left this room," the chief said. "We are all here. Unless it was a shapeshifter, or a night rider."

"Maybe another Ravenmocker," said Stalking Turkey.

"Damn your superstitions. Someone has the ear of Halifax, he's spilled a bad word against me. Bringing up all the debts incurred from Ostenaco and the riots he stirred two years ago."

"We cause no trouble. We sit in this room all day. We would like to stretch our legs, but stay inside," Chutatah protested. "Are we guests of this nation or its prisoners?"

"No, no one leaves. You hear me? No one." Henry's voice rose. He turned to me. "Make them understand. English. No Tsalagi."

But should these people commence a war and scalp every encroacher to revenge the ill treatment they received while coming in a peaceable manner to seek redress before they had recourse to arms, let the public judge who must answer it: I must, however, lay great part of the blame on certain parties, who possessing the ear of Lord Halifax, made such an unfavorable report of me, that either his Lordship, believed, or pretended to believe them imposters, or Indians brought over for a shew.

Timberlake

During that first trip with my father, the Cherokee were like magpies, Timberlake said, their eager eyes caught by any shiny trinket. Ostenaco, Cunne Shote, even Woyi, he had feted them to sherry and port, meat pies, great feasts, attentions of the masses and high lords and ladies. Shopping along Savoy Row, the French tailors who cut them gentleman's suits. Medals and beads, spectacles, ribbons. The shillings flew from his purse. He was bleeding gold and silver along London's fetid streets.

Henry signed for all the expenses, anticipating that the Royal Treasury would reimburse his investment in peace and diplomacy for the good of the realm. Until he learned how penny-pinching were the Scots who minded the Chancellery and kept the king's accounts. His Majesty did not grow wealthy by paying his common debtors.

Two years after the first fiasco, creditors, once they learned Timberlake was back in town, surfaced with their liens and letters, demanding payment with interest.

The last of the Virginia Bright purse emptied quickly, he was obliged to part with some plates and linens from poor Eleanor's hope chest, even a dress or two (though I kept one of her gowns for myself, the proper uniform to pass as a lady in the streets of London and even the royal courts.)

Henry would have been rich, if he had only bowed to temptations, collected a half-penny from each gawker, each turned head from the walkways and alleys, the armies of small children and loose women who followed in the wake of our peace part. Chutatah at the head, merely nodding at their appreciation, his warriors casting strange sharp looks, their hands on the hilts of knives, clutching their war clubs and tomahawks, their moccasins treading the cobblestones, and sidestepping the steaming horsepats.

We found ourselves in the back room of a small tavern, the Star and Garter, where men sloshed tankards and yelled loudly, while a dwarf kept making the rounds, pulling at sleeves, collecting coin, and ugly barmaids kept drawing more beers for the crowd.

On a small, raised platform, the spectacle to be performed made its entrance. A motley of dingy feathers likely collected from the molt of the dirty swans that paddled around the public parks and shit on the banks. Loud glass beads looped around his scrawny neck, and his face was painted with ash in the shape of circles and lightning bolts that meant nothing, like a child pretending to be grown-up and wise had doodled a poor idea of a warrior.

Chutatah pulled at my arm. "Who is that fool?"

"They are all fools. They think that imposter is you."

"I am Chutatah the Conqueror. Look upon my savage visage and shiver, you English scum," the imposter kept yelling at the top of his lungs, over the roaring crowd while the dwarf danced off with a grin on his giant head, his short arms piling the coins across a counting table.

"Look at the crowd," Henry shouted into my ear. "Sumter kept saying we could have charged money. I should have listened to the Sergeant. This is exactly what they accused me of."

The imposter's entourage spoke in a gibberish, that wasn't Tsalagi. They pranced about the boards, whooping and slapping their hands against their kicking heels, while one of their number beat out a rhythm on an upturned kettle with a wooden spoon. Heyeh,eh hey, ho. See the Indians, see the savages, they sang.

"I am Chutatah the Great," the imposter shrieked and waved his chicken wing fan.

"You are no Chutatah," I shouted from the back of the room, and the white pasty faces turned in our direction. I could not hold my tongue.

"Here is the Real Chutatah. We are the Real People," I shouted.

"The hell with thee, damn your eyes. Go on with ye," the crowd yelled back.

The English wouldn't know real Cherokee if we ran through the lanes at night and scalped them in their beds. They prefer these mimes and dumbshows, these spectacles and pranks.

"Shouldn't we put a stop to this farce?" I asked Henry.

"All of England is a farce and a dumbshow," said my sad Virginian.

***

At our leased lodging, Trueheart grew fainter, he coughed up blood into his fist, and staggered to sit on the bed. He held his head heavy in his hands and rubbed his tired face, putting only a little more life into his looks. "God save us from this City," he whispered. "We should sail while we have our dignity, our name."

"Bear with us, Mr. Truelove. I will make this right," Henry insisted. "We will win our case. Chutatah will have his say. We will have our money."

***

Henry had been put off by secretaries and undersecretaries and exchequers and the dozen men in periwigs who stood between a proper ambassador of a friendly nation and an audience with His Royal Majesty. He had tried Halifax to no avail, waiting in the antechamber.

He aimed for an audience with Lord Jeffrey Amherst. Perhaps his former commander, Conqueror of Canada could put in a good word for him, at least honor the debts he had incurred on behalf of the Crown, as a field-commissioned lieutenant and would-be diplomat.

Dressed again in his regimental uniform, Timberlake this time took Chutatah in all his regalia, a white stroud hunting shirt, black leggings, a red loin cloth embroidered with conch shell, a silver gorget at this throat and hammered bracelets for his arms. I had slicked his scalplock with pork lard. Chutatah complained there was no bear meat to be had in London. He wore an eagle feather and his face painted Blue like his clan. The British soldier at his best, the Great Chief of Citico, waiting their audience with Amherst.

I came as well, wearing my best outfit, proper clothes for the Councilhouse at Chota or an audience in London with a Lord Commander. I had combed out my long black hair and braided it with red and white ribbons that hung over my left shoulder. I had my best long shirt made of calico from Charleston, a wraparound skirt and leggings made of the best wool stroud sewn with silk ribbons. And my best buckskin boots with their fringed and beaded tops.

But the yoneg made me nervous as well. Secretly, I still had the stone flaying knife that Cat Walker had given me on that last day in the Overhills. I had slid that sharp blade down my legging to rest against my warm thigh. Men carried their blades in open, but a woman should keep secret but close at hand her own means of protection.

We waited in the great cold hall of the stone house. High on a mantel above the sputtering fire hung a great painting.

"Who is that?" I nudged Henry.

"Amherst. The man who will set things right for us," he said hopefully.

Lord Jeffery Amherst, conqueror of Canada, commander of the King's Army in North America. In his picture, Amherst was arrayed in plated armor like a knight of old, thin shoulders bulked with hammered steel, greaves likely on his shins, his helmet a useful prop for his elbow and his hand to thoughtfully stroke his chin. Storm clouds gathered at his head.

I understood my father following a portrait of the king to meet the Dragon-slayer himself across the ocean, but I was not sure why we were seeking an audience with Amherst.

"Do you know this man?"

"Not exactly, though I served under him. He does have some pull with the court and may be able to get us in to see the king," Henry said. "We can hope."

Candlestubs flickered in the wall sconces. Wallpaper darkened by the oily heads of too many supplicants in these uncomfortable Chippendales, cooling their blistered heels in buckled shoes, all at the pleasure of milord. The men in their powdered periwigs and velvet tails came and went, flitting like strange birds in the tangled branches of power. Each came with bound portfolios stuffed with parchments and letters and portfolios and instruments of power, dividing families and nations and lands and kingdoms.

"Lt. Timberlake?"

Henry rose before this new fellow greeting him and smartly saluted. The rank on his collar showed the gold bars of a captain, to accompany a gold sash and a fine sword.

"Captain Carrington. You would do well to remember my name," the officer said.

"Should I know you, sir?"

"No, but I know you. You were at the Long Island signing with the savages. You made that ill-advised trip into their dens, their infestations."

"I found them quite hospitable, sir."

"And what they did to Demere?" the captain said slowly.

"Unfortunate incident," Henry stammered. "Terrible things happen when men wage war, but the Cherokee sued for peace. I have traveled among them. They may have strange customs, but I have found them true to their word."

"Demere was my cousin."

"My condolences. I'm sorry for your loss."

"If you were offering a true apology, you would not accompany these Savages. They don't even speak a decent language, and you would bring them before the court?"

Timberlake was blushing red to his ears, the blood rising to his gorge, his fist tightening on the handle of his sword. I, without thinking, put my hand on his, staying any rash answer.

"I see you brought one of the Harpies themselves. My God, what those women were capable of." The man glared at us.

"I would watch your tongue, sir." Timberlake was trembling with rage. "You need not insult my companions."

"I would watch your head. Wild animals will eat you alive when you least expect it.

Good day, lieutenant." Carrington turned smartly on his heel.

Henry took his seat again.

"You know that fellow?" Chutatah asked, cupping his deaf half ear.

"No, but he knew Demere. He acted as if what happened to that poor man was my fault."

"Hunh," Chutatah snorted. "Demere a bad man, even for a yoneg. He died the death he deserved for the way he treated the living."

We watched the clock tick away, the English have measured their days, sliced it into small pieces that they rush about and lose. The majordomo would appear at the great doors, dismissing all who did not make the audience for that day.

The perpetual petitioners go out into the gloaming and make their way to rented rooms, to wait out the long nights and resume their seats in the antechamber on the morrow. Officers and Indian chiefs, veterans of forgotten wars and their widows have likely whiled away their years, waiting for a man to change their pensions, their positions, their prospects.

But those doors were closed to him, and debts counted against him, chiefly from Capt. Carrington's opposition.

"Whatever did I do? How have I crossed this man that he should slander my good name?" Henry would clench his trembling hands into futile fists.

It seemed obvious to me. "He is looking for blood," I said. "Ours."

Looking back, even as Carrington was insulting the honor both of my husband and my people, I could hear Cat Walker's voice in my ear. Hadahisdi. Kill. If I had snatched the stone blade from inside my legging and sliced Carrington's throat then and there in the antechamber, would it have changed this terrible story. I likely would have been hanged at Newgate Prison, but it might have saved Henry from his fate. But I stayed my hand and let fate take its course.

***

On the sixth of November, Mr. Trueheart passed away in a fit of coughing, the innkeeper wrapped his body in the soiled linen and carried him down the stairs, to be thrown into the ocean of humanity, the pressing waves of flesh that was London.

With Trueheart's life and purse spent, we followed his corpse with heavy hearts. The beadles and the undertakers turned right at the lane, taking Mr. Trueheart toward a pauper's grave, but we parted ways. Down from Long's Court in Leicester-Fields, into even meaner streets and lesser rents into the Cheapside. This time a room, smaller, colder with an odor of sweat and despair seeping into the thin walls where mice scurried.

Chapter 10

London, 1765

On a second application, Lord Halifax agreed I should be paid for the time the Cherokee remained in London and that he should take care to have them sent home. I was allowed two guineas a week for the month they stayed afterwards in town, but from Mr. Trueheart's death, what in cloaths, paint, trinkets, coach-hire, and other expenses, including the bill for their late lodging (for which I was arrested and put to a considerable expense) and the time they had lived with me, I had expended nearly seventy pounds, which I must inevitably lose, as Lord Halifax has absolutely refused to reimburse me.

    Timberlake

We took rooms in Grub Street in a tenement that leaned hard against its neighbors. For two shillings six pennies a week, Chutatah and his warriors wedged themselves in one flat. Across the tight hall, Henry and I had a half-tester bed with brown linsey-woolsey spread, itchy to lay beneath but better than nothing against the damp. A small table, two creaky chairs with cane bottoms about to collapse. A glass in a red frame gave you your face each morning when the London light broke through the window after you threw back the curtain.

In the corner squatted a rusted iron stove, attended by a poker, tongs, and fender. We had an iron candlestick, a quarter bottle of water, a tin pot, a vial for vinegar, and a stone white teacup to keep your salt. The plaster had cracked on the walls, darkened by the grate of coal. Firewood was scarce in this England where they only had legends of an ancient forest, long since cleared for pasture for beef and milk cows.

Henry counted out the coin, and the landlord pocketed it. "First of the month, mind you."

"You may depend upon it, sir. My word is good as any gold."

The man was in no mood for good manners. "Don't be spitting your cheap talk in my hand. Put the coin in my palm first of the month, and we'll be good."

***

I began to know Henry finally, love his little habits, how he craned his neck against his collar, at the same time tightening the tendons that hinged his jaw, setting his teeth, his mind, on some course of action.

When he sat in an armchair, he would list to the left, his head about to rest on his drooping shoulder with a faint smile, as if all his good thoughts outweighed the ill. Jolting himself awake, he would drum his fingers on a tabletop, deep in his thoughts, one fingertip then the next in a roll against the wood. Suddenly, he would snap his fingers and clap his hands, welcoming an idea, a fancy that had come to him. He would lean his elbows on the table, bend to his task, the quill scratching away at parchment, carrying his thought. He was good with his letters, schooled as a child in Virginia, and knew all his numbers, even when he could not resolve his many accounts and the bills that came so constantly.

He read his speeches, the petitions he made on our behalf, our people, our family, the Real People to princes and powers and principalities to reconsider our fate of a people who lived far across the water, behind the mountains a month's march from the coast.

They have many of them a good uncultivated genius, are fond of speaking well that paves the way to power in their councils; and I doubt not but the reader will find some beauties in the harangues I have given him, which I assure him are entirely genuine. Their language is not unpleasant, but vastly aspirated, and the accents so many and various, you would often imagine them singing in their common discourse.

Timberlake

Each day in his room, Chutatah practiced his audience with the king. He had by heart what Ostenaco had said, hearing so many times the Mankiller's speech passed from ear to ear, around the fires of the Nation throughout the Overhills. While women nodded, men recited my father's fine speech again and again.

But Poor Chutatah was tongue-tied, and often stammered. He was no orator like Ostenaco to make men shout or women cry.

"Mighty dragon-slayer, Father of the Yoneg …" He faltered. "Do you think he really slew an Uk'tena with his own lance?"

I shrugged. "That's what Ostenaco said. Timberlake will return soon. He'll know. But do you know what you will say to the king?"

Chutatah cleared his throat and began: "My good lords of the English, I have traveled far over my mountains and across the waters that belong to no man, into your river and your lands and halls, to pose the problem. The world out of balance, the relation of our nation at risk. I come before you to ask your responsibility to set things right, to honor the words of your wise king that was given to us only two winters ago, but now melted away surely as snow."

"Not that I've seen much snow this winter, more rain," Chutatah chuckled to himself, the old man's fascination with the day's weather, how much sun, how much clouds.

Later that afternoon, Henry's weary booted tread came up the backsteps and he entered the rooms with hat in hand, his brow deeply furrowed. He sat on a creaky chair and sighed, then put his face in his pale hands. The last of the coal crumbled in the grate, and the draft that Henry had brought with him wrapped around us, a chill in the air.

He said not a word, and I knew not to ask how his day had gone.

From the streets below, the passing cries and curses and hubbub that doesn't seem to cease with nightfall. The lanes lit by lanterns in the long dusk, by men with long staffs to lift the burning wick. Sometimes screams of women, sometimes that of men, curses and oaths. I wonder how anyone sleeps through the London night, surrounded by so many living, and people dying constantly.

In our bed, even in my arms, Timberlake would sometimes tremble in the middle of the night. He had dreams of drowning.

Henry was a brave man but not in all elements and aspects.

He had come down the long arm of the Long Man, the river whose head was in the hills and his legs ran down to the sea, our town safe in the crook of his bent elbow.

A fortnight in a wobbly, leaking canoe, clinging to the sides with M'Cormick and the hotheaded Sumter took turns with the paddles. His wool clothes dripping. They had gone to water about every crook and rapid of the river, upended. The river pouring out of their boots when they made land, and built fires on the banks, fended off bears. Their guns nearly useless, their powder damp, the triggers broken.

They went under, but fortunately, the river didn't run deep. They found their footing in the swift currents and gasped at the air again. Henry had never learned to swim in the dark swamps of Virginia, and in the wilderness, he panicked at the thought of falling into a pool where he could not stand, only flail in the dark, swallowing the water until the light went out of his eyes.

But they had not drowned. They were found and were escorted to Tomotley, guests of the nation, their blood kept warm and ready to shed at the women's insistence, if the English did not honor their pact.

Henry remained deathly afraid of drowning someday. Part of his hesitation in making a second voyage to London with another Cherokee delegation was his horror of the open sea, how fragile the barks and argosies that set sail on the waves, dark fathoms under the creaking timbers of the hull, a toy made by men against the forces of Nature.

But there is more than one way to drown.

He had visions of a floating corpse in a river bottom, his eyes sucked out by whiskered catfish. He would wake on his pallet with a start, eyes bulging, in a cold sweat beneath his thin blanket.

I know. Many a night, I would hold him and rub his back, calming him. A man is an overwrought boy in the dark, while he gathered his courage again. And he often did the same for me, when nightmares of the U'ktena made me start in our shared bed. We held each other against our worst fears.

About the beginning of March, 1765, I accompanied the Indians on board the Madiera packet, in which they returned to their own country, leaving me immersed in debts not my own, and plunged into difficulty thro' my zeal to serve both them and my country, from which the selling of twenty pounds a year out of my commission has rather allayed than extricated me. The Indians expressed the highest gratitude and grief for my misfortunes.

Timberlake

A gray day that still felt like winter. We stood on the dock, the wind blowing across the North Sea, and rustling the feathers we still wore in our hair. Henry was hunched in his greatcoat, the same campaign issue that had seen him down the river to Tomotley and on two voyages to England.

Chutatah never had his chance to see the king in the flesh, to make his case that Tsalagi life is as precious as that of the yonegs breaking their sovereign's own oath. Instead, George the Dragonslayer had delivered to the docks the usual goods, gifts, and trinkets that traders said the Red Tribes favored. Chests now made of hammered tin and ribs of polished wood, filled with peacepipe, blankets and axeheads and medallions and gorgets and bright medals stamped with the likeness of the Great King.

Chutatah was tired and ready to go home. He scratched his ear.

"You stay with Timberlake." He held his palm out, stopping us from moving, like a conjurer staying the pox or some sickness that crept overnight into your belly or ear.

I had not felt well. I had been throwing up my breakfast and blamed this on the gruel served in the latest rooms Henry had found to let for us. The English were such poor cooks, their meat too salty and boiled, and most all of what they had too bland. I wished for a comb of honey dripping in my hand, I hankered after Cat Walker's yellowjacket soup made from the nest and soft grubs before they grew their wings and sharp stingers.

I rested my hand flat against my belly. In that moment, I had felt it inside me, the quickening I remembered with you, Richard.

.

I remembered Eleanor's greenish face as the light left her eyes, the blood and worse issued with her miscarried child, that I had delivered to the sea. I would not risk my child's life crossing the ocean and its wild storms. I would wait until she was strong enough. I felt the girl growing inside me. She would be the fire I carried home upon my return.

"What would you have me say to your father?" Chutatah asked.

I knew I had to stay with Henry, until I had seen this child safe, even here in England.

I had failed my son in the Overhills, I could not fail my daughter conceived in this alien land. She was not ready to risk the sea and a perilous voyage. I was between two worlds, two children.

I opened my mouth, then clenched my teeth, uncertain what to say.

"Heya, well said." Chutatah nodded at my silence. "I think the Mankiller will understand your message."

He saluted me with his upraised palm then crossed his fist across his heart, a sign I took as a blessing. Go in peace but be brave.

The headman of Citico limped up the gangplank to begin his passage home, and that was the last I saw of Chutatah.

Henry raised his greatcoat and took me under his battered dripping wing, held me close against the English drizzle. We turned as one, like a couple in the great dance, and went on our way toward the terrible City.

Chapter 11

Wood Street, London, 1765

Looking back, we only had a single season in the city to ourselves, perhaps only a fortnight in a single room before we were chased out with unpaid bills and fewer linens. We descended to smaller accommodations, fewer meals, a little less of Henry's purse. We surrendered the rest of his wardrobe, his linens, his shirts, his plate. But we were together for a time.

"Our fortunes will improve. You'll see."

Our fire was meager, just a faint glow of the coal, and London was a cold place, the rains lashing those cracked glass panes. We wore all our remaining clothes by the grate, sipping weak tea from cracked cups. No bearskins or buffalo robes to keep us warm. We lay under his great cloak that he'd worn down the river into Tomotley. We sheltered and took our pleasure and thought ourselves fortunate indeed as Henry said.

He stroked my belly and whispered to our new child.

"My love, my Indian lass," he whispered his love to me, his hand bringing the sure touch, pressures that brought forth cries of pleasure. We learned our language with our tongues, and we didn't speak. I'd heard the quiet couplings in the winter houses, children listening to their mother taking the man's seed, like the moon coaxing up the corn from the dark fields, the rhythmic beating of bodies together like drums and panted breaths that make the lovers' song.

***

We were together until Carrington's collectors hunted us down. They would not be bribed this time or satisfied with a pair of shirts or fine stockings, the last of Eleanor's plates, or even Henry's coat I had mended with steel needle and silk thread, a more delicate seam than those Cat Walker had showed me with sinew of deer and a bone awl.

Carrington's cruel men wanted Henry and no excuses.

They rushed Henry down the narrow steps, pummeling him as he tried to fight them, holding on to the railings. "Skitty, Skitty, our child. Take care, girl."

I followed Henry and his captors, down the lanes and up the crowded streets. Henry lost a boot along the way, barefoot in the cobblestone, they were stripping the poor soldier of everything, about to take his pants as far I could tell.

The jibes of whores and drunks, pressed out of the way. One poor soul complaining, "It's not fair, governor," and down the man went with a crack of the truncheon. I saw him white faced and retching in the gutter, blood trickling out of his earhole.

The blackguards pushed and shoved. And I followed on behind. "We'll take you as well, dearie," a whore pushed her toothless mouth into my face and pulled at my petticoat. "They've got a whole room for the worthless women up at Wood Street, and the bailiffs take their turns."

I punched her face and ran after Henry. I turned up a lane and saw his bare head bowed and his white shirt coming off his thin shoulder, as the blackguards pushed him into a brick building. The stout oak door swung on its rusted hinges and slammed shut with the sound of bolts shot into their latches.

I banged at the entrance, my fists against oak. "Henry, Henry!"

A slot opened like a mouth in the door. Through the slot, a yellow eye studied me and blinked. "What's your business, bitch?"

"You've taken my husband."

"You have his debt in hand, you can have his person. Until then, to hell with you."

That bloodshot eye winked, the slot slid shut, and all hope was lost. I ground my forehead against the door that refused to open, to give me back my Henry.

***

I took our last belongings and blankets and left the crowded tenements to what little sun and grass the town promised. In Hyde Park, a few trees still stood, survivors from the ancient forests the English had long since slaughtered. Clean water flowed from the fountains, and I found a hedge of evergreen shrubs to hide myself from the passing public.

My stomach rumbled and complained. I picked at the weeds that stubbornly worked their way up in the cracks of walls and cobblestones. Green life was fed by perpetually wet lanes and avenues, the mud puddles that glimmered in the short afternoons.

I boiled potherbs over a small fire I struck with Cat Walker's flint knife and a steel bolt I found in the gutter. I huddled under my blanket against the chill. When the sky threatened rain, I tried singing the song that Walking Mountain had tried to frighten away the storms at sea. The words did not work on the wet English weather. The rain fell into my cup but tasted of metal in the morning when I drank and washed my face.

I walked across half the city from the park to the prison, wary of attracting undue attention from bailiffs or Carrington's blackguards.

In Wood Street, I pulled a barrel from the alley and stacked a couple of crates, building a platform. My hand and cheek against the rough brick as I climbed higher.

"Henry. Dear Henry!" I called up to the barred window.

Once we nearly touched our fingertips, but I could not see his face. I heard only his voice.

"Be brave. Our fortunes will improve. I am writing harder."

He was deep in his sorrows.

Inside, Henry was writing his memoirs, his message to the world, explaining himself, defending his actions and the gambles he had made with fate and fortune. In his dark grief, he recalled Eleanor and the son she had carried in secret for so long. He dared not tempt another crossing back to Virginia, but he would make his stand in London Towne, fight the slanders of Carrington, fend off the bill collectors. The army owed him a pension for his bravery. He had saved countless lives, kept the Cherokee on their lands, and not raiding eastward, burning cabins into the Carolinas, saving sons and daughters, both yoneg and of the Real People.

I reminded him that he was saving his own son, home in the Overhills.

But he could not save himself.

In Wood Street, the walls were damp and there was no heat for the inmates. He shivered in a thin blanket, blowing on chapped hands with what little warm breath he could muster, until he coughed up trickles of phlegm and even blood.

He left behind a book, but he never wrote me a love letter, no paper bearing his soft words, or how he compared my dark beauty with a flower or a lowering sky. His words are long fled, with his last breath. His brave heart stilled.

But still and forever, I could feel his heart beating close to mine, our warm skin touching beneath the bear hide a world away or beneath the thin sheets of the Cheapside lodging.

Chapter 12

Gin Alley, Hyde Park, 1765

Richard, mark the passing of your father.

The day before Michaelmas and Henry, my husband, was dead, the brave man who accompanied the feathered delegation, the savage chiefs who toured the town.

Notices came in gazettes; he did not go unremarked in the Fleet Street postings. Died Sept. 30, 1765, Lieut. Henry Timberlake of the 42nd Regiment. He arrived with the Cherokee Chiefs and attended them at court. He was twenty-nine years of age.

No survivors were listed, no mention of me.

My Henry lay in a pauper's grave at St. Giles, piled in with the dead, arm in arm, covered by English dirt.

You never met the man. I've told you what I could. He is perhaps as mysterious as the Uk'tena, a tale told to children, but he was a real man, and brave like your grandfather.

Ostenaco was old when I left the Overhills. My father was no longer painted red or primed for war against the foe he had seen firsthand. The years passing, his strength waning, but he was still powerful enough to lift you up overhead, dangle your kicking legs. You laugh, lowered again into his lap, fondle his long ear lobes wound with wire and feathers, the handsome features of a handsome man. He was not painted with ocher from berries, or the ashes of the sacred fire, not decorated for the war party. A few gray hairs floated through the black mane of his scalplock. He had kept his head through raids, skirmishes against the Catawba, pitched battles with the English and their allies, our enemies. He had seen enough.

He likely wore the wired frames over his fading eyes, the spectacles that he brought in a velvet sack from his London tour. The cunning tool of the English in which glass pieces can be worn like a mask over an elder's fading eyes to bring the world closer and sharper again.

Perhaps Ostenaco brought your face close, studied your features. Did he wonder about your slightly finer, lighter hair, the green flecks in your eyes, features that come from your father?

Did Ostenaco also see me, his daughter, in your face, my nose, the high cheeks I gave you? Did he think you fuss too much, not like an Overhills native, but like the white stranger who came floating down Ostenaco's river, into his town, his home, to take his only daughter away, leaving him with a grandson?

I still see you, Richard, across so many years, so many leagues that separate us. Even if you can't imagine me after all this time, I will always see you, my son, as my little baby. Someday, I swear I will meet the man you've become in my long absence.

Book II

Chapter 13

Star and Garter, Boylston Street,
London, 1766

The boy came first, wringing his wool cap between dirty hands, then a man with his hat cocked squarely on his block head.

"Is she for real, Da?"

Father steadied son's frail shoulder. "Get your shilling's worth, laddie. She ain't going to bite." He pushed the chap forward for a better view.

"Can ye speak?" the boy asked me.

I smiled my strong teeth. The young'un hid his fearful head in the rough cut of his father's coat. The crowd laughed. But the boy stabbed my heart. He would be about the same age as my Richard.

I was the show that season in an upstairs room in a public tavern, reached down a dark alley of the city. A rope stretched from corner to corner, frayed ends of hemp nailed into the plaster walls, dividing the close room in twain, me on one side, paying customers on the other. Dozens of them every day, mostly men in their powdered wings, but women of the lower orders, giggling and painted themselves. They climbed the stairs for a paid peek at a real live savage as promised by the broadsides posted on this public house. "Audience with an Indian woman, See the Cherokee Chieftain's Consort."

They came to stare, to gawk, to jeer. Their pale and pocked faces, guffawing open mouths with their few and crooked teeth. Many were drunk. One man vomited in the corner. The sour stench lingered. Those in the back had to stand on tiptoe to see me. The crowd grew so big, pressing against the poor rope, that the nail was pulled from the plastered wall. The barrier separating me from them fell to the floor. A collective gasp, they stepped back. I rose from my chair, bent to pick up the bight, pushed the nail back into its hole. I resumed my seat, a rickety ladderback with a broken cane bottom that groaned and creaked. My head swam with the White Drink whenever I stood too fast.

I stared between my bare feet at the grain of the rough floors, trees that once grew in forests, hewn and hauled to this terrible city. Sometimes I studied the gaping crowd. Fools, one and all, I could tell them to their faces, but they would not know what I said. They would take Tsalagi as gibberish and part of the show.

***

I had lost myself after losing Henry.

Without board or bread, roof or room. Sleeping in the greens fenced beyond the great houses at the city's edge. Eating heels of bread loaf, molded rounds tossed in the streets. Looked for herbs and plants in ditches. Slept in the arms of elms by the stream. Hand always ready on the stone knife, the only trusted companion from Overhills. Cut a thick quarter stave to walk the streets. Yobs lurching out of dark and behind corners, grabbing at my sleeve, tearing at my sleeve, wanting more, their slobbery mouths pressed against mine, their hands wandering. A quick knee up between their legs would bend them double as I made my escape. I could have scalped many a man, but I let them live. They sought to harm me, but I wanted only blood for the husband.

In the park, a beggar had mercy on me and gave me the White Drink from his bottle purchased for only a pence over in Gin Lane. One draught and I was gone. A woman on the street, huddled in a worn blanket, pulling from a dram of spirits, waiting for the Uk'tena to slither my way. Content to drink more and scratch my flea bites, as the rains of London fell on my roaring head. But there would not be enough water to make me clean. I was drowning as Henry had feared.

Until the dwarf came to find me. I thought he was one of the Yvnwi Tsunsdi. Cat Walker had told me tales of the Little People who would steal children walking unawares in the mountains. The English tell old wives' tales of evil dwarves with an appetite for human young. These stories serve to scare little boys and girls, make them mind their elders and say their proper prayers lest the dwarves bake them into meat pies.

John Coin was no fable, but flesh and blood, if only four feet tall. A huge head and hard-knuckled hands attached to his strangely stunted body. He could cuss, fart, and fuck, he claimed, with a man twice his size, and once slew a giant in Northumberland, or at least bit his knee in a poor sideshow. He had brains to go with his big head, and Coin ran his own tavern in Giles' Court. Bitters and gin served downstairs. Upstairs, tired trollops and scurvy scullery girls spread their chicken legs for the plucking of paying customers.

He found me in the nick, because the child I carried was close to arrival. But the pallet Coin gave me, I could not squat in a proper position and was not strong enough to push out my daughter into this world. If I'd had a conjurer or even a good root woman like Cat Walker, it might have gone better.

The dwarf kept feeding me the strong white drink, and I would vomit, turning my head, the draught burning my lips, my throat. Their faces swam overhead. The dwarf's large face bobbing next to mine. Rough women's hands parting my legs and telling me to push. A terrible pain tearing my body in two. After I quit scream-ing, there was only silence afterwards. The two crones shaking their frowning faces. "No luck there, John Coin." They took away the remains of the daughter I couldn't safely deliver, my little girl.

Like Eleanor in her terrible passage, I turned my face to the wall in my unkempt bed, and waited to die, but Death was not so kind.

The dwarf had not delivered me. I was Coin's captive.

After a time, he began to admit guests into my room. I could hear their steps up the creaking staircase, the coppers drop into the wooden box outside. The lines were long. They had never seen my likes.

The first crowds were look-only, touching not permitted at this price of only five pence. As I gathered my strength and they wore down my soul with the white drink, Coin would likely raise the admittance and started collecting for individual audiences with an Indian, when I would not be dressed in these lice-infested hides. I would be a rare fuck indeed.

***

One day, the door admitted a gentleman in a frock and wide-brimmed hat, followed by a blackamoor, evidently his manservant. He pressed through the gawkers, shouldering aside men a head taller. He leaned over the forbidden rope that marked my boundary and the spectator's safety. He touched my arm.

"Might thou be Mrs. Ostenaco Timberlake?"

I heard my father's name, my husband's name, my beloved.

"Yes," I said.

"I am a stranger, but rest assured I come as a Friend," he said, then turned to the jeering crowd.

"Shame and fie upon thee," he shouted. "This is not bear baiting, nor a gaudy show. If ye be Christians and decent souls, leave now, let us be."

The crowd was not amused. I thought the muttering men might strike my slight rescuer, any one of them could have likely thrown him over their shoulder or heaved him out the window. But the gentleman paid my bill to the dwarf and his housekeepers and dismissed them curtly. "Consider yourself fortunate, sir, I do not report this to the constables nor the Board of Trade. Thou are taking liberties with a foreign ambassador to the king's court and the penalty is harsh for such transgressions," the gentleman said.

"Ambassador, my arse. She's naught but a cunt from another country." The dwarf spat and took the shillings in his outstretched palm. "Don't be parading your Quaker thou's and thee's before us."

The gentleman, along with his black manservant, hoisted my weary arms about their strong necks and carried me down the narrow stairs. I went blinking into the broad daylight.

Chapter 14

My rescuers bore me to another chamber, more spacious than Coin's garret off Cheapside. A fine room with an upright bed with four posters and my world was tied to that bed for a fortnight.

Sweating, shivering, rising only to throw up or shit in the porcelain chamber pot, then swoon again into the sheets. But when I fluttered my eyes again, the bed would be clean, the pot emptied. The gentleman and his black manservant guarded me, nursed me, gave me broth instead of the white drink, until I could stomach bread soaked into milk.

I awoke, the morning light of another London falling through a clear glass window on my face. I slipped from the coverlet over the soft featherbed. I was dressed in a white shift like the yoneg dressed their dead, and I wondered how I had passed to the darkening land, but why was it so light on this side.

Barefoot, I crept out the white door and down the creaking staircase, slowly, seeking a way out into the street, but down the front hall, I passed by an open door into the parlor.

"Aho, our lady is awakened." The gentleman who had saved me sat in a Windsor chair, smoking a clay pipe. "Come in, dear one." He folded his crinkly paper and stood, beckoning me to a chair.

"Frank, Frank, our guest has been resurrected," he called into the back of the house.

"Coming, Squire Wolfe."

"We're so glad to see thee up and about. Ghastly experience thou must have had at the dwarf's quarters. Frank and I fretted mightily."

The manservant appeared with a tray of glasses and bottles, but Wolfe waved him away. "None for the lady. I think we have safely weaned her away from the ardent spirits. It was quite the test like an exorcism of the demon rum. We need tea, Frank."

Frank returned with a tray of tea things and poured a libation into a fine cup. It was almost as good as the teas that Cat Walker used to steep.

"I know thou only as Mrs. Timberlake. Prithee, what would be thy first name?" Wolfe asked. "Pardon me, I mean thy Cherokee name."

"Skitty."

He motioned very gently. "I am Wolfe." He patted his chest. "Thaddeus Wolfe."

By my puzzled look, he quickly apologized. "I'm sorry, the language barrier must be tiresome. Thou speak our tongue passably well."

I nodded, my lessons learned well from M'Cormick and then Henry.

"Speak thy mother tongue, please," Wolfe asked.

"My mother died when I was but a baby. I'm not sure I remember her voice."

"I mean, thy own language. Say something in Cherokee."

So I began to sing, closing my eyes, taking myself away from this England of dwarves and louts and evil dreams. I sang an old song of Tomotley that Cat Walker had hummed when she gathered plants in the spring, the sun dappling through the first green leaves. We sang as we filled our baskets with the good greens that made the bone strong, and the blood run sweet in our limbs.

Squire Wolfe bowed his head. "Why, that's lovely a hymn as I've ever heard in any chapel."

He rose and went to his credenza.

"Mrs. Ostenaco Timberlake, I have something I believe belongs to thee."

He placed a parcel upon my lap, hide-bound, soft, and tanned, inside filled with paper leaves covered with script. "It's thy late husband's memoir, and the proceeds are rightfully thine."

Richard, I must tell you how my eyes filled with tears. It was the first I had seen of what Henry had done with his short time in the pauper's prison. He had always been one for words, filling page after page with his fine writing, though I could not make out the marks. He had tried to write his way to freedom before his untimely death.

An accountant by profession, Wolfe had been charged by the courts and creditors with settling Timberlake's estate. The memoir had come out to much acclaim, with several hundred copies spreading through the coffee houses and clubs along the Strand, and even rumored to be read by the powers in Parliament and in the ministries and Board of Trade.

My claim to whatever revenues the book had produced remained unclear since my legal status in Britain was questionable, Wolfe tried to explain. I was one of the Real People, but not according to the English. No parish office held my name, nor a ship's manifest. As a woman and even as a proud Cherokee, I was invisible, unofficial. It could be argued by barristers in their old-fashioned wigs, their wobbly chins and their stuffy voices that I was a ghost, a figment of the colonial imagination, an outlier. I was certainly property, but there was the rub, whose, exactly?

As a Christian, Henry was legally bound to Eleanor. English law didn't recognize a man and woman pledging their souls to one another by the banks of Tomotley.

But it could be argued that I was part and parcel of Henry's unfinished business, his estate in escrow. If I had landed a year earlier before Lord Henley's Act of '63, I might have been sold off as a slave. But people bought elsewhere were perceived to be freeholders setting foot in England. Free but stuck. I had no permission to be here, nor passport to leave. I was a babe in limbo as the Papist would have it, a soul swimming endlessly in between, Wolfe said sadly.

"Frank had been in much the same situation, before we were able to get his legal rights assured," Wolfe explained.

Frank, the handsome youth from the sunny climes of the Indies, who found freedom in this rainy island, and could walk the streets of London without fear of slavedrivers with chains. In gratitude, he made himself indispensable to Wolfe's mission, which I would only begin to see as compassion. To settle the estate, Wolfe determined he must find Henry's surviving heir.

A Cherokee woman alone in Londontown, a settlement of five hundred thousand souls, the largest city on our world, was not so hard to find. Wolfe traced a yearlong trail from Leicester Fields to Grub Street to Hyde Park and Wood Compter. There were no signal trees about the streets, but playbills pointed the way to my abode. Wolfe, or more accurately, his man Frank, got wind of a raree-show at John Coin's celebrated tavern, a new peep show.

***

In the lodgings on Fetter Lane, I sat by the fire, regaining my strength. I held Henry's book on my lap like a baby. I scouted the pages, trying to wrestle the strange markings to the paper.

If you could read the trail, you could follow a man's mind through the world.

But the markings could take a different trail, and it wasn't as I remembered.

"Friend Wolfe, could you teach me to read and to write?"

"I would be delighted, Mrs. Timberlake."

He pulled over a Windsor chair beside mine and leaned over to point out the words on the page. Thus began my long tutelage.

The letters were hard to hold in my mind as I made the words of English with my tongue, the strange sounds that make your tongue swell behind your teeth, some words like things you spit out, a fleck of tobacco leaf caught on the tip.

Wolfe tutored me well through the seasons, reading and rereading Henry's book to me, as I told him what was true and what was Henry's misapprehension. I had heard every story that Henry had told me, and there was nothing he said that I wasn't there to see or had heard from the mouth of Ostenaco or Sumter, who were in Londontown before me.

Wolfe read me other volumes, slicing the leaves loose with a silver penknife, and he would go over the words carefully with me until I could say them correctly.

"Thou are becoming a good reader. This will serve thee well in London."

"Can I take this book home to Tomotley and teach my son to read?"

"Oh dear, my poor Mrs. Timberlake." Wolfe looked over his flashing spectacles. "I'm afraid that would be impossible now until we find the means for a passage. I was able to track down the despicable dwarf, but I have not been able to unlock Timberlake's estate. All the proceeds that could pay for ship have been tied up by creditors, mostly a Col. Carrington. Do thou know such a man?"

"I met him once. I will not forget him. He is responsible for my husband's death, my child's death."

"Ah." Wolfe shook his head. "We won't be able to argue that in any court, I'm afraid. Some things we must leave to divine judgment."

"My father's clan was Wolf," I said. "How did an Englishman like yourself earn that name?"

"It was my pater's surname. I inherited it, along with his estate, such as it is."

"But I see you have a strong animal spirit, very like a wayah. That's our word for wolf." I lifted my face to the empty ceiling and let fly from my throat the wolf howl heard on the lonesome mountain.

He laughed. "Well, no. I'm not that beast, though I may be in sheep's clothing. There's been no wolves in England since the first Tudor took the throne," Squire Wolfe said. "And it's spelled with an 'E' on the end, but the vowel is silent, never mind."

He closed the book. "We must think about thy name, my dear."

Chapter 15

In the chapel, a pipe organ bellowed a bitter tune, sounding like a storm trying to blow you off the mountain. I missed the deep beats of the drums of Tomotley, the soft flutes of the Real People, sounds that swayed your body. I was drumming my fingers against the wooden seat until I saw a woman in the pew ahead turn and scowl at me. I knew my place. Hold still, don't fidget, lest I faint again.

That morning, I had nearly swooned as Frank laced me into the whalebone corset for the occasion. "Hold still, Missy, ye are not helping matters here." Ladies in England can scarcely breathe, let alone move. They must sip at the air like the hummingbirds.

Wolfe had ordered the Indian cotton and the lace for my communion dress, took me to a dressmaker to be measured. He meant to change me, make me official in the eyes of the English. But, inside this starched dress and corset, beneath the petticoat against my thigh, I secretly kept the stone-cold flint that Cat Walker had given me when I left my homeland.

Someday, and I hoped soon, I would pass Carrington in a London street, the man who had thwarted poor Henry at every chance, hounded my poor husband into debtor's prison and an early death, the villain to blame for the loss of our baby. I would take my revenge, honor my family, and slit his throat.

Today, I pretended to pray as the English. With my eyes shut, I could see Indians everywhere, people with my skin, my face, my features, not the washed-out faces, the limp fair hair of these slope-shouldered, thin waisted women.

Imagine war party paddling canoes up the Thames under the full moon. They break into Westminster with torches and tomahawks, cutting down the hapless Beefeaters in their velvet berets and ruffed necklaces. They run into Piccadilly Circus, burning the taverns as they go. Naked, painted warriors, singing death chants for their enemies, swinging war clubs, their knives severing ears and noses, relieving the English of what little hair they have beneath their powdered wigs.

***

"Now, my dear, it's thy turn." Wolfe elbowed me.

I went and knelt before the white robed rector facing the small congregation.

The sad-faced man intoned a long list of questions that echoed through the chilled chambers. Wolfe had given me the words to answer. If I faltered, I glanced at him for guidance. He nodded and mouthed the words "I do."

"Do you renounce Satan and all the spiritual forces of wickedness that rebel against God?"

"Do you renounce the evil powers of this world which corrupt and destroy the creatures of God? Do you renounce all sinful desires that draw you from the love of God? Do you turn to Jesus Christ and accept him as your savior?"

I said a dutiful yea to these enquiries as instructed by my guardian.

I knelt, a captive before the rector. I opened my mouth, ready for my tongue to be cut out. The man placed a white wafer, tasteless, into my mouth and proclaimed me neither male nor female, neither Jew nor Gentile, but English through and through.

They gave me the blood of this Jesus, and I became a cannibal.

They anointed my head with the clear cold water from the stone font. And I was brought to my senses at last.

The congregation took their hymnals and sang through their noses in their joyless way, their faces frowning, sad with the suffering of their Jesus, who they torture each first day of the week, relieving the pain of the god who dies.

I was Christian now, baptized, a new creature in Christ, this white man said. He had only splashed a little water on my head, not at all like the cleansing and cold pool that Cat Walker made me go under. What do these unwashed yoneg know of going to water, of being cleansed?

While he was wetting my forehead, I held fast to the prayer I said every morning in Tomotley, wading into the cold water, feeling life spring in my limbs, warm blood in my face. Washed away all those thoughts that separate me from this world in which I am created. Washed away all those evil thoughts that separate me from my brothers and sisters and all animals.

***

Coming out of the chapel into the feeble English sun, still escorted on Squire Wolfe's arm, I had to ask: "What have you done to me?"

"One need be official and documented. This dumbshow is an unfortunate necessity, I am afraid. Please do not think this a matter of belief or conscience. Believe me, the vicar is in for the purse, rather than any desire to save lost souls. The church needs all those candles because they are blind to the True Light within."

At the registry office, Wolfe paid the vicar and the parish scribe to put my name, Helena Ostenaco Timberlake, in the rolls. "God save us and St. Martins-in-the-Field Parish. It's not the book of Heaven, but it will do. Thou are now a legal Englishwoman, but I believe thou can be a proper gentlewoman yet."

***

"That man said my new name is Helena?" I asked Wolfe. "Helena, where did it come from? What does it mean?"

"Perhaps my predilection for Pope." Wolfe laughed and waved his hand. "But it befits thee. Helen was a famous beauty. Men went to war for ten years over her hand. A city was besieged and finally burned for her honor."

They cried, "No wonder such celestial charms

For nine long years have set the world in arms;

What winning graces! what majestic mien!

She moves a goddess, and she looks a queen!

Yet hence, O Heaven, convey that fatal face,

And from destruction save the Trojan race."

When Wolfe recited that lovely speech, half of which I could follow, but the music in it was lovely, I was moved that he would associate such beautiful words with a poor and abandoned woman such as myself.

"The Trojans, were they a tribe conquered by the English?"

"Oh, no," the Squire Wolfe laughed. "It's all ancient history but perhaps thou come to aid the salvation of your race. I only hope to be of some assistance if that is the Lord's will."

"Helena, she sounds more like a bitch than a beauty if she can't decide between two husbands and a whole people are slaughtered on her behalf."

Many an evening in the drawing room where we retired after our dinner, he read to me from the man he always called the Mighty Shakespeare or a hunch-backed poet named the witty Pope, or even one of Dr. Johnson's latest essays in the Rambler, and I with my sewing, my stitches, the flash of the needle in the fabric, drawing the sleek thread with each dive, like a fish silvering in the shallows, which gave me a good feeling, that Cat Walker would still be proud of me, even if that old woman would never admit it.

My favorite of the books that Wolfe read was Defoe's Robinson Crusoe, about the adventurer marooned alone on a South Sea island, forced to fend for himself without aid of any crew or clan, no country to call his own, but the alien palms, until he found the man Friday, the savage.

I am not sure who I more resembled, the man Crusoe or the man Friday. Civilized or savage, both dressed in ragged furs, and none of the fine ribbons, the colorful plumage. What a sad tale. I thought of it often.

I am the Indian, I am the outcast, I am the exile.

I am the stranger you jostle in the street and perhaps look back at, wondering who is that strange woman, before the rain drives you on, turning up the collar of your greatcoat, hastening away to your own burrowed life, your secret sorrows.

Chapter 16

With so few groves still standing in the city, the English enjoy no signal trees to show the trails in London. Plenty of finger posts point to public houses and taverns and places of commerce. Wolfe seemed to know his way about the streets and parks which we walked each afternoon. Wolfe was not a man who would pay others to cart him about the streets like the haughty gentlemen in their post-chaises. "God has given us two strong legs. Let us use them to see the glories of his world," he would say.

So off we ventured, once circumambulating all of London in eight hours' time, beginning in the morn at Moorfields to Newington Green, Hackney, Bethnal Green, Limehouse, New Cross by noon, through the hamlets of Peckham, and Stockwell to Battersea, Chelsea, Knightsbridge, through Hyde Park, round Tyburn to Paddington, up the road to Islington and along the new City Road, making Moorfields, tired but in ample time for a good spot of tea.

Life is London, the smoked air choked with coal. Tea leaves littering a white cup. Smells of fried fish and chips, beef tripe, boiled cabbage from a dank scullery. A wide-eyed child, the apples gone from its sunken cheeks, peering down from a casement until shooed away from sight by a female hand. Shawled women in alleyways, drunkards sleeping on cobblestones. The horse guard passes in the night, the clop of steed's hooves on stones laid first by Romans. A beggar advances on two crutches, swinging one leg forward, the empty pants leg flapping like a flag for a lost cause.

A river of tears that fill the Thames under a new moon. The tallow candles gutter in the lamp posts, making a multitude of shadows in an already dark city. Distant bells peal out the short hours into the long night. Any hush that descends is broken like glass. A woman screams. There are always screams, cries, a city of sorrows.

The town crouched tight on the banks of the black Thames had sprawled into a city over the years, as the empire fattened itself across the waters, both to the East and West. The East India Company was expanding trading posts in India, hiring guns to terrorize the brown skinned Bengali and loot their fabrics, their spices, and of course the tea that the English guzzle almost as much as their home cooked gins. In what they called America, once mistaken for the Indies, though still calling the inhabitants Indians, the English traded slaves for tobacco, smoking up their coffeehouse. Deer hides and beaver fur, occasional nuggets of gold, silver, and other precious stones. If it had value, it washed up in England. Ill-gotten loot, even stolen goods were seen everywhere, glistening in the gold buckles on shoes, swishing in the silk of the ladies. Money was the root of all evil, and the taproot was in the Thames, Wolfe used to complain, his voice growing ever higher and pinched at the rampant immorality.

Yet on the other hand, he saw nothing but Progress and Light beating back shadows of ignorance and folly, depending on where he focused his gaze on our promenades about the city.

I walked proudly on the arm of Wolfe, who a whole head shorter than we, steered us around the mudpuddles and the obstacles of the gravel paths. He strode confidently down the streets, standing his ground against the traffic.

"By your leave, sir."

"No leave here." He would sidestep as the sedan chair and its burly bearers came jogging along, the unseen gentleman tucked away in the fabric carriage between the stout legs of two runners, long armed men who could jog between Whitehall and the River in a moment's notice.

A respecter of no titles nor of the Quality, as the rich called themselves. Wolfe was a lover of all souls. All lights made equal in the eyes of the Creator he called upon.

***

One day, we walked over to Tower Hill and the city's most ancient fortress. He escorted me through the iron gates, the stone bridge, paying the blind attendant five pence for admittance.

We watched a bear on a chain, a morose, matted beast with rheumy eyes. It had scarcely any teeth when it opened his mouth to whimper rather than roar at the crowd on the parapet above. We leaned over the side, and some threw apples and other crumbs down. Likely captured in the Casperians, crated up and shipped across the Continent toward this castle, the beast looked little like the Yona who roamed our mountains. In olden days, mobs would watch the beasts tormented by packs of dogs or prisoners sent in to be mauled by the half-starved monsters, while the crowd would yell their wagers who bit the dust first in the gladiatorial contests. "Thank God, we are not so cruel in our more enlightened society," Wolfe informed me. He had all manner of secrets and knowledge and history crammed under his Quaker hat, where he would stuff bits of paper, scraps of notes to himself to transcribe, a quill in his pocket, penknife, and a vial of oak gall ink for a quick enquiry.

We glimpsed a dusky bulky creature in the dry moat. A startling monster, like a great bear had tried to swallow a Uk'tena, the long tail and tusks from its mouth, the flapping wings at the sides of the head. "Elephant from Asia," he read from the pamphlet, a guide he had bought from some enterprising urchin at the gate. Kalama, I thought, Butterfly ears, I thought he was beautiful.

How you would have marveled at that great beast, Richard. I could not wait to tell you, but then my heart always sank. I could picture you, no longer a child, but a lanky youth, standing by the river of our town, perhaps slinging rocks across the surface, perhaps aiming your anger at the mother who had abandoned you.

Perhaps Ostenaco, my father, comes to comfort you. Don't turn away.

Listen, Richard …

***

I would not see my father in the flesh again, but I did meet with his likeness. Squire Wolfe took me to a hall of amusement, where artisans fashioned man-sized replicas, not just the face, but the whole body of famous personages, past kings and queens, poets and statesmen, and celebrated visitors such as my father, Ostenaco and his famed tour of a few winters before.

The hostess was a simpering woman with a heady aroma that made my nose wrinkle. Even the Squire Wolfe held a handkerchief to his nose as she showed us to the back.

"Mon mademoiselle, come see." She ushered us into a storeroom of shadows. My eyes adjusted to the light. I could make out the three of them, standing next to a headless Tartar, and a Roman centurion. They stood in the corner, resting against one another like wood stacked for a fire, or leaning poles.

"Remarkable," whispered Wolfe. "Ostenaco."

I knew him at once, the slight resemblance, the proud bearing even done in candlewax. He smelled funny of course, not himself, the scent of pine and water and sinew that I knew from my earliest dreams, but of tallow and lye.

Moths had eaten his shirt and his leggings. The gorgets were not beaten of silver, but a thinner tin. The scalp knot at his rounded head drooped. His head was too large on his shoulders, his feet were not really feet, but blocks of wood that filled his moccasins. His arms held no sinew, his hands had no fingers, but were blobs of flesh fisted about the peace pipe he carried and the folded blanket over his shoulder. The paint had faded on his face. His eyes were dead, like pebbles you see glinting on the bottom of the sunlit river, only to turn dark if you scoop them up, dripping in your hand.

"The Chief Ostenaco was among our most popular attractions. The people could not get enough of him in the flesh when he was here or in the wax after he departed," the woman explained.

"Does it favor him at all?" Squire Wolfe asked me.

"There is no spirit to him." I shook my head.

He looked more like a doll he fashioned for me out of cornstalk.

I remember my father's face was splotched, beneath its wild paint, the bronze of his skin pocked by the illness that had afflicted the tribe before I was born. Scars left by another type of war, waged and lost by so many of the People, who went into water, time and again, and shivered to death, unable to shake off the smallpox that the English had brought with them.

"His visage caused many of our patrons to flee screaming from the hall," the woman said proudly.

"English are too afraid of what they don't understand," I said and turned away.

Ostenaco once told me never to be afraid, that Pretty Women, the ones who tied back their long hair and painted their faces red, went to war with the best of the men. They showed no fear. How? I asked.

Fear has to do with hate, my father said. You cannot hate anything, but start with the worst days, the ones you say you would hate. Why hate the storm that howls out of the hills, the hail that rips through the corn and tender squash, the rain that raises the river and floods our fields? What is there to hate or fear? Rather say this has happened, what we did not want or wish for.

Learn instead to love what is, every day, love again the rattlesnake coiled underfoot, the yellowjacket that stings and swells your arm. Learn to love the hail, the thunder, the fire that burns you, the snow that freezes you, the rain that chills you. Like the hailstone in summer, the white ball of ice melting at the foot of the beaten corn plant. The passing storm that arcs the many colors in a bow over the mountain. Everything passes in this land, even the Real People.

Remember, Richard, I pray. Don't be afraid. You will see my face someday.

Chapter 17

Camden, 1767

Squire Wolfe took lodgings close to the dealings of the Inn of Court, the medieval back alleys where men in white wigs and dark robes argued and rewrote laws to suit themselves and their clients. A man of the City, Wolfe at his Welsh heart was a child of the countryside. Aside from the long explorations of dense books and dusty tomes, the consulting of precedent and court papers, Wolfe also loved to roam along creek streams and pastures, beneath the shade of proper English oaks and elms, what few remained in the countryside surrounding Greater London.

One summer when the business of law had slowed in the season's heat, he rented a cottage in the nearby village of Camden and pretty Primrose Hill, where we had a three-mile walk into the city. I was glad to see trees and fields and even sheep out here, though there were no commons. The summers were cooler and shorter, and we never got the heat that sweltered over the mountains guarding Tomotley and the Overhill settlements, the screech of the locusts in the trees and the dry grass. Nor did we see the lightning storm that would shatter the high ridges, only a steady drizzle and the sodden grass we trudged on the old Roman Road into London Towne.

***

We were whiling away a late afternoon at summer's end. The sun was slanting lower and the shadows coming up this season. Different days. Soon we would leave this cottage and resume our life at our city flat.

A soft tap at the drawing room door.

"Squire Wolfe, Mrs. Timberlake," Frank announced. "We have a caller, a Mr. Griffin, who says he has business."

Our guest entered hat in hand, no periwig, but his natural curls tied back in a black ribbon. He sported a white waistcoat and red cravat neatly tied. His dark stockings showed little of the mud from the long walk to Camden.

"Thomas Griffith, at your service." He flourished a half bow and quick salute with his large hat before handing his topper to Frank for safekeeping. Fishing about in a cloth bag he had brought, he set upon the low table a delicate vase, its lip decorated with ceramic roses.

"Handsome work Mr. Wedgwood accomplishes these days, with French enamels," Wolfe observed, handling the vase and turning it within the light for a closer look.

"A good eye, sir. Mr. Wedgwood is a stickler, an artist when it comes to his jasper cameos, the stoneware. His apprentices shape and fire the dishes that the king eats his kippers from," Griffith said. "He demands only the very best materials from would-be suppliers like myself."

"Beg pardon, sir, have thou come into our house, seeking to sell us some wares? Rather forward, I must say." Wolfe set down the vase.

"You will find me a forward and forthright man," Griffith said. "But no, this is a gift for the lady." He asked Wolfe to interpret. "Can she understand? Could you, sir, express my desire?"

"Sir, say it to her face. No cat has her tongue. She has her own and ours very properly." His eyebrow arched and Griffith paled.

"Mrs. Timberlake," Griffith tried again, but I held up my hand.

"Mrs. Ostenaco Timberlake. Don't forget my noble father as well as my brave husband. Helena is my Christian name."

He frowned. "You are Christian?"

"Aren't we all, sir?" I smiled. "Baptized the same as you, Mr. Griffith."

"I read your late husband's memoir. Quite the brave man to venture into a recently defeated foe's territory. A hostage almost," our visitor said.

"My husband was a brave man, who saw the injustices done to the Real People and took up their cause twice before the King of England."

"Yet your husband died penniless in debtor's prison. And you nearly disappeared, Mrs. Timberlake. I've had a devil of a time tracking you down."

He had scoured all of London in search of me, evidently. He had followed the
reports in The Gentleman's Journal, checked ship manifests in Gravesend, hunted
the parish hall where Timberlake and Eleanor had signed their troth two years
back. He had deciphered Chututah's passage in the ship manifests, checking the
records in Gravesend and Bristol. He traced our lodgings from Leicester in the
Field, to Grub Street, to Wood Compter and Hyde Park, to John Coin's ill-reputed establishment, and then caught me again in the parish rolls at St. Dunstan's
church, where the witnessed seal was one Squire Wolfe, a Welsh accountant with
lodgings on Fetter Lane and now a short summer lease in Camden.

"I wanted to show you a treasure." Mr. Griffith produced from an inner pocket
a small box, sliding across the low table beside the vase.

I lifted the delicate lid. Inside was something wrapped in a rag of red stroud. I
set the box on the table and unwrapped the mysterious bundle. The smell was
instant and familiar, a chunk of white clay, still damp to my fingers as the day it
was dug from the bank of a mountain stream.

"I see you are acquainted with this piece of earth. A lump of dirt to most people,
quite valuable to others with the right knowledge. This came from a Quaker potter
in Savannah, in the lower Carolina colony. Upon further enquiry, we found the
raw material had been traded upon a place called Cowee not far from the Anoree
mountains."

"What does a lump of my homeland have to do with me?"

"The secret to Wedgwood is the clay, of course. You may be our key to the
clay," Griffith allowed. "My investors are most interested in acquiring exclusive
rights to such clays as could be dug in the Cherokee mountains. We seek only safe
passage into a savage land."

Again, always that word, savage. Applied only to my kind and never to the
yoneg.

"The Tsalagi seek only to defend themselves, to live in peace. My father has
given his word that we will not fight against any English," I insisted.

"Yes, but my agents aren't brave enough to believe such assurances," Griffith
said. "The Cherokee killed off the last trader in the valley just last year, making
normal trade dangerous."

"What would thou desire of Mrs. Timberlake?" Wolfe interjected. "She has not indicated she is ready to return to her homeland as of yet, nor has she the means to make a safe passage for a single lady."

"If you can't go, perhaps you could write a letter of introduction under your name, then," Griffith said to me. "Any assistance you could offer in negotiating such matters would, of course, would be amply rewarded."

I replaced the poor lump in its shroud, replaced it in its small box. The two men looked at me, waiting for an answer.

"I know a man, a Scotsman named M'Cormick, who trades on the creek. I could write him a short letter. He would show you how to get to the mountains for your clay."

"It seems we have reached an agreement," Wolfe smiled. "Let me draw up some papers."

In exchange for my letters of introduction, I would receive a percentage of whatever shipments of clay dug out of Cowee and shipped to England, as witnessed by Wolfe's red dripping wax and notary seal. Griffith's more practiced signature and the flowing marks that Wolfe had taught me, my English name signed in oak gall and the fine quill.

But holding the quill thusly always cramped my fingers, more used to awls and needles, yarns and ribbons. I rubbed my hands.

"I envy you, Mr. Griffith. You get to see the best land that men and women have ever called home. Deer Town. Cowee. My grandmother had relatives there we used to visit. Tell them you saw me, the Mankiller's Daughter. Tell them you have my blessing and best wishes."

***

I can drive a bargain as well as any man.

I watched Cat Walker strike deals with M'Cormick with baskets of bright corn ears when the trader first opened his Overhills outpost. But within a few seasons, men forgot how to deal with females, and the market down the mountain had lost its appetite for something so common as corn ears.

The yoneg wanted only fur and more fur. For every fifty deerhides, a Tsalagi man could trade bow and arrow for a new gun, black powder, and lead shot, which allowed him to go kill another fifty buck and doe.

Besides guns, they promised glass beads and ironwares, woven blankets and pretty ribbons for our hair, guns and powder for the men to find and slaughter more deer, the herds growing smaller and scarce, driven farther into the mountains. The trade that made us girls all so lazy, unlikely to weave our baskets or coil and bake our own pots when an iron kettle was dumped in the coals.

Cat Walker thought it was blasphemous to trade deerskins for new instruments, white men's toys that would make us into children.

"See the iron pot that Pretty Girl has in her house?" I had marveled. "I saw her drop it on the rocks by the river and it didn't break. It will never break."

"Like you did with my mother's best cooking pot," Cat Walker reminded me. "What happens when women, foolish as yourself, know only how to stir hominy in the yoneg's skillet, and forget how to make yellow jacket soup in an earthen pot — the way things should taste."

I pressed my eyetooth into the softness of my lip. Why did she have to be so old-fashioned?

"I want to wear a dress like Little Deer's."

"We would need to change that girl's name to White Tail, the way she flounces her scent about the men. She even walks with her legs wide open," Cat Walker said.

Once my father told me of a hunt at night, where the men ran through the forest with burning torches, driving the deer toward the river where other men shot them by the dozens, herd after herd. How the blood ran over the rocks that morning as they butchered their kills, food enough and hides. The women pounded the brains and cured the hides and stacked them as high as their heads, enough to bring guns and petticoats and iron pots and hoes, the conveniences of our modern days versus the wooden bows and arrows and flaked arrowheads, and deerskin dresses, fired but fragile clay pots.

Even before I left the Overhills, the deer had been driven farther back into the high ridges, away from our towns. Men could bring down more deer with the guns we traded with the English and French, but the noise had chased them away. Hunters were gone for the duration of a moon, before they came back skinny and gaunt with the haunches hung on poles. The deer were getting skinnier too.

Fewer deer meant less to barter for. Now with sassafras and clay, I meant to make my fortune.

Later, I revealed my hopes to Wolfe. "With enough coin, I can go home, can't I?"

I saw myself riding into Tomotley, bearing treasure and trophies for my people. I would embrace my son at last. My father and grandmother would shout my name. I would be treated as Ostenaco and Attakullakulla and even Chutatah had been celebrated with song and dance. I would be the spider crossing the waters, bearing fire on my strong back, home at last.

Chapter 18

Two years later, I had nearly forgotten the visit with Griffith and the deal I'd made with the Lincolnshire man with his nose for earth. We received a post that our cargo had arrived by heavy-laden barque direct from Charleston.

Wolfe and I hired a skiff to take us down river to the wharves at Gravesend.

Every English morning, the wharves are stacked with crates from India, smelling of cloves and cinnamon and human sweat and even a whiff of shit. Inside were bolts of muslin, gingham, chintz, the dazzle of the Orient. From the Americas arrived hogsheads of tobacco, rice, indigo, naval stores, pallets of fur and deer hide. Goods and wares pouring into their island from around the world, England was building an empire on which the sun would not set. The English counted Indians both in the East and in the Americas as but their lackeys and suppliers.

Wolfe signed at the customhouse for the receipt of delivery, before our cargo was transferred to another ship to be ferried upriver to the Bollingsgate market, along with another ticket to be taken to the Exchange. Paper traded for paper, giving us legal ownership of the casks and barrels, pallets and chests, furs, stacks of timber still smelling of a distant forest, the clay of course that Wedgwood wanted, but a last barrel too.

The longshoremen pried open the lids fastened with the rusted nails. The smell of earth, and then the fragrance of my childhood. The hogshead packed with root and stem and drying leaf.

The yoneg called it Sassafras, potent for the French pox and other diseases that men will pick up tupping the wrong wenches in Gravesend or the back corners of Covent Garden, or most any city or village, men always following the compass of their lusts and their pointing cocks.

I knew it by the name Kan'sta'tsi. I could see the three tell-tale lobes of the leaf, like mittens ever waving in the Overhill woods. I snapped a stem, felt the fine dirt still on the damp root, the sweet rich fragrance that nearly made me swoon.

Mother. Summoned by a scent from years ago and a distant grave. Not Cat Walker, nor my father, or Woyi, but her sweet ghost.

I no longer saw the wharf or the Thames or anything of smoggy, smelly London.

In an instant, as if I had taken a draught of the old Black Drink, I felt myself transported to Tomotley. My mother lay me down in the soft moss under a hemlock, giving me a stem of sassafras to suck on. The women were moving across the hillside, a soft herd of them, bent to graze the forest floor, gathering the wild onions, the first shoots of greens, the best roots. I was safe, singing to myself in the babble of babies before they have their mother's words in their mouths, when all is a smile or tears, joy or hunger, plenty or hurt.

I couldn't see her face, but I knew she was close by, the warmth of her words, speaking softly with her mother, Cat Walker. "Here, ah, a big one."

"It won't budge."

"Here, let me try."

They dug their fingers into the rich earth, harvesting the roots. That sweet smell was in all the teas she gave me to drip, the various medicines she rubbed with her fingertips across my lips, even the milk from her warm breast smelled of Kanasti.

***

The seven barrels of sassafras came accompanied by a leather pouch of receipts and letters, including a tattered post from Tomotley.

"Lord knows how long it's taken," Wolfe frowned at the page. "It's from last fall, a year ago now. It's signed M'Cormick."

A sharp pain in my side as if my knife under my skirt had cut me to the quick. I had the English that Wolfe had patiently tutored me to decipher, but I did not trust myself to make out the meaning, fearing perhaps what this cipher from across the ocean and from my forgotten home might portend.

"What does it say? Would thou read it for me?"

Dearest Skitty, first daughter of Ostenaco

The town still talks of you and your exploits. Chutatah wears his spectacles and Ostenaco his fancy medals with the king's likeness, even little Attakullakulla is hopping about, but you are still there among the English, seeing the wonders, the sights.

Some said a mere woman, even a Tsalagi girl as strong as yourself, could not survive such a passage, let alone life in that island, among such strange and powerful men, but I have known your mettle since you were a little girl. If any were to make her way safely among the haughty English, I'd bet on our little Skitty to surprise those lords and ladies.

There are women, I won't say who, but who whisper among themselves that you should have stayed in the cornfield, by the cookfire, but not playing a man's role, talking before our enemies or distant nations.

Make peace if you can. The Americans have not honored the treaty, pushing on the tribe's gamelands and abilities to hunt deer for their food and to trade for more necessities.

Griffith's agents have brought us word of Timberlake's death. I am very sorry for your loss, knowing the affections you had for the lieutenant. Ostenaco himself looked shaken, speaking long and loud in the council of the brave Timberlake and the pains he had taken to advance the People's welfare to the king.

I kept my eye on young Richard. He has often asked me if I do think you might return. I pray for your return.

Yr humble servant

Patrick M'Cormick

I had never known M'Cormick to be an eloquent man, but his words in his rough hand had reached across an ocean and gripped my heart.

Oh, Richard, you must have felt yourself an orphan, your father buried in a pauper's grave, and your mother lost in a hostile land.

Why had I stayed behind for so long? I had been a lost woman in John Coin's dark rooms. I had carried my stone knife in secret upon my person, but never deigned to slash out at that little man. The dark grief I carried for my daughter, Henry's child. I would have called her Sarah after Henry's own mother. I would have nursed her, cherished her, taken her back to our mountains to meet you. But all that was a dream brought on by the drink that washed away all my memories, my fears.

"I must go home," I told Wolfe.

He was tallying our receipts and profits.

"Another few shipments as rich as this, and perhaps thou may," my guardian said. "Not just yet. Pray for patience, Mrs. Timberlake."

Chapter 19

London, 1769

As to the Southern Indians, they are evidently the descendants of the ancient Carthaginians, who in their days as the greatest Merchants of the universe, discovered by their Trading Vessels many Islands, and sent Colonies to the Cultivation and Improvement of them; Probably some of their Vessels in the Pursuit of their discoveries recognized the more Southern Shore, fell in with the Trade Winds, not experienced in sailing upon the Wind, were blown over into the Gulph of Mexico, which Carthaginian navigators carried with them the Knowledge of conveying their Histories to Posterity by Hieroglyphics, from which northern Indians have learned to leave their particular adventures and Exploits with red and black on trees nearest by, as evidences by the truth of these ancient hieroglyphics, the Author has met with in the American Forests, especially the Appalachian Mountains, representing Figures executed with such art, as appear on the Coffins of the Egyptian Mummies.

William De Brahm's Report of the General Survey of the Southern District of North America

Fascinated by the indigenous tribes of what he always called North America, Squire Wolfe collected all matter of research and any kind of correspondence regarding my people, even the most outlandish tales which I suspect were fabricated by authors who had never met a living Indian outside a London sideshow.

"I would trust this De Brahm fellow even if he is German. It's my understanding that he had seen your particular country," Wolfe explained.

De Brahm had been at Fort Loudon, helping build its fortifications, until he had a falling out with Capt. Demere and departed. Good for the sake of his own skin, since those defenses would fall before Ostenaco's onslaught, and Demere would be made to dance for his life by Cat Walker and the Pretty Women, but I was loathe to tell Wolfe that part and what I had seen.

"So, he has been to the Overhills, but who were the Carthaginians? What are mummies?" I asked.

Wolfe would sigh, but he was very patient with my constant questions and encouraged my curiosity. He produced the small globe on a spinning axle and a wooden base, which he said was a true representation of the known world.

"The Carthaginians would have been here in northern Africa. Cross the desert over here, and you will find the Egyptian mummies, which are well preserved corpses in bandages, are found in giant pyramidical monuments, here." Wolfe would spin the great ball with its maps on its axis. "Over here are the American colonies, disgruntled as they are, and farther on your Cherokee Mountains if you look very close."

I couldn't help but spin the little toy just to watch it whirl, until Wolfe stopped its orbit with his pointed finger. My Quaker friend insisted that our world was like a giant ball suspended in the infinite sky revolving around the sun. "Put aside all superstition and understand that the world is round."

I had to laugh. "Cat Walker told me the world is a great bed tied with rope to the Four Directions."

"So, we are all in bed together?" He blushed furiously. "I think not. It's a ball, not a bed."

In Wolfe's way of thinking, we were spinning willy-nilly through nothingness, like a rawhide ball hurled skyward by God in a game, but no netted stick would ever catch us, no sweat-slicked player run us to a goal. We kept spinning until we were dizzy or all of life would be shook off the sides of the Earth.

Wolfe had read all the books, reports and dossiers and scientific papers on the Aboriginal Americans. My guardian had a theory. The Real People and indeed the other tribes thereabouts, whether Shawano or Catawba, Mohawk or Iroquois were likely descendants of the Lost Tribes of the Israelites as related in the Book he revered above all on his desk.

"You had an ark after all, much like the Israelites, carried through the wilderness. There's our proof," Wolfe exclaimed.

I had told him what Cat Walker once told me, about the earthen pot with the coals of the sacred fire that the medicine man carried on his back into battle.

"The ancient Hebrews bore the Ark of the Covenant, a box of gold similar to your healer's basket, containing mighty powers against their enemies." He scribbled greedily away, his quill pen flying across the parchment as pages dropped from his lap desk to the floor at his feet. "There's also how thy People handled the menses of the women, sending them out of the town."

I have never known a man so curious and prying about the monthly things of women and their particular ablutions. The men among the Real People kept their distance, and sacred things were not so spoken of, that was only the way things were done among us.

But Wolfe found that our sojourns by ourselves with that blood that came with each moon matched the habits of Hebrews, governed by the laws and hygiene that Moses had brought down from his mountain. Evidently, the Mighty Jehovah prescribed rules and conduct for his Chosen People.

"Another thing, Mrs. Timberlake, I have been pondering. Did the Cherokee ever practice Circumcision?"

"Circumcision," I tried the sound on my tongue. "Prithee, good Wolfe, tell me the meaning of your word."

He explained how priests would cut the foreskin from the penises of young boys as a sign of holiness. I shook my head, perhaps those people liked to torture the newborn into the hell of the world. Test courage of the coming man by tailoring the manhood. Who is the savage, and who are the civilized?

He seemed taken back by my shock. "It depends on your point of view. Some consider it barbaric how scalping has become so commonplace in those wild frontiers.

"One wonders who invented scalping. I've read arguments that the savages look upon it as a strange mercy, letting the soul of their victim make its way from the chambered skull of our mortality to the Great Creator. Others say the Indians, a cold, cruel race, murderous as descendants of Cain, perhaps lack all soul that could be assured a home in God's heaven, that taking the bloody hank of hair from their still breathing victim was but a satanic gloating, a last mortal indignity and a taste of the hell to come." He looked at me, and his face flushed. "Not that I believe that of thou."

But I had never told Wolfe of what I had watched Cat Walker do to Demere, not just the hair of his head. I had closed my eyes as a young girl when the flesh began to come off the bone, but I could not stop the screams in my ears. I could still hear the man howling an ocean away and years later. I shuddered.

"The only man I would think of either circumcising or scalping is Col. Carrington."

"Who?" Wolfe wondered.

"The officer who blocked our audience with the king. Didn't Henry mention him in his book?"

"I don't remember any Carrington mentioned. There's only a Greek name Kaxoanthropis," Wolfe said. "It's Greek for 'bad man.'"

"I wonder why Henry did not call him out by name?"

"I imagine your husband was not unwise," Wolfe said. "He wanted no retribution for slander. Carrington is evidently a crafty foe."

"All the better to slice his throat."

"Ah, but Mrs. Timberlake, thou swore off those evil deeds when thou were baptized with holy water into the Church and made a real Englishwoman."

"When I was tricked," I retorted. "Do men not kill monsters? I've seen pictures of your St. George plunging a lance through a dragon's heart."

"Those are just stories to scare children and peasants. Myths and metaphors. We must slay the dragons and demons that haunt our dreams," Wolfe said.

Here was a man trying to talk to me about fear and revenge and morality. I was afraid that forgiveness was simply an English habit of forgetting the harm a foe had done to your loved one.

Chapter 20

If Wolfe was a meek and gentle man, Frank was one to trust in a fight.

Frank was born in Jamaica, bastard son of a sugarcane planter, who distilled his own rum and possessed by his desires, visited his slaves' quarters at night for his pleasures. A mulatto, Frank's skin was hardly darker than my own, but his hair was curly compared to my straight locks. Wolfe explained that Frank's people originally hailed from Africa. Frank's forefathers had worn lion skins and sat on the bone thrones of elephants, the same behemoths we had seen on our tour of the Tower of London.

The Quality folks were pale as spirits, but pretended anyone darker, a person who shoveled their coal fires, or rowed the wherries, or climbed up their chimneys or served their teas, all those were invisible. Darker folk kept to the shadows. Unseen, unremarked, but always underfoot. In the back kitchens and back rooms and downstairs in the cellars or stuffed up in the top garrets where the rains came through the ancient roofs, they had been taken in chains and shipped to the coast. King George had ended the trade in human souls, be they black as Nubians, four years before I set foot on this island.

Officially a freedman and a full legal subject of the English king, Frank remained black in a world of whites, while I was a red woman. "It matters not," Wolfe insisted. "Jesus loves his children of all different colors."

"Amen, amen," Frank said loudly, but I also heard the undertone that followed. "Then why do they always make Jesus so white in the colored windows of the church?"

Frank was soft spoken, but beneath his double-breasted coat and under his tight breeches, you could see the hard muscles bequeathed by generations of slaves, men who had given their bodies to build great houses, to harvest great fields, to amass great mansions for small white men who could scarcely match their strength.

Roaming the Strand and the dark steps down to the Thames, walking to the
end of Drury Lane where the brigands would club you and pull you into a side
alley in St. Giles.

The fishmongers and the flower girls, dirty faced urchins pawing at your side,
not just begging, but putting their sticky little fingers into your pockets if you did
not slap their little arms away. Mind the footmen with their chairs, bearing unseen
personages through the muddy streets, out of the way, watch ye self, they shout,
their boots kicking aside the idle and the bystanders, the crush of so many lost
souls in this soulless city.

Once Frank and I were walking back from Market Street, our baskets filled
with fresh hen's eggs, potatoes and onion, a green topped bunch of orange carrots,
even a stewing hen to pluck for the night's pot. Down the lane, a gang of toughs
came tumbling out of the local tavern, already staggering at noon from the white
drink. One of them bounced into Frank, and he shoved the drunkard into the
gutter.

"Watch yourself, boy." The drunk righted himself, brushing the filth from his
frock coat. "You darkies need to go back to wherever you came from."

"We come from Oxford Street and Soho Square, not from the Gomorrah of
St. Giles," Frank said in his most measured tone.

"Ye bastard ripped my best coat," the first fellow said, inspecting his sleeve.
"What do you intend to do about it?"

"Go about our business, as I would suggest you scoundrels might."

"Ah, brave words from a nigger's mouth. And what of your wifey? She looks a
little too dark to be a real Londoner."

I heard this hard talk before in John Coin's ill-reputed establishment and my
bad days loitering and worse along Gin Alley. I was ready with my reply. "Aye, ye
are a true Cockney, but your cocks are nothing to crow about, I can tell already."

The drunkards were riled and rushed us with their hobnailed boots and their
meaty fists.

Frank cracked the first rogue's kneecap with his walking stick. And out from
my girdle came Cat Walker's flint knife, and I sliced the other man's nose. He held
his thick hands to his face, blubbering that I had murdered him as the blood
dripped through his fingers.

Frank and I ran down the cobbles and doubled back to the house on the other side of Soho Square, out of breath, and bolted the door.

And I had dropped three of the six hen's eggs we had bought that morning, dropping potatoes and onions in our path.

"Should we tell Squire Wolfe?" Frank wondered.

"He'd want us to forgive," I said. I cleaned my knife with a rag at the table and slid it beneath my dress again, smoothing out my appearance. But then I burst out laughing.

"He'd say we should pray for those men."

"Pray he don't bleed to death with no nose." Frank laughed.

"Pray the other with the knee-capped knee won't limp too long."

***

Frank was always the gentleman, and I liked his build and his demeanor more than most Britishers I would meet in all my years on that forsaken island. I missed the warmth of a man in my bed, and sometimes dreaming like a widow, I would close my eyes and pretend that my hand was Henry's, but then I would weep even after the last gasp of a forced pleasure.

Even though Frank slept in the back and my room was upstairs, and Wolfe was in the middle, I dared not creep to his room, though I often closed my eyes and let my fancy roam.

I overheard them once, a soft murmur, a little laughter, and in a bedroom where I should properly have knocked at the half-closed door, I burst in unawares. Wolfe humbling himself, kneeling before the manservant seated on the bed. Frank's breeches were pulled down about his strong black calves. Startled, they both looked at me, wide-eyed like boys caught in some naughtiness.

I shut my eyes, unable to unsee what I had witnessed. I closed the door and left these two dear souls to what they needed from each other. We take what we can, love is a small trade, pleasure so rare in this life for so many.

It was a secret we never talked about in our house of three — white, black, and red.

Chapter 21

Aside from his moral education of a naïve arrival to these shores, Wolfe had other ambitions.

His treatise, A Study of American Aboriginals and Their Affinity with Ancient Hebrews, based on his study of Holy Scripture and confirmed by the stories handed down to me by the wise Cat Walker, was to be the work of his lifework. But he could find no willing publisher along Grub Street or up and down the Fleet.

"Indians and Jews? Not a likely market," said the ink-stained gatekeepers as their penny pamphlets flew off presses in their back shops.

Still, my Quaker friend longed to see his manuscript set in type and published for the betterment of learning, added to libraries of peers and fine gentlemen. He desired not only to distill his collected knowledge but wanted the best minds of his time to read and applaud his worthy effort. Out of a vanity he would never admit, Wolfe paid himself for a single copy, and bound it with a silk ribbon and boxed it in its own little crate.

"Looks like a coffin. As if you mean to bury your book."

His face was crestfallen.

"I'm teasing with you, sir." I laughed to make light of the moment, but it was if I had blown out the Light of the Spirit within the poor man with my unfortunate jape.

My tutor had taught me another hard lesson: Words are serious matters, and those who would be writers are serious souls. But the rub now was how to get his self-made volume into the hands of an authority, beneath the keen eyes of a learned observer, a great mind, such as the famous Dr. Johnson.

Wolfe had been screwing up his courage for an encounter with the Great Man, the best speaker in the whole land, the most learned and fierce of critics. He followed faithfully every missive signed by Johnson in the Rambler and then the Idler, had subscribed to the massive project of The Dictionary. And poured over the Lives of the Poets.

"He that wishes to be counted among the benefactors of posterity must add by his own toil to acquisitions of his ancestor and secure his money from neglect by some valuable improvement. This can only be affected by looking out upon the wastes of the intellectual world and extending the power of learning over regions yet undisciplined and barbarous; or by surveying more exactly our ancient dominions and driving ignorance from the fortresses and retreats where she skulks undetected and undisturbed."

"What Johnson said ..." And he closed his old copy of the Rambler. He nearly genuflected.

"So is the man saying that Ignorance is a woman?"

Wolfe ignored me.

"Without doubt, his is the greatest Mind in England, and I would hazard, the Continent, which would make up the whole of the civilized world. He must be a prodigious reader, all of Shakespeare, and his Dictionary. He knows every word in our language.

He had even planned a witty repartee, "What God had wrought, Johnson already wrote."

If only Johnson would read Wolfe's words.

***

We had our opportunity one afternoon. We were taking the air in the close London lanes near Wolfe's offices in Temple Bar, when my Quaker friend halted and yanked on my elbow, pulling me around the corner.

"Oh, Lord, it's him," Wolfe said. "In the flesh."

We dared to peek around the brick corner. There was indeed plenty of flesh to behold, a man not nearly as big as The Mountain as I remembered, but very wide for a yoneg. His appearance was very similar to a toad with his bloated and poxed face, his eyes askew. Unkempt for a gentleman, not as well cleaned as Wolfe. He wore a wig, much too small and crooked for his large head. His brown suit shined with use, his shirt neck and the knees of his breeches were loose, his black worsted stockings ill drawn up, and he had a pair of unbuckled shoes.

"It's him. Johnson," Wolfe whispered in awe.

If his appearance was uncouth, his words were polished, his voice sonorous, even beautiful. Even I, not a native speaker of this language, could hear him talking in a different tongue than the usual yoneg.

"Good Lord, he's composing an ode in Latin. I hope someone is writing that down," Wolfe whispered.

"Go ahead and speak to the man." I pushed at Wolfe, but he resisted.

"We look like beggars." He came away from the wall with the back of his best stockings covered with black soot. My skirts were marred as well. We retreated to our lodgings where it would take days of washing and bluing to make those clothes presentable again, and not the motley attire of ragamuffins, urchins, and the be-grimed chimney boys and coal haulers.

Wolfe wondered if he would get another encounter with the Great Man. He did not want to accost the writer at The Club where he would be seen through the high windows carousing and talking the great talk with the accomplished men (but no women, of course.)

But Wolfe was not a Club man. In his household, Wolfe did not serve any strong spirits perhaps on my behalf after he and Frank had saved me from the English White Drink and the bad days I had been in Gin Lane. On our household, he allowed himself only small beer and perhaps shandy, but much preferring strong tea, rather than the black-brewed coffee that could be found in the various houses up and down the Fleet and over into the Strand.

But drink lubricated the tongue of men like Johnson and did not dull their sharp minds.

What I had heard of the man in the street, Johnson was very melodious in his manner of speech, even after a few drinks. In that regard, he reminded me of At-takullakulla or of my father. Yoneg usually consider us to be a people of few words and thus thoughts as we keep our own counsel and do not betray our ignorance or endlessly boast. But the chiefs making their great calls for war or for peace in the council house, they could make rivers of words, waterfalls of words, their thoughts directing the flow of the whole nation. Words are like water; I had come to learn under Wolfe's tutelage. You come to words the way you come to water, letting them wash over your head, cleanse your thoughts. Some men's minds were like stagnant ponds or bare trickles of dried stream beds. Others were like oceans.

I believed Johnson was such a man, and on behalf of Squire Wolfe who had done so much for me, I resolved that we would speak to the Great Mind should opportunity present itself again.

Chapter 22

Not all our outings were edifying.

One Execution Day, we walked over to Newgate to see the hangings. Wolfe said a condemned female was to receive her just desserts, an unusual occurrence that would draw a curious crowd.

A woman in a plain woolsey gown was led to the gallows, her hair let down in public and the rope placed around her pale neck. She wept and cried and prayed for mercy, but the crowd only hooted. She had been convicted of stealing a silver plate from a tavern. A loose woman, she had pled her belly was with child when she was thrown into the prison, but as she grew thinner and not thicker, and her tale was soon seen as a lie. The only fate worse would be a sentence of transportation to America. At least, the gibbet afforded a quicker route to her final Judge, rather than having to face the terrors of wilderness, savages, and wild beasts.

"May God have mercy on your soul," intoned the cleric with his frowning face, signing an unmerciful cross over her bowed head. The executioner pushed her unceremoniously off the stoop, her last ground. She kicked frantically a while in midair until her body stilled.

The crowd applauded and cheered. We waited as the platform was cleared for the next appointment.

"I know it seems barbaric," Wolfe allowed. "I wish cruel punishments of all sorts were outlawed. Vengeance should be the Lord's and not a cheap entertainment for the lower classes."

The English seemed to behave differently from my People. They vindicated their actions as divine judgement, rather than readily admit the human appetite for revenge.

Wolfe explained the English used to burn heretics and witches and generally anyone that came afoul of their ministers and kings. They used to draw and quarter traitors, a lengthy process of knives and ropes and fire.

The other week, there was a French spy who was hanged, drawn, and quartered, my good Quaker friend explained. The man who had passed state secrets it was said was hanged by the neck for a good half hour, slowly choking, until almost unconscious, then he was cut down into the sawdust, and the executioner turned the knife on his belly, pulling out his entrails like long ropes into the fire, then the poor soul was finally disposed of his head, and then his limbs lopped off with a heavy ax. His head raised to the roars of the crowd. "Here be the head of the traitor."

There was quite a crowd, hundreds of men, women and children, lusting for blood. "Barbaric." It's a marvel that we don't hammer them up onto crosses, crucify them if that wasn't reserved for our Lord Christ.

I watched as the executions went on that morning, the crowd cheering. I did not turn my eyes away, but there was no blood shed, only the jerk of the rope about the thin necks of those poor souls extinguished of their one precious life. Justice, I suppose, was served.

I had been raised to believe that blood was required to restore balance in a world too easily rocked by wrong word, the thoughtless action, the surge of red that cut down a kinsman and set up the right of blood revenge, the whole clan called to take a life for the one lost — that was the way that the Real People lived and breathed in this realm. A grandmother clubbed while watching the corn fields, a child swung by the heels and brained against the closest tree trunk, a warrior for a woman, a babe for an old man, all lives equally lost and revenged in the scheme of things since this troubled world began.

The only man I could see executing was Col. Carrington. I still carried Cat Walker's stone knife, strapped to my naked thigh beneath my petticoats. One day, I planned to use its sharp edge.

"Remember what thou see here, Mrs. Timberlake. Men and women can be cruel as children at times." Wolfe led me away, blowing his nose, catching another cold, that delicate man.

"At least they hang the poor bastards these days. Less a bloody mess of lopping off their heads or sawing off their scalps like — "

He cut his eyes at me, but too late. I had caught his thought.

"Like Indians? Savages?" I could feel the blood hot in my face. I shut my eyes and shook my head, but years later, I could still hear the trilling tongues of Cat Walker and the Pretty Woman butchering the cowardly Demere down by the river.

"Helena, believe me, I meant nothing by it. Not thou certainly."

But even my guardian saw only my Red Skin and my taste for blood. He knew I carried a stone knife on my person. I could live in London the rest of my days, and I would never be as white as Wolfe.

Chapter 23

St. Stephens Church, Gravesend, 1772

Our agreement with Mr. Griffith for continuous trade in Cowee clay and sassafras went well, drawing me an annual allowance of two hundred pounds. I may never be properly English and accepted by Society, but I would not be poor again, living in the gravel paths and hedges of Hyde Park. With Wolfe's encouragement, I would save up an inheritance for you, my son. Someday, these bank notes and silver pieces will mean more than the deerhides and bushels of corn that Ostenaco and Cat Walker wanted to trade with the yoneg. More money meant that someday I would be a lady of means able to book my passage to America and return with honor and trophies to Tomotley.

Every few months, we would hire a lighter down to Gravesend, the oarsmen slicing the dark Thames with the wooden blades, while Wolfe and I sat amid ships, watching England and its houses and villages slide by on the banks. Waiting on the wharves ahead was another shipment of clay dug from the Cowee hills, sassafras, hands of tobacco packed in hogshead. We had become exporters and padded our purses. No need to count the coin, we took promissory notes, more scratches of paper.

With each reckoning, I asked Wolfe if I had enough fortune yet to book my passage home.

"Not yet," he kept saying, his spectacles flashing as he looked down the tally of figures. "Maybe the next shipment will do the trick."

He folded the papers and put them into his breast pocket of his coat.

"Shall we stretch our river legs a bit, see the sights?" Squire Wolfe suggested.

My guardian and I strolled Gravesend's High Street to the St. Stephens church. Not a churchman, my faithful friend found the naves, chancels, and altars unnecessary for his religion. Still, Wolfe admired the architecture.

In the portico hung an oil painting depicting St. George Slaying the Dragon. The artwork was on loan from another church that bore the Saint's name, but was undergoing a renovation, Wolfe said.

I was struck by the dragon. The English had their own Uk'tena, by the looks, the scales and the wings, but I couldn't see any crystal imbedded in the beast's small horns. The dragon looked more like a great lizard with leathery wings, threatening the praying damsel and the knight in armor sitting his steed, lowering his lance.

"Myths and romance. Fancy and lies," Wolfe said, a practical man who wanted to know the truth of things.

"You mean dragons are not real?"

"I've never seen one with my eyes, though I've read reports of large reptiles on the isle of Komodo, but none native to England. We don't even have the poisonous snakes that populate your mountains."

We walked out into the yard among the graves, in the drizzle that had blown in from the narrow sea. The dead lay beneath single slabs with their names engraved in their custom. Back in Tomotley, I remembered the rough cairns, rock that the Real People would pile on the bones of the fallen warrior or the beloved woman, letting their names be whispered into the woods.

"All this is new, rebuilt since a fire razed the church back in '42. In the chaos, they mislaid her grave, but she's here somewhere." Wolfe tapped his cane about absentmindedly, it seemed to me as if sounding out the hollows of the crypts and the bones within.

"Who?"

"Mrs. Rolfe, or her remains, I should say. She was like thou, an Indian princess."

Her name was Pocahontas, the daughter of a chief who fell in love with an Englishman named Smith, a soldier who was both captive and guest of an Indian nation near the Virginia coast. She begged that his life be spared.

"And she married the man, her true love?"

"No, she married a friend of Smith's, a man named Rolfe, who brought her here. She became a good Christian, or at least she converted and was baptized. She bore Rolfe his babies, but she died young. Only twenty and one, I believe she was."

Wolfe had brought a penny pamphlet from a rack inside the church, an old-fashioned likeness printed therein, which he showed me. Mrs. Rolfe's face was white, her head narrow as if severed and served on a lace ruff, a strange bird with her tall hat, but her eyes were dark, familiar.

"It's a tragic tale, romance gone astray. True love parted, early graves."

"What happened to her people back home?"

Wolfe shrugged. "They were Powhatan, I believe. Have thou heard of that nation?"

My turn to shake my head. I studied the likeness of the poor woman, who looked so unhappy even a hundred years ago. Her dark eyes even in a poorly printed engraving stared off the crumpled sheet, over the centuries, finding mine.

Had she been searching for the fire, or had she turned her back on her tribe, followed a husband across the sea and forgot her past?

"What happened to her child?"

"I have no idea. What happens to most children these days?"

His question brought a terrible vision. I could see you, Richard, staring dejectedly into the cold waters of the river that flowed by Tomotley. I saw the bundled body of the daughter I could not safely deliver in John Coin's evil garret. I saw myself, a lone woman wandering the streets of the city only to throw herself from London Bridge into the dark Thames below.

I shook away such thoughts and pushed the pamphlet at Wolfe. "I am not her. We are not the same. I am alive, and she is dead."

But even dead women hold terrible power. I could not shake her cold grip upon my thoughts.

He draped his greatcoat across my shoulders. "Thou are shivering. Come, Mrs. Timberlake, we don't want thee taking a chill."

Chapter 24

London at night

In the midnight, when the bells of London strike, an eerie sound I have heard so many nights now living in this burning land, the anthracite crumbling red in the grate. I can hear another noise I've not heard since leaving Tomotley, and I catch my breath icy in the air over my bed.

There comes a slithering in the streets of the district, a glint of scales in the night, and a blinding light from the crystal on the horned Uk'tena's head. The forked tongue tests the smoggy air, the foul fogs. A lantern beam glancing against the dirty glass windows of the tenements where men are gobsmacked by cheap gin, snoring their troubled dreams, and cold children whimper in crowded beds, their swollen bellies beginning to rumble, or the girl with her legs raised high, screams bloody murder, bringing another of the brood to this troubled world, and still the snake passes by, mile upon mile, coiled around Piccadilly Circus, and stretching toward Westminster Abbey and Parliament, angling its crystalline light here and there, down alleys and empty streets, into the courtyards while rats skitter away at its approach.

The Uk'tena searches for me, the baby who escaped the rattlesnake's wrath an ocean away, my mother cursed to be bitten and die.

I awake with a start, bolt upright in my bed, clutching the clammy sheets. Pale Wolfe stands with the tallow candle in the doorway in his nightshirt and his thin, sad knees.

"Thou were screaming, madam. Gave me quite the scare."

***

In London came reports of a new plague, a bloody flux and ague making the rounds of the poorer quarters, cemeteries stacking up with bodies like cordwood. When a man's cough in the streets struck fear into others, many went about with kerchiefs tied about their mouths and noses to avoid the stench of shit, vomit, blood, the reek of death as fading flowers hung in wreaths and black crepe nailed to heavy doors.

When Frank dropped the tray of tea things, Wolfe and I helped him up and put him into his bed. Frank was pale, his lips blanched, the eyes yellowed, coughing.

"We may have to call a doctor in to bleed him."

I hurried north of town where the cobbles gave way to the dirt roads and fields where greens still grew. In the Overhills, a practiced healer like Cat Walker would gather the green medicine. She would paint a salve of certain bruised leaves and roots, the saps drawn up from the life force of the earth itself, to restore the balance of congested chest, aching limbs, troubled bowels. The salve required a magic song, the right words that would correct the wrong that had befallen.

I had been Helena too long, and Skitty was just a girl who didn't always pay attention in the woods. Could I make the tonic that would save Frank from the barber's blade? At least we had sassafras to give it flavor. In the kitchen, stoking the fire, stirring the pot. I had seven plants, the sacred number, but couldn't be sure of the formula. I certainly didn't have the words.

At his bedside, I raised his head and put the cup of tea to his lips, but he turned his head. I tried again, forcing the fluid into his mouth. He spit it full into my face. I slapped his hot face.

"Don't be such a child. Drink this if it kills you."

Feverish, he drank and swallowed it down. Frank had saved my life, along with Wolfe nursing me from my dreams and delusions with shandy, small beer and lemon water, and then only strong tea. Save for this man, I would have been a trollop with my skirts hitched, my legs splayed open for any business on Gin Alley, all for a swallow of cheap liquor.

He must not die. It was my turn to save him.

In the branches of the willow tree in the back garden, I set a demon-catcher as an added precaution. I once watched a Conjure Woman, even more powerful than Cat Walker in her medicine ways, make such a snare.

She had bent a slender shoot into a hoop, lacing the circle with sinew and adorning it with the proper feathers and formulas chanted under the breath, as she waved her creation to the four cardinal directions.

These were snares to catch nightmares, the Ravenmocker, that shapeshifter who played as your father or mother or sister only to grasp your beating heart and eat your soul. Or the nightrider who could fly by dark into a town and carry off a baby's breath leaving only a stiff dead bundle by a mother's side when first light came.

I had brought the Uk'tena to this island. No telling what other monsters had followed me here. I had to set a snare for any spirits who were haunting Frank with his shaking body.

***

On the third day, I heard a laugh from the garret. Frank was sitting upright against the wall, and Wolfe was holding his hand, seated on the bedside. The worst seemed to be passed.

"Look who's back from the dead, Helena, thanks to thee."

I drew back the drapes and threw up the window sash. "Let's allow some daylight in amid all this gloom. A little air. Let the vapors out. It smells like men in here or swine. It's about time you got out of those dirty bedclothes and let us clean the linens. Up and about."

Wolfe grabbed my hand to stop my bustling about the sick room. "Stay, Helena Timberlake. Plenty of time for that." He held onto Frank and to me with his small hands.

"God help us, I'm not sure what I would have done if we had lost dear Frank."

After such a long time on his back, the manservant made his way unsteadily to his feet, but also made a pained face. "Good Lord, just don't make me drink any more of her Indian tea."

Outside the window, the demon catcher swayed from the willow branch, having worked its proper medicine.

Chapter 25

Frank regained his strength once more and was able to accompany me to markets when Squire Wolfe was in court.

One day, we rounded the corner and nearly collided with Dr. Johnson. He had come from Clifton's eating house on Butcher Row, picking a nail at his good dinner caught in his teeth.

A younger man was at his ear, arguing loudly. "What say you, sir? Why are some men created lesser than others? Why are some men black and some white?"

"Depend upon it, sir," Johnson slowly allowed. "It has been accounted for in three ways: either by supposing that they are posterity of Ham, who was cursed; or that God at first created two kinds of men, one black and another white: or that by the heat of the sun the skin is scorched, and so acquires a sooty hue. This matter has been much canvassed among naturalists but has never been brought to any certain issue."

"Excuse me, kind sir, I could not help but overhear your conversation." I pushed myself forward. As I made my curtsey, I made certain he could see the tops of my warm brown breasts. He was a man like any other, enamored of the female form.

"My friend, Frank, here is a blackamoor who hails from Jamaica. And I am not white, but red, what has been too often labeled American aboriginal. Where would I fit into your argument, sir?" I asked in all my feigned innocence.

Dr. Samuel Johnson seemed speechless, perhaps for the first time in his conversational career. He had been ambling along his usual London route, arguing the ethics, when a stranger had accosted him. Two strangers, not even of his own race. And one, a member of the fairer if lesser sex.

"Johnson, I do believe she has you by your horns." The younger man laughed. "Rousseau may be right. The natives of the Americas may be more noble than our own kind."

"Rousseau? Don't speak to me of that Paris pimp of the mind, extolling the nobility of savagery," the great man tutted. "For my part I would never surrender London, the life of learning, indeed the love of civilization, to be blissfully ignorant in the wilderness."

"Johnson, your idea of wilderness is a tree in Hyde Park. There have been cultured gentlemen who lived for a time in the wilds of America, free and unrestrained, amidst the rude magnificence of Nature," the younger man insisted. "I could envision such a life, say with this Indian woman by my side, and a long gun with which I can procure food when I want it."

The young man who grew handsomer by the second took my arm in his.

"Do not allow yourself, sir, to be imposed upon by such gross absurdity," Johnson argued. "It is sad stuff; it is brutish. If a bull could speak, he might as well exclaim, 'Here I am with this cow and this grass: what being can enjoy greater felicity?'"

I interrupted. "Did you just call me a cow, sir?"

The handsome companion laughed, taking my cause as well. "I believe she is right, sir. You have slandered this beauty as a bovine. And you insinuated I am brutish, if not quite a horned bull."

I saw my opening with the Great Man. "Your sudden rudeness aside, Dr. Johnson, I've been told you are the greatest mind of England, perhaps the Continent, the soul of our wit, the Doctor of Dictionaries."

"You flatter me, madam, which I recognize as a vice, but I would let anyone as lovely as yourself speak her mind."

"We have not been formally introduced, but I have followed your wise words since the Idler and the Rambler."

"One follows only in the shadow of the Bard. I am but a hack, madam. A scribbler, a speechifier, but I seem to have a reputation of sorts."

"Well-earned, that reputation," I said. "I've been told your Dictionary is the finest achievement of our time, fortifying for once and for all the importance of the language, correctly used."

"Again, I must ask, do I know you, my dear?"

"Her name is Mrs. Helena Ostenaco Timberlake," Frank piped up.

"And this is Mister Frank Jones," I returned the favor of these formalities.

"Mrs. Timberlake! I would not take you for such a good English name." Johnson's young companion smiled.

"Ah, where are my manners." Johnson made a short bow. "Mrs. Timberlake, meet the impetuous James Boswell, better known to his friends as Bozzy."

"That's Bozzy to you, and you are more than a bit bossy yourself." Boswell took my hand within his own warm grasp. "Charmed would be the common term. Enchanted would be much more accurate, Mrs. Timberlake."

"Mrs. Henry Ostenaco Timberlake," I corrected him.

"Mrs. Timberlake is the widow of the late Lieut. Henry Timberlake. You may be familiar with his memoir of his adventures among her people, the Cherokee," Frank said.

"Ah, I have read the late lieutenant's report," said Boswell.

"Mrs. Timberlake's father was the war chief, Ostenaco, who toured the town," Frank added.

"Sirrah, I remember the riots when the Indians took London by storm," Johnson interjected. "Quite the spectacle if I recall, pickpockets and cutpurses made their mark while the mobs pressed for a look see. Live Indians, dead Indians. When they will not give a droit to relieve a lame beggar, they will lay out ten to see a dead Indian."

"That's Shakespeare." Frank nudged me.

"Small wonder, Johnson wrote the book on Shakespeare," Boswell said. "He can quote the Bard in his sleep."

Mr. Boswell would not let go my hand until I pulled free and turned again to Johnson.

"Our guardian and benefactor, Squire Wolfe, has written a book of sorts. Perhaps you would be interested?"

"A book, fancy that." Johnson's face twitched.

"It is a project Squire Wolfe has undertaken with my help. His thesis is that my people are none other than descendants of the Lost Tribes of Israel. Squire Wolfe is but an amateur but believes that Royal Society could be interested in its thesis. That is to say, hopeful."

"All writers are hopeful. It is their delusion. Tell your guardian and master Squire Wolfe to deliver it to my quarters. I am overwhelmed in manuscript and correspondence, but as a favor to you, madam, I will offer an opinion."

"Let me come collect it for you," Boswell said. "I am somewhat of a writer myself, not of course like Johnson, but I would be glad to peruse it. You might be able to explain the finer points of your history to me, Mrs. Timberlake. I'm sorry, Mrs. Ostenaco-Timberlake."

Chapter 26

The missive had arrived in the post the very next morning. A declaration of intention again to call on me, signed in the most extravagant hand by Mr. James Boswell:

"If you ask of Boswell, I would be glad to tell you. A most excellent man, of an ancient family in the west of Scotland, upon which he valued himself not a little. At his nativity there appeared omens of his future greatness. His parts are bright, and his education has been good. He has traveled in post-chaises, miles without number. He is found of seeing much of the world. He eats of every good dish, especially apple pie. He drinks old hock. He has a good manly continence, and he owns himself to be amorous. An infinite vivacity, yet he is observed at times to have a melancholy cast. Rather fat than lean, rather short than tall, rather young than old."

"Anything of interest, Helena?" Wolfe asked in passing, seeing me deep in study of this letter.

"Nothing of any great matter," I lied, folding the pages and slipping them into my pocket for safekeeping. I was in possession of what the French would call my very first billets-doux.

In all the foolscap that Henry filled, the reports to his superiors, the urgent pleas to the Board of Trade, to Amherst, to central command, to the Royal Court, even in the memoir he fashioned from his adventures in the Overhills, in all his writings, he had never written me a love letter.

Across all of London, young hearts write out their rage on scented sheets, press their painted kisses into the pages, sprinkle and seal their fate with eau de water and French colognes. They trust these intimate communiques to scullery maids and periwigged footmen, to slip beneath the sills of locked doors. They pine, waiting for some return word, a declaration of true love.

But papers can be lost, burned in the fire, dropped into gutters and puddles, the ink running like blood. The words can be lost. Or ripped into shreds like a forsaken lover.

There is no paper in Henry's hand, mentioning my name, only what he whispered in my ear in the winter house of Tomotley by the pure river, or in the tenements of Grub Street where he spent our last month as married couple. What remains I carry with me forever.

Back home in the Overhills, we used to chant a formula for the love that leaves. The rest of the formula I have nearly forgotten, so many years away from Tomotley and my first tongue. I dream only in Tsalagi, the soft syllables in my sleep.

And now you have rendered the woman blue. Now you have made the path blue for her. Let her be completely veiled in loneliness. Put her into the blue road. And now bring her down. Place her standing upon the earth. Where her feet are now and wherever she may go, let loneliness leave its mark upon her. Let her be marked out for loneliness where she stands.

If Henry had only said the proper words, seven times in the right order, how to mark a woman as your own, he may be with me even now.

***

A few days later, Wolfe had gone to his office, and Frank was out to market.

I had the house to myself and was surreptitiously reading Mr. Sterne's latest and most amusing installment of The Life and Opinions of Tristan Shandy, Gentleman, a book that Squire Wolfe felt most inappropriate, even cheeky to read in mixed company. I was chuckling to myself in the front parlor when there was a knock at our front entrance. A visitor at the front, rather than some delivery at the back.

I found Mr. Boswell, hat in hand, bowing on the threshold.

"Mrs. Timberlake, forgive the intrusion."

"You just missed Squire Wolfe."

"Did I now? Fancy that." My handsome caller smiled. "No matter. The manuscript is here, and so are thee. May I presume to impose on your company?"

"The manuscript, yes, of course. Do enter."

I went into Wolfe's study. The fair copy of the manuscript lay on the corner of his desk, bound with a red ribbon, next to his squibs and inkwells, the candle shield by which he wrote most nights.

Mr. Boswell had followed me, inspecting the books, the desk. "Is this where your guardian does his deep thoughts then? And you keep him company?"

I clutched the book like a shield to my breasts, feeling somewhat and suddenly warm even in this normally chilled room. "Yes."

I thrust the papers at him, as if to push this man away.

"Squire Wolfe is so appreciative that Dr. Johnson is willing to invest his time in reading."

"I'm certain Dr. Johnson will appreciate the work as I appreciated its subject and muse." He held the manuscript, but I felt it was not all he had come for. Nor did I particularly want our company to yet part.

"Where are my manners? I must make you tea." I brushed his hand as I fled to the kitchen.

But he trailed after me, not at all a polite man who would be confined to wait politely in the parlor. As the kettle boiled, we talked.

"I do have some sassafras tea from my homeland. You must taste it. It reminds me of my homeland."

"I was looking through your late husband's memoirs after our encounter on the street. Fascinating. Timberlake was quite the hero in my estimation, taking a journey into the unknown, to find such treasures as you."

I felt my face growing hot as the stove.

"I recollect hearing of the Cherokee chiefs who came to town years back, the great spectacle they presented. You are related to the Chief they called the Mankiller?"

"I am his daughter. We do not have kings and princes among the Real People. I'm no princess then, just a woman who grew up in Tomotley."

"Tomotley, what a charming name to trip off the tongue." Boswell's smile grew whiter.

When the kettle finally whistled, I poured the boiling water over the ground fragrant root, one of our last shipments. He followed me as I brought our tea out into the parlor, where a lady could more properly entertain a gentlemen visitor.

He saw my copy of Sterne's novel on the settee, raised his eyebrow, but said not a word. I spread my skirts as I sat. He chose the Windsor chair by the hearth, a discrete difference from me.

"Wolfe would do better to write a novel, something that women like to read. You would make a fascinating character in a popular novel. You sound just like Pocahontas."

"Squire Wolfe and I were down at Gravesend and saw her grave. He told me of Mrs. Rolfe's sad story."

"Poor Indian princess changed her name, married the wrong man, died in England." Boswell crossed his shapely legs, sipped his tea. "Now there's a story worth writing. Squire Wolfe would find a ready market for that, I wager."

"But he has spent years on his study, Origins of the American Aboriginal."

My visitor looked at me over the rim of his cup, held so daintily between the first knuckle and thumb of his hand. His right leg kicking merrily, crossed at the knee.

"Seems Squire Wolfe had his thesis before he met you, another cock-and-bull story that the lost Tribes of Israel wandering through the desert mysteriously wound up a world away in the Americas," he said. "You look dark to me, milady, but you have not the Sephardic nose."

"Beg your pardon, sir?"

"You don't look like Shylock's tribe to me." Boswell tapped his fingers on the thick portfolio of Wolfe's best efforts. "I don't quite understand your relationship to the man."

"He has been my protector, a legal guardian, an advisor after the death of my husband."

"And it seems he has been purloining the best of you for his misguided philosophy."

He smiled his fine white teeth, such a rarity among the English. He was a most handsome man. I decided to change the course of our awkward conversation.

"How long have been acquainted with Dr. Johnson?"

"I have known him for years, once went to the Hebrides in his company. I do get annually to London for a visit, to see the sights. Johnson is right, of course: when a man is bored with London, he is bored with life."

"Dr. Johnson reminds me of my father," I said. "He talks like him. Like a waterfall. My father could make men go to war and women cheer them on. He could say anything, and everyone listened."

"I'm certain you take after your father in courage. I saw how you walked right up to Johnson and spoke your mind." Boswell laughed.

"I'm sure Dr. Johnson is a fine man. He does like to talk about London."

"Johnson. Good God, if there is an England, it runs like hock in his veins and he would not have you forget that the English subdued the Picts, threw out the Romans, took on the Welsh, scoured the Scots, and have planted their plantations among the inferior Irish. Little wonder that the British Empire is expanding like the sun itself. Keep up this rate, and the sun will never set on what lands belong to good George's throne, the domain of Britannia and our rule will know no end."

His voice thickened into a burr as he talked, a snarl of the vowels that hailed from his Scottish Highlands. I lowered my gaze. Cat Walker taught me it is impolite among the Tsalagi to interrupt anyone, even a fool. I was foolishly swept in the flow of his voice. I was going to water, his words washed over me, like I had shed my dress, and stepped into the pool to let the waterfall rush over my long dark hair, the roar in my ears. I was going to water, I was praying.

"Your eyes are closed, milady. I hope I am not putting you to sleep. Johnson has said bluntly that too often I'm speaking and saying nothing."

"Are thou married, Mr. Boswell?"

"Call me Jamie. My friends do, except for Johnson. Bozzy, he always calls me. He, of course, is the bossy one, but brilliant."

"I asked a question, Jamie. Are ye married?"

"Yes."

"Happily?"

He sipped at his tea and stared at me over the rim of his cup. "This is quite good. What did you say it was called again?"

"Sassafras, we called it kanasti. It has the sweetest taste. Every time I drink it, I think of home. My grandmother said it could be used as a love potion."

"I believe your grandmother." Boswell set aside his cup and saucer and joined me on the short sofa before the hearth.

"You bewitch me, Mrs. Ostenaco-Timberlake." But he wasn't smiling now.

I was warm all over. He closed his eyes and I mine and venturing into that thin space between us, we found each other's lips, as my fingers intertwined with his.

***

Wolfe was most surprised that he had just missed Boswell that evening when he made his way home for dinner. Of course, I had made sure that the Scottish lawyer had gone out the back gate into the garden and across the courthouse after our pleasant interlude. The bright Scot turned and blew me a hearty kiss on the other side of the loo and cocked his hat on his fine head.

"I thought he had come to collect my manuscript." Wolfe frowned, finding the papers on the table in the hallway.

"He must have forgot. We, he was carrying on such a conversation. Lord, how that man could talk. Here, Frank, hurry!" I shoved the papers into the manservant's arms.

"Deliver this at Dr. Johnson's rooms at the Anchor Brewery in Southwick. He keeps a late hour, so he would understand the intrusion," Wolfe said.

"Yes, Frank, hurry!" Both of us pushing the poor servant out the door for perhaps different reasons, Wolfe for desire, and me wishing only to hide my own. I would need to go upstairs and tidy my tossed bed, lest these two males suspect not foul play, but the fairest of play between swains and maids.

***

Poor Wolfe, his long wait had just begun. Anxiously checking the posts for some positive word. Pacing the parlor floor, trying to anticipate the wise Doctor's every cutting critique.

"The chapter on circumcision," he fretted. "I'm sure it needs more documen-
tation."

Poor man. I stared into the fire, with my sewing on my lap, my teeth in my lip,
keeping my secret. Words will fail you. Writers hurl their noiseless scribbles out
into a void and wait breathlessly for universal applause. Wolfe's hopes and eye-
brows were raised with each knock at our door, with each arrival of the post, but
no word was forthcoming from the Great Man.

And I awaited the word, a true declaration, from my handsome Highlander.

Chapter 27

During those days of my dalliance with Boswell, I would also enjoy the company of other friends of Dr. Johnson's set.

I once sat for a portrait by Sir Joshua Reynolds, the president of the Royal Academy. Through Dr. Johnson's good graces, I made his acquaintance outside their Club, which met every Monday at seven in the Turk's Head in Gerrard Street, Soho. Poor Wolfe had always hoped he would be invited in to share his writings, his theories of the Natives of America with the best minds and talkers of our day. Pity, how he would stammer in any company other than my own.

One evening, we passed the gentlemen in front of their favorite pub. They were going in for their pipes and port, already arguing out on the street after their dinner. "Sir, your claret was lacking. A man would be drowned before he is drunk," Johnson was saying. "Wait, I know that woman."

The men, swaying on their feet, stopped us in the street.

"Ah, my dear Reynolds, may I have the honors of introducing you to the fetching Mrs. Helena Ostenaco Timberlake, she of the royalty of the Cherokee and the widow of a brave soldier, Lt. Henry Timberlake who wrote the most interesting of memoirs about his adventures among her people."

"Mrs. Timberlake, I remember painting your father, Ostenaco and his friend, Cunne Shote. I, of course, did not understand a word your father said, but his noble bearing, his air was undeniable. You can tell men of quality, even if they are unchristian and heathen."

"Yes, my father was a great man. Most happy to make your acquaintance, sir." I nodded, then inquired most innocently of Johnson. "And where is your boon companion, Mr. Boswell?"

"Old Bozzy is up in godforsaken Scotland, probably feasting on the sheep's intestines and the other delicacies those kilted heathen would be eating, that is when they aren't blowing them up with pipes to play their bags. He gets down to London for life only infrequently. I do not see how the man survives."

Poor Wolfe interrupted his idol. "Sir, have you had the opportunity to peruse the papers I delivered some time ago?"

"Squire Wolfe, yes, I remember. I thought you Friends were still silent. I see you found your voice, not in the Spirit, but in the public after all. Your book, why yes, I'm sure it's in the batch I have at the house, sir. I will see to the correspondence." He swayed and belched a bit. "But now, Mrs. Timberlake, I want to hear more about your America where the colonists seem most insolent these days. What is the name of your town?"

"Tomotley, by the banks of the river we call Tanassee, beyond the Cherokee mountains. Tsalagi, what you have corrupted and call Cherokee."

"Tomotley," Johnson repeated, savored the word. "How exotic. What a disappointment, I'm sure, to come to this sprawling slum by the dark Thames. Depressing some days, but mind you, never boring, all this humanity packed into its lanes and tenements, the paupers stewed in coal ash and fog. One wonders if the Italian Dante might not have had London in mind as a lower circle of his hell. But then turn a corner street and you meet a fine lass like yourself, an exotic Indian. A glimpse of heaven. Would you not agree, Reynolds?"

"Prithee, Johnson, what would you say the color of her skin would be?"

"I am but a scribbler, Reynolds. I do not deal in the petty pigments of your craft. But the poets would perhaps venture the phrase 'Dusky,' think you not?"

"Vermillion and ceruse, how much amber would it take to capture her?"

Reynolds was swaying on his buckled shoes. "Could you turn about for me, my dear?"

He motioned with his hand the pirouette I was to perform. He applauded when I did.

"I must paint this pretty," Reynolds said, his powdered periwig askew on his flushed forehead. "Come to my studio on the morrow. Alone. I'll make it worth your while."

The writer and the painter staggered inside, for more port and Spanish sherry.

"I do believe those men were drunks," I said to Wolfe.

"Nonsense, they are artists and allowed a little license," Wolfe said. "They certainly took some license in their talk with you, Helena Timberlake. If I didn't know better, I'd say you were on the rise in Society."

***

As the neighboring church bells chimed, striking the appointed hour, I knocked on the oaken doors of Burlington House in Piccadilly. I had hurried up Richmond Hill, a long walk this morning, but the hem of my dress was not too dirty, out of the slums of Westminster, and Thieving Lane, into the gentle folk's tall brick houses and the open fields.

A woman with a long face and a pinched mouth answered the door. "You're new, and what's worse, you're late."

"Helena Ostenaco Timberlake. Sir Joshua wanted me — "

"Don't you know enough to use the back door?" The horse-faced woman looked up and down the street as if someone of Quality might see me at the front stoop. "Next time, let's not have any foolishness, mind you, not that you're guaranteed a next time."

I followed her inside, but in the foyer a familiar face of my Overhills childhood peered at me from the wall.

Cunne Shote, or Stalking Turkey, as he was sometimes called by the English, watched me. His portrait, of oils and pigments brushed onto a stretched canvas, hung in a gilt frame.

The egret plume in his scalp lock, his broad shaved forehead and crown. The long earlobe wrapped in wire, dripping with a strand of bright red beads. A hammered gorget hung around his throat against the white linen of his hunting shirt. A red trade blanket draped over his left shoulder. His right hand holding his scalping knife, upright. Cunne Shote, my father's boon companion who accompanied him on the tour of London. I hadn't expected to see his face again, not in this life.

I instinctively spoke old Tsalagi to him, "Siyo," or hello. I thought of you, Richard, speaking my mother's tongue by the river at Tomotley. I ached to go home.

"Let's go, missy. Mustn't keep milord waiting." The housekeeper hurried me up the back stairs to a freezing cold studio with pale curtains diluting what light London gets this time of year.

"Milord will be with you momentarily. Undress now and slip this on."

"Beg your pardon?"

"For the painting. You are a model, aren't you?"

The housekeeper gave me a worn gown, dressing in the back, there were stains on it from other women, other wearers. I held the folds to my nose and took a deep whiff; there were others who had marked the territory. But I shook off any revulsion and did as she commanded.

There was a Negress with me. Against the chill of Sir Joshua's studio, she had wrapped herself in a clock. "Not seen you here before, lovey."

"My first time," I said. "You have posed previously for Sir Joshua?"

"He's very generous but fussy when it comes to the poses." She glanced at the door and lowered her voice. "He likes to pinch. Watch for his hands. Sometimes he likes a private audience. Be sure to keep clean down there, the old hat. He's very particular."

I stiffened my neck. "I'm not like that."

She laughed. "Any girl a shade past white is always like that to these men."

Sir Joshua made his entrance on a cloud of eau de cologne, wiping at his mouth with a handkerchief. He wore a dressing gown with a sash, and a turban in place of his public periwig. His slippers were silk, and their toes pointed and curled like those of a pasha.

He sipped at his tea. "Mrs. Jennings, I believe this lacks enough sugar. How many times do I have to tell you?"

"Very good, milord."

I saw the housekeeper retreat to the doorway and take a flask from the side table, splashing into the teacup.

"Ah, that's much better." Sir Joshua licked his lips with the new draught, adding to the insistent crimson flush of his nose. "Now, where were we?"

He took up his flimsy painted shield against his arm and daubed the badger-haired brush into a blue dot of coiled hair. Wolfe had said that painters were half-crazed, breathing in the minerals of the ground rocks they favored for their best colors.

The housekeeper clapped her hands loudly. "Milord needs you to be still. You must hold your places."

"Mrs. Jennings is quite right. A lack of motion is key. Hard enough when the fidgety children come in for a sitting. I rather envy Stubbs who does only the horses." Reynolds stirred his brush until the tip bled crimson red. "So lifelike. The secret, of course, is that the horses are quite dead. He props them on rods to achieve a simulacrum of life. Then he sends his models to his butcher, I'm told, for steaks. Why I rarely dine with Stubbs."

Reynolds came over to position my right arm. "Here," he said. He gave me a knife to hold and lifted my chin just so. He nodded. "One more thing." He reached into my gown and lifted my one breast for display. I was too stunned to protest. "Now, stay very still."

"Perfect," he said with a firm squeeze and a wink. He returned to his station at the easel and raised his palette like a shield, his brush like a sword, the heroic painter in hot pursuit of half-naked nymphs, red and black.

"I do wish that you ladies would stop your shivering. For God's sake, goddesses don't have goosepimples!"

***

An hour in the freezing cold, I could feel the black girl's breath on my face, her breast only inches from my face, while my fingers tired, clutching the edge of her golden girdle as arranged for Art's sake. I could hear her black belly rumble on toward lunch time.

Sir Joshua complained that the hour was late, the light was failing him, the Muse had departed. He put aside his brushes on the table for Mrs. Jenkins to clean up.

After the painter had departed our company, the housekeeper returned with a set of chipped cups and a pot of tea. "You may get dressed now. Sir Joshua is done for the day." She made a show of biting a crownpiece and placing the payment on the pewter tray beside our cups. "You can see your way out when you're done with your tea."

I poured out the tea for my partner. We sat with the shawls and blankets drawn back over us, trying to warm ourselves.

"What kind of woman are you, lovey?" My black companion smiled her fine teeth at me. "You're not colored like any English as I've laid eyes on before, nor a Nubian that I can tell."

"Tsalagi from what is commonly called America."

The model said her people were Ibo from Africa. A proud tribe, but her village had been overrun by slaver parties, and her world ended as a young girl, snatched up by a mustached man in flowing robes, who had chains for children. From scullery maid to nursery, to lady in waiting, to paid companion, she had bought her freedom.

The housekeeper returned.

"You, you can get dressed," Jenkins said to me, then turned to the black girl, and she hooked her thumb. "As for you, milord calls for a private audience."

The ebony girl stood. She gave a curtsy and flounced her skirt as she went to the door, as practiced a hitch of the skirts as the trulls on Drury Lane, advertising their honeypots.

Alone in the studio, I dared glance beneath the sheet that Mrs. Jenkins had draped over the canvas. I recognized the black girl, her small, pointed breasts that the painter had lovingly lingered over while her face was a still blob of black paint. In the painting, my likeness was ripe and red and unnatural as if the painter could not quite master my flesh tone. I stared into my dark eyes as he portrayed me and saw such hatred.

Two Amazons, one black, one red, half naked. Titillating and sensational, a picture that would hang in a men's exclusive club, but never any Academy or lady's drawing room.

Even drunk, Sir Sloshua could see through me. I was Cunne Shote again with a knife in my hand. He knew the edge I carried under my skirts, blood calling for blood, biding its time.

Chapter 28

1776

Soon after crossing this large branch of the Tanasse River, I observed descending the heights at some distance, a company of Indians, all well mounted on horseback. They came rapidly forward; on their nearer approach, I observed a chief at the head of the caravan and apprehended him to be the Little Carpenter, emperor or grand chief of the Cherokees. I turned off from the path to make way in token of respect, which compliment was accepted and gratefully and magnanimously returned, for His Highness, with a gracious and cheerful smile, came up to me, and clapping his hand on his breast, offered it to me, saying, "I am Attakullakulla." And he heartedly shook hands with me and asked me if I knew it. I answered that the Good Spirit who goes before me spoke to me and said that is the great Attakullakulla. I added that I was of the tribe of white men, of Pennsylvania, who esteemed themselves brothers and friends of the red men, but particularly so to the Cherokee, and that notwithstanding we dwelt at so great a distance we were united in love and friendship and that the name of Attakullakulla was dear to his white brothers of Pennsylvania.

Travels of William Bartram, 1776

We heard of another Quaker's journey through my mountains, and Wolfe eagerly awaited the full report of Bartram's travels, rumored to be in the works. Our American correspondent's initial field notes made the rounds at the Strand coffeehouses that Wolfe liked to frequent even if he found the black drink made his hand tremble and his heart race.

It did my heart good to hear that Attakullakulla was still alive, making the whites smile with his diplomacy, trying to keep an uneasy peace.

***

I believe I know why Bartram changed his mind, how he changed direction and journeyed no farther into the Cherokee Mountains. He sat his horse on the trail through the Nantahala gorge, the poor animal burdened with parchments and notes, and plant specimens and one shaken Quaker. The dust was still settling from the passing of Attakullakulla and a contingent of his warriors from Chota headed down the trade road toward Charles Towne. Painted ponies, warriors, the fringe of the buckskin, their arms, and shields, ready for a raid or for peace, depending on the omens, the signs, how the medicine played out in the medicine man's fist of crystal and beads and feathers.

Attakullakulla had shaken the Quaker's hand, given assurances of his safe passage into the Overhills, but Bartram hesitated. Perhaps the woods grew too close, the mountains like walls on either side, the dark river on his right hand, he was in the west in the darkling land, and perhaps the white man felt the darkness growing ahead. Only seventy miles, four days walk or three by horse, following the river north and northwest, through the green passes, to reach the first of the seven Overhill towns.

Behind him, a hundred leagues east, lay Charles Towne, wainscoting and tallow candles and bead board and brick hearths, and the comforts of the civilized world.

Ahead the winding track, the dripping trees, the river that seemed to rush and say his name. A white man, alone, could lose his way, could lose his scalp. He studied his surroundings, suddenly afraid now of shadows behind trees, and the leaves waving at him in the still air, even when no wind was blowing.

An unknown path ahead, behind him the winding way he had traveled. A man must always choose. He turned his horse and went home. He knew the war was coming. And its casualties would find us as far away as London.

***

I had been away from my homeland for a dozen years on a mission to bring peace to my People.

I had not forgotten the strife we had seen at Tomotley, the battles we had won and the ones we had lost. That first year my father brought back bloody kilts from the Scotsmen who fell at Old Estatoe, and I remember Cat Walker wearing one as she danced around the fire, her tongue trilling with delight.

That next year, Montgomery's men returned, this time with fiercer and cunning Choctaw, real warriors who knew how to fight against woods savvy Tsalagi. The Choctaw went through the dead, rolling the men on their backs, tugging at their scalps, severing their topknots from their skulls, hanks of bloody skin and matted hair.

The British forces followed their scouts. They found a woman among the bodies, her beautiful haughty face gone with the brain splatter left in the wake of the musket ball. They cut her teats off as souvenirs and sliced the scalp from her broken skull. They cursed this tribe of savages who would send Amazons against them. They were afraid to fall into our hands.

The soldiers rode into Nikwasee, pissed on the sacred fire in the council house. They found a white woman in her house, atremble. She wore feathers in her blonde hair and red stripes on her pale cheeks.

"You're free of these savages now," the soldier said. "We've come to take you home to good Christian folk."

She wept and wailed and clung to the threshold of her hut. She didn't want to go. And these blue-eyed, fair-haired men, who looked like her, had slain all her people, her loved ones. She was Tsalagi now. A little girl swept away in a gingham dress years before. She was fed and well-treated and learned to speak and dyed her hair black as she could with the soccham berry. She danced each year in the Green Corn Dance with her sisters and mothers and grandmothers.

And these bloody men would have her declare who was her true family.

A girl caught in the middle, like myself.

She had lost two worlds.

***

That year brought other reports that the colonists on the coast were growing restive and even hostile. Mobs rioting in the streets of Boston, dressing up as Indians and raiding merchant ships in the harbor, dumping crates of tea overboard to protest having to pay any tribute to their king, which set all the fine gentlemen aflutter in London, the ones who counted the commerce flowing unimpeded across the main into their bank accounts while the ladies fluttered their folded paper fans, like angry hens clucking at the effrontery, the audacity of these once loyal subjects, now boasting themselves as a new breed of people — Americans.

Final proof of American insolence reached London the second week of August via the Mercury packet ship, which sailed with important correspondence from General William Howe. The London Gazette, the official Crown organ, reported Howe's missive: "I am informed that the Continental Congress have declared the United Colonies free and independent States."

Later that day, Wolfe read to me from the London Evening-Post: "Advice is received that the Congress resolved upon independence the 4th of July and have declared war against Great Britain in form."

He let the broadsheet fall in his lap, and his jaw was agape. "This has gone much too far. They still are subjects of the king, despite their temper tantrums. If they have grievances, they should follow the proper order to have them addressed rather than threatening violence and uprising."

What truly worried Wolfe was the potential wounds our import business could suffer. The British navy protected most of our cargo, but the rebellion had disrupted our trading lines, the pack trains of pulverized sassafras and Griffith's white clay dug from around Cowee no longer flowed freely from the green mountains to the wharves at Charleston, meaning no crowns were added to our purse at Gravesend.

"War is always bad for business if you're not running guns," he said.

Poor man tallied our amounts, and re-tallied, double columns of his quick figures, his nose bent over the ledger, his quilled pen flicking like a bird flushed from the brush. He would chew the vanes wet and set to figuring again, muttering all the while. "Bad business. Bloody fools." It was as close to cursing as I had ever heard issued from the prim mouth of my pious friend.

My ambition of returning home with proper treasure and trophies would have to be postponed until the English could put down the American uprising and restore their colonies to proper order.

Meantime, I feared that my People were paying a terrible price, sticking to Ostenaco's oath to not attack the English. Armies were marching through the mountains, laying waste to Tsalagi towns. News of blood washing down the rivers came to us in gazettes and broadsheets passed around the Strand coffee house and Fleet Street's taverns.

***

Wolfe returned to the house one day, badly shaken. Missing buckles and buttons, the noble brim of his black hat broken and bent. His face was paler than usual, his breeches dirtied and torn at the knee, a gash over his head. His cane was shattered, the steady staff that had carried him through Tottenham and kept him safe in Covent Garden's darker alleys. I helped him through the doorway and sat him in his best chair. He was clammy to the touch. I mopped his brow.

"Frank. Frank, oh poor Frank," he kept mumbling.

"Where is he? Is he coming?"

It took time for me to swab his cuts and a restorative cup of sassafras tea to settle his nerves before I understood the battle they had been through.

The king's Navy needed able-bodied seamen, and where there was need there was money to be made by some toff in this England. Mobs of recruiters went through the back streets of the city and into the parks. They looked for men of good age, not much station. Frank and Wolfe were perambulating the street, stopping by a stall to look over fruits, apples, and pears, when the men came.

"Out of the way, old man." And they fell upon them.

A crack to the back of the knee, and they brought Frank to a kneel, a blow to the side of the head, and they had the irons on him.

He had been pressed into the King's Service. They rounded up a replacement crew for the scullery and to wait on the officers below decks of the HMS Victory. Quick marched down to the docks and down river to Gravesend where the fleet rested at anchor.

Frank was at sea, to wake up again in chains, below decks, back to his slave days, but again a slavey. They would pay him in rum and rations. He had been born on a ship; he would likely die in the passage again. So many of his kind, the constant trade of bodies, white, but more and more black. Human ballast below the timbers of the waterline.

"All we can do is pray for God's will."

The quiet Quaker began to tremble, but he did not hide his face from me, unafraid to be unmanned and weeping.

Wolfe had lost his beloved man, and I had lost a true friend.

Chapter 29

The ravens hopped across the green grass, blackguards under the ramparts of the Tower.

At our approach, the birds took flight, but they did not leave the Tower, circling back to sit on the high stones, cawing down on us.

When those winged witches left the grounds, the English believed their empire would be doomed. But the ravens remained, pecking at the lice in their ebony pinfeathers, staring at us with their gimlet eyes. They may have been Ravenmockers, witches as Chutatah once suspected, beings that would fly off with your soul come night, leaving an even darker shadow at your feet when the sun rose.

We walked across the bridge over the moat where Wolfe and I once paused to observe the oliphants. Kamama, I called them in my old Tsalagi tongue, or "big butterfly" with their great ears like giant wings. But the great beasts were no longer on display.

Inside the fortress, we made our descent down a worn staircase, lit by a tallow candle I carried in a tin shield. The stones wept along the dim passage, like the cries of long dead prisoners, women led out to have their heads lopped off. Wolfe huffed beside me, stumbled against my side.

"Are thou fine, my friend?" I worried about Wolfe. He was short of breath often and flush of face, slow in his steps, something vital drained out from within, that inner Light of his dimmed by Frank's absence.

"Never mind, I'm fine," Wolfe gathered himself, taking my arm. "Lead on so we may see our enemy."

We had come for an audience with a captured American.

The turnkey unlocked the door and showed us into the keep where the prisoner was housed, not in any high Tower, with views of the river, but down in a dank cavern, still with the smell of gunpowder where munitions had been stored. Inside, a writing desk and papers, a neat cot, and a tea table. He could pay the porters well, for his own tea. After all, Henry Laurens was a man of means, a planter from Charleston where my father and Attakullakulla once walked the cobbled streets.

An ambassador to the Dutch, Laurens fell afoul of the wrong people when his ship was captured in the North Sea last year. But Wolfe had it on good authority from his coffee house klatches that Lord North and the Prime Minister's government were in negotiations with the rebellious Americans, a prisoner exchange in the works.

"I receive so few guests." Mr. Laurens bowed. "This is most kind, madam, and most Christian of you, sir."

He went to shake Wolfe's hand like a gentleman, but my friend was not in the mood.

"Christians are commanded to visit the prisoner. It is only our duty, if not often our pleasure," Wolfe said in a surprisingly sullen manner. He motioned irritably toward me. "She is the one you should be addressing, sir. Not I."

He offered me the only chair, and I sat at his table, while Wolfe kept tapping his cane impatiently against the flagstones, an irritable rhythm. "Do I know you, Mrs. Timberlake?" Laurens asked politely.

"Only too well, I fear. And it's Mrs. Ostenaco-Timberlake if you please," Wolfe refused to be silent. "You fought against her father, Ostenaco, at Old Estatoe. Then you trooped up to Nikwasee, burned out their towns, slaughtered their old, infirm, and babes suckling at their mothers. That book that Timberlake wrote will give you the full account of their suffering."

"That is enough, Friend Wolfe. I can speak for myself," I insisted. "Yes, I have brought a copy of my husband's memoirs. It may help to explain the story of my time here, and well as pass your days before your own return home."

Laurens flipped through the book. "The pages are already cut, I see. Thank you for that consideration. My guards do not allow sharp implements lest I attack them, or perhaps do myself harm."

"A man can be most resourceful if he wants to end his life," Wolfe allowed.

The folded and sealed paper within the book fell to the stone flags. "What is this?"

Laurens held up the letter I had slipped into the pages, to avoid search by the lazy Tower guards. He read the address on the front. "Sumter?"

"Britain is still at war with the Americans." I lowered my voice. "I cannot very well send a correspondence to the king's enemy without arousing suspicion."

"A war that you started," Wolfe interjected once more.

"Sir, I have wept at the thought of independence from the Motherland," Laurens rejoined. "But agents of the king have no right to make themselves Caesar. They have abused his loyal subjects to the length of their patience."

"Did not Christ say to render unto Caesar what is Caesar's? Don't seize it and throw it overboard, dressed like mock Indians," Wolfe said in exasperation, tapping his cane with a loud point on the flagstones. "And what kind of poisonous people would choose as their flag a rattlesnake under the motto: Tread Not on Me?"

"We merely insist on our rights to liberty."

"How is it that we hear the loudest yelps for liberty among the drivers of Negroes? Don't you yourself own some two hundred souls of black men, women, and children?"

"It is a peculiar institution, but I need workers for the rice," Laurens said. "We have brought them out of Africa and gave them food and clothes and even the Christian gospel as well as meaningful labor."

"You talk of their afterlife. Yet you have sold men to be broken, women to be bred, children to replace their stock. You have made money as a peddler of flesh and monger of abomination," Wolfe shouted.

"I've seriously considered granting them their freedom upon my passing, if it doesn't happen here in this terrible tower, where I am kept against all laws of nations."

"Do not talk to me of injustice, sir," Wolfe sputtered. "Not just a traitor to your rightful king, but to God's natural law, an ally of the Devil himself."

"Since you don't like my company, sir, you can go straight to hell," Laurens fired back.

I thought Wolfe was about to strike the prisoner, our host, with his cane, until I put my hand on his arm. "Give us a moment, dear friend. I won't be long."

"I'll be out on the grounds, then, Helena Timberlake."

"Tetchy fellow," Laurens allowed after Wolfe exited.

"Forgive my friend, and his outburst. He mourns for our manservant who we fear is lost at sea with his ship. He was an unwilling recruit, the sweetest of boys, pressed into service for His Royal Navy."

"My condolences then."

We sat in an awkward silence, not the quiet of a Quaker meeting, but feeling Wolfe's outburst still reverberating about the room.

"How is Sumter? The last time you saw him."

"I've not seen that old banty rooster since Charleston."

"I've not seen the sergeant since Tomotley," I said. "My hometown. Sumter escorted my late husband on their expedition to the Overhills years ago."

"Oh, he's a general now, commands the Second Regiment of the South Carolina Line. He's been a terror to Lord Cornwallis, his irregulars picking off the red coats. They've borrowed more than a few tricks from your people, hiding in the trees, picking off soldiers, none of this face-to-face, man-to-man, volley stuff the Brits all favor. He's a tough bird." Laurens paused.

He shivered and drew his shawl about his shoulders. "It takes a tough hide for a Carolinian to get used to this English climate. Always so damp and chilly. How long have you been on this godforsaken island, Mrs. Timberlake?"

"Twenty years now, I'm afraid. I've gotten used to it."

He walked around the room, stared out the window onto the keep where I could spy Wolfe in his black frock coat, hands behind his back, pacing as stiff-legged as the ravens pecking the grass for worms.

"It sounds funny, but do you know what I miss? I miss mosquitoes." He laughed sadly. "I miss being hot and sweaty. The smell of the marshes. I am tired of fighting. I want to sit in a good chair on the dock by the river and watch the water just roll by. A drop to drink, a little bread, perhaps a good tobacco to smoke in a pipe. That sounds like peace, doesn't it?"

He looked at me. "You look like a lady who has known loss. What do you miss from home?"

"You have children, Mr. Laurens?"

"I do, Mrs. Timberlake. And grandchildren as well."

"I have not seen my son in a great while, longer than I had ever expected. I am hoping that Sumter may be of some help in restoring our communications. The letter, Mr. Laurens?" I tapped the sealed envelope on his writing desk.

He returned to his chair, looking at the letter simply addressed Sumter. "This is highly irregular. I could be searched at any time by my captors."

"The risk is mine. If they search your person, my person is imperiled. Correspondence with a rebel officer could get me hanged as a traitor, or transported to America, if I were lucky."

He tucked the papers among his portfolios. "I think we are not foes, you and I."

"We are not friends, either. But perhaps your people and mine will someday live without war between us."

***

After my audience was ended, I found Wolfe out in the keep of the castle, seated on a crude bench. He looked haggard, his stocking legs splayed, his chin propped on the crook of his cane as he eyed the ravens hopping about the green, pecking at worms and what not.

"I assume you are over your pique of anger. What got into you?" I scolded.

"A tiredness of spirit, a lapse of discipline. I am just an old man fed up with this war."

Wolfe rose stiffly, slowly. His ankles had been swollen as of late. He did not look well. "Will the American convey your message? Not that I'm sure you can trust that rebel."

I shrugged. "I trust no man but thou, dear Wolfe. But I appealed to his sense of honor and his feeling as a father. We can only hope."

***

I was visited with dark visions, nightmares from that summer twenty years ago. Ostenaco lost the war and sued for peace, the corn stopped growing but the harvest of the best of our nation was terrible.

The bodies kept coming down river, through the passes of the Twenty-Four Mountains trail, from the Middle Towns to the Overhills. You would go to water, to find the Long Man defiled with the dead, bloated bodies, you could no longer tell man from woman, bloated, floating, caught in tree snags, or beating their scalped, brained heads against the rocks. The worst were the children, the babies that arrived, not from the darkening land, but from the East where the sun should rise, but a new darkness was coming. I wish I could unsee what I saw that summer.

Dispatches in the London gazettes echoed my dreams. The war had not gone well for the British since the summer. They had routed the unruly Americans, but then the always problematic French had sent reinforcements. A surprise maneuver and Cornwallis had been forced into surrender. The king was said to be livid, but also crazed, a mad man in St. James. All this Wolfe had on good authority, chatting at times in the smoky taverns, waving away the clouds of tobacco, and the offered tankards of strong ale or tumblers of whisky and gin. He would not dim the Light within with strong spirits.

My messages to M'Cormick in the Overhills had gone unanswered for years now. In my mind's eye, I saw these frail papers like wings flying over the main and blown like dead leaves up the mountains, but no one read their intent. My son was across the enemy lines, across the sea, and across a hornet's nest of swarming American rebels, burning down their British forts, slaughtering the empire's Indian allies. I did not know if my son, my father, my grandmother, if anyone was left alive in the smoldering ruins of Tomotley.

Chapter 30

1st of April 1781
London

My dearest Sumter,

We have not had opportunity in these swaying motions of this world to meet since your stay in the Overhills. Forgive this bold intrusion into your affairs late in life, during wartime, but I beseech thee to consider your bond to your ensign, my only husband, Henry Timberlake.

You may have heard of my husband's passing. He always spoke highly of your courage, and your exploits on the river figure prominently in the memoir of his adventures among our people, which he was able to complete before his untimely death, lo, now these many years past.

You remember me as Ostenaco's daughter in the Overhills. By the banks of the Tanasse on the ball field, I could not help but catch your roving eye upon my girlish charms. It was only love's happenstance, a maid's whim, that I chose Henry for my suitor, instead of you, old friend.

But be not hardhearted toward me nor toward my people.

I have heard of campaigns into our mountains, Americans marching into the Middle Towns and burning fifty-two of our towns. The Overhills under assault, and the Lower Towns long abandoned. We will soon have no territory to call our own under these constant and unlawful excursions. You may consider my people as enemies, but we have broken no bond, nor the oath my father Ostenaco gave to your former king. We have waged no war on the Carolinians and the new country of America as often claimed.

I wish only to restore the communications broken by this war with my son, Richard Timberlake, who is under my father's care in the Overhills. It has been too long since I've had correspondence with my people though the skills of M'Cormick, your companion in that long journey to our towns that brought me Henry, and to you, fame.

If you have any word of Tomotley, or of Timberlake's true heir, I would be forever in your debt. Please convey a mother's love to a young man who may have forgotten that first face to smile upon him, the breast that suckled him, the arms that ached to let him go.

Yrs. In fond affection

Helena Ostenaco Timberlake

Chapter 31

The other evening, Wolfe removed his spectacles and rubbed the stained knuckle into the pale blue of his eye until it turned bloodshot. He set his seeing glasses upon the pile of papers rising steadily on his desk, pages splattered by ink and wax from the burning candle. He had not given up on our accounts, but there was an unseen drain toward which all that was liquid in coin and worth had gone.

"Oh, my poor lady, can you forgive a poor fool?

"What is it, dear Wolfe?"

"I fear I've lost thy fortune."

We were poor. Our investments lost at sea. The lines of trade had been cut off by the American rebels and their French allies. Our last shipment of sassafras had sunk somewhere off Newfoundland in a sudden squall. Other ships had been commandeered by privateers. We had not seen a ship safely with our cargo into harbor for years now.

What does a man who swears off killing of any kind, who lives for peace, know about making a money in a time of war?

Wolfe was always trying to make his fortune on his book studying the Native Tribes of America. "No paying gentleman or refined lady wants to read about savages a world away," came the rejection at printer after printer up and down Fleet Street.

Without his beloved Frank to serve as ballast, Wolfe was dangerously unmoored. He began to gamble recklessly, and he had been snookered as badly as if he had sat down in a gentleman's room late at night and lost hand after hand of faro and other card games.

He had put his money on stock, explorers in Egypt, the secret route of the Northwest Passage. He invested in International Geophysical Society, tracing the lien lines that had transported the twelve Tribes from Mesopotamia to America.

He put more money in missions to seed Quaker colonies among the savage tribes in Africa or the Americas.

But all those schemes advanced by idealistic dreamers came to naught. The poor souls who went to their deaths, killed by plague, starving to death, slaughtered by mercenaries, and more than a few who blew their brains out with pistols, or walked back into the sea they had crossed.

And all the crowns and sovereigns that had come with the shipments of my sassafras and fine porcelain clay, all the money that had filled our sails and our coffers, had been bleed away from our bank account with Wolfe's unwise investments.

"I must go home," I insisted.

"This is home now, Helena."

"Don't call me that. I am Skitty. I'm going back to Tomotley to see my son."

"There is no money. I'm afraid there is no safe passage. The price is too dear."

"You kept me here as a captive. You are no better than that dwarf, John Coin. He put me on public display, but you have kept me for your own sideshow. Your own collection."

"Do not be so harsh, Mrs. Timberlake. It was for your own good, the sake of your immortal soul and your mortal body."

"You have stolen my spirit, my life. How long have I wasted my life in this terrible city, this cold cruel island?"

I glared at him, then turned my flushed face to the fire. We did not speak in that charged air. I was lost in my rage, staring into the glow of the coals on the hearth.

Back in Tomotley town, I used to sit by the fire, leaning against one of the solid four posts that held up the rafters.

You could see the stars at night through the smoke hole, that peephole into the universe, but in winter, the sky often showed gray with rain or even snow coming through, a drop or a flake on your upturned face. The winter house had a small door that big men had to crouch to come through, but was the perfect height for a child, keeping in all the warmth of Cat Walker's fire and her corn mash on a cold winter's day. We huddled on the beds, the creak of the sleeping bodies on the river cane, and the grunt and hastened breath of lovers in the dark, beneath the bear hide. Keeping warm, planting seed for new children come next fall. We counted the long winter nights of the Snow Moon, the Cold Moon, and the Bony Moon, before the days grew longer and the sky cleared overhead, and the snows melted into mud along the river, and greens sprouted under the bare hardwoods on the mountainside. Come spring and warm weather, we moved our blankets and furs to sleep in the summer house with the thatched roof.

But the storms brought lightning and loud thunder, and we shivered under the thatch roof of the summer house, watching the black clouds come over the mountain.

"Agasga." It is raining. "Daganani nigohil." It will rain forever.

Now, when I was not fixed by flames, I was rapt with rain. When the evenings grew wet in winter, I watched the night's tears streaking the glass, the hiss down the flue into the meager fire.

I used to love the smell of fresh rain in Tomotley and its sound when we slept in the summer houses. The soft patter on the thatch roofs and on the green leaves across the mountains. Rain splashing for joy on the river.

Cast away on this northern island, I learned to love rain, drizzle, downpours, deluges, showers, mists, fogs, haze, miasma. The English had many names for what fell from their gray skies.

Rain sounded different in England than back home. Here, it came down in regiments, divisions of downpours, like soldiers who marched before the palace, their boots stamping against the stones. Rain was an army in England, invading the crowded dirty streets, pounding on the glass and the shingles, trying to get in, like the bailiffs coming around to arrest you or the merchant's debt finally coming due. Yelling and pounding. Pushing you to the door with your arm twisted behind your back. Henry, oh Henry. Where have they taken you?

Wolfe got up from his chair with a creak of his knees. It was time for him to retire to his chambers.

"Can thou ever forgive me, Mrs. Timberlake? I have been a fool." And he looked shaken with his pleading eyes, as if I had cut him with my faithful stone knife, that I had used for little more than a paperknife to cut the pages of the books he read.

"Good night, sir," I said at last, but would not say what my mentor so desperately needs to hear.

***

So, in our reduced circumstances, I sold my finer skirts and blouses, some shawls, bits of silver service, even the Wedgwood teapot and cups that we had been given, made from that first shipment of fine clay from my Cherokee mountains. The two-hundred-pounds annuity that Wolfe said I could always count upon was long gone.

We moved from a brownstone townhouse, farther afield from the din of downtown London, the Fleet Street and Courts. We were bumpkins, out in the countryside, which I did not mind. But it was a ten-mile walk into the city. Our fare at the table with more gristle and bone as we often were late with our bill to the butcher.

Always I was afraid to hear a knocking at the door, or to be stopped in the lane leading to our house by a bailiff with a notice for Wolfe's arrest. Back to the poor house until his debts could be paid.

I had been a rich woman in England, now I was a poor wench in this cursed isle, so far from home. Why have I remained so long in this burning land of smoke and fog? I hate the tight houses, the slops on the cobbled streets, the smells of a million outhouses in the courtyards, the stench of death wards in charity hospitals. Women selling themselves on the streets, children left outside the gin houses.

I have missed the taste of bear roast, or turkey, or the corn my granny hoed by the riverbanks, or the sochan and jellico gathered in the damp woods come spring, potherbs that made the blood jump again with the sun, the body stretch from the cramped winter house hibernation. Here, I have been living on thin gruel indeed, greasy fish and chips, starchy potatoes, stringy meat, small beer, where water is not to be trusted. I have become slow as the cows that mill across the thin pastures.

Neither English nor Tsalagi, I have two tongues yet cannot say what I feel in either. But I am my own woman. What I chose is my path. If I make a fist or extend my hand, if I raise Cat Walker's flint knife or sign my name with Wolfe's clipped quill pin, my shadow follows suit. I chose.

We live the life we are given, not the one we plan. And perhaps I have been telling not just a story, but a lie to myself.

I could have taken passage on many a ship that brought me riches and clay and sassafras and returned to Tomotley in those years before the war. I could have come home with my riches, yet I was seduced not just by a fine man like Boswell or a fine mind like Johnson's. I loved the feel of silk on my sin, and the color of jewels. I loved the smell of the streets, the humanity packed into its houses and halls, and parks. I thrilled to the spectacle.

I kept telling myself the story of the spider who brought back fire, but I may have missed my father's lesson. It only counts as a heroic journey if you return home.

How was I any different from Mrs. John Rolfe, the woman who was Pocahontas? She had given up her tribe and followed her husband to this cold island. She had followed her love. And she had died. She brought nothing home to the poor orphans, the widows of her people, driven from their homes and towns by the greedy yoneg.

What if the spider had not returned, bearing the gift of fire, branding her own back with the burning coal? What if the world remained cold because she had fallen in love and lost herself in a distant land, among a strange people? Does not the spider often devour her young with her own appetites?

Remember me, Richard: But I cannot blame you if you have sworn to forget me.

Chapter 32

Charleston. Jan. 1783,

My dearest Helena Ostenaco Timberlake,

I must admit to my great surprise when I received word from across the ocean that you still live and all your many adventures. It took, of course, time for Laurens to return to the Charleston and before he was able to deliver to me your correspondence, I wept at the news that you were still alive in faraway London, and the passing of my old comrade Timberlake so many years ago.

I have not seen you for twenty years now, but it seemed like only yesterday you were laughing at me playing games at Tomotley. I saw your crestfallen look when I told you that Timberlake had not accompanied me back to your fond arms but had instead married otherwise. I wish I had better news for you now.

After our fateful trip overseas with your Cherokee kings, I returned to South Carolina a poorer man. I petitioned the Virginia government for reimbursement of the sizeable expense that I had accrued along with Lt. Timberlake in transporting and entertaining the Cherokee kings in a fashion becoming to their rank. But those stiff necks up in Williamsburg plainly stiffed me. Roaming the streets, I was set upon by ruffian bailiffs and thrown into their debtor's prison.

It wasn't until my friend Joseph Martin came to visit me, smuggling in ten guineas and a tomahawk. No, I didn't raise any Cain nor shed any blood of those Virginia ruffians but following Martin's sound advice, I simply bribed my way to freedom.

I returned to the High Hills of Santee and married a pleasant woman, a widow named Mary Jameson. With my soldiering days I thought behind me, we planted our fields and opened a few profitable mercantile stores.

But the British, of course, would not leave us be. When the war for our freedoms came about, I had no choice but to take up arms. I led the brave lads of our district against those redcoated mercenaries after they burned my house to the ground and scattered all my slaves and livestock. If they wanted a fight, by God, I would give it to them, and we harried those troops out of the woods for years until they cried uncle and left our lands.

I ran into General Griffin Rutherford during our battles. He had led the troops against the Valley towns and burned fifty of your old towns a few years back. He did not have that high opinion of your kind and had no kind words for what he called atrocities and scalping and the like. I like a good fight as well as any man to get your blood up and to feel alive. But I also know war is a terrible thing with sights that would make any feeling man weep. I am sorry for your losses.

I know not what happened to the Overhills, but I did meet with that old trader M'Cormick, who was trading down in Ninety-Six along the old trading path. We shared a laugh about our adventures down the river, fighting off bears and the water itself, and that lark living among your people for that season. I still can taste that nasty Black Drink and sometimes dream of the furred and feathered fancies, the booger dances that your people put on for us.

M'Cormick said that your grandmother had passed, and Ostenaco led the tribe and his people from Tomotley down the river toward Chickamauga, putting a few more mountains and breathing room between your people and our restless Americans.

M'Cormick said your son is a handsome young man now and a brave warrior who stands at your father's side.

I am sorry for your situation. I know that you always fancied Timberlake over me, but I would be a liar if I didn't say I thought you were the most fetching woman I have ever met, whether white or red, American or British or Cherokee. I wish I had better news for you, and I hope that someday perhaps we could meet again and talk over the old times in Tomotley, which was a capital adventure.

Perhaps we are official enemies now, given the postures of our people and the hostilities between our nations, but I count you as a good person and a true friend of my heart. I hope this letter will someday find you still, our Lord willing, alive and well.

Most sincerely,

Brig. General Thomas Sumter

Chapter 33

December, bitterly cold. A small snow fell in general upon the capital but was shoveled onto the curbs into great chunks that turned black with soot, as if draped in mourning crepe. All of London was weeping.

Dr. Johnson was dead.

Wolfe and I paid our respects to the Great Man laid to rest among kings and poets under the flagstones of Westminster, beneath the battle flags that hung with dust motes in the amber air of the English's great spired Council House.

Exiting in a long procession of black crepe, we made our way to the Academy. A queue of mourners and curious stood, waiting to inspect the last likeness of the Great Man, the Talk of the Town, or our times. One by one, we signed our names in a register to record our last respects.

In a small room, they displayed his death mask, made immediately after the last breath had departed and the shroud covered what remained. His head and shoulders had been coated in a plaster slip to make a mold of his features. The resultant bronze cast captured his features, dismembered of his limbs, his stomach, his desires. An uncanny likeness, it stood on a carved wooden base.

I recalled mainly an ugly man, a mass of twitches, the pocks of his living face, the thick jaw ready to brain you. The bust made him seem more noble, even shorn of hair, and minus the usual wig. I was afraid that the frozen face might at any moment open those lidded eyes, part those thin lips, see through me, speak to me again.

I thought again of the lifeless wax likeness of my father, how the candlelight fell on his painted face in the museum. The blanket that hung lifeless from a stick shoulder, the leggings lank on his wooden shins. No light in the marbles that recreated his eyes.

"We will not see his like again," Wolfe said, biting at his lower lip, his chin a'tremble.

"He could have at least read your book," I said.

Squire Wolfe had waited years for Johnson's approval, made calls upon the Doctor of Dictionaries, but did not find him often at home, but more often in the clubs and eating houses, his lazy eye traveling after women, holding his court.

We paid our respects and went out into the cold London streets.

"There, isn't that his great friend, Mr. Boswell?" Wolfe pointed.

My heart did a strange leap. Yes, my sullen Scotsman, Jamie. He looked more haggard, the light banked in his fine blue eyes, but it was the same man who had come to me in more than a few dreams since our tea together. We went over to renew our acquaintance.

"You remember me, Mr. Boswell?" Jamie, I wanted to whisper, but not in front of Wolfe.

"Ah, Helena, I mean, Mrs. Timberlake, it has been much too long."

We did not embrace as mourners or shake hands as men might. He bowed. I briefly curtseyed. It was proper and English.

"I am so sorry about your loss of your great friend."

"I am bereft, madam. Johnson liked to jape that when a man is bored with London, he is bored with life. London and my life will not be the same without him, I fear, whenever I'm in town."

"I haven't seen you in ages," I said.

"I lead a narrow existence, work, family, duty," he said. "Everything my father, the lord of Auchinlink, would have desired for his wayward son. His idea of exile, I'm afraid. Not at all London."

"Your wife and children, they are well?"

He donned his hat again. "Ah, yes, decidedly."

But poor soul, he was decidedly not. The man looked ashen, lost.

Wolfe interrupted. "I never did hear from Johnson about my book. He didn't by chance ever mention my work in your long conversations?"

"Ah, your book. I'm sorry sir, I don't recall Indians coming up too often in our talks." Boswell tapped his silver-tipped cane on the curb in a most mournful tattoo. "And you, Mrs. Timberlake, where is your book?"

"I am but a woman. I am no writer nor warrior, like my husband."

"Ah, but you have a story to tell. I think you are the most enchanting of story-tellers."

"You flatter me, sir."

"I fondly recall your talk of Tomotley and that delicious tea. What was the name again for the sassafras?"

"Kan'sta'tsi."

"Kan'sta'tsi. What a wonderful word. I love the taste in my mouth."

Again, he tapped his cane. We had so much to say to the other but could not in this public place so full of mourning.

"Mrs. Timberlake, do you ever think of home?"

"We are in Stepney these days. Not far from the bustle of the city, but we are content."

"I mean home, America. Do you miss it?"

His hand reached for mine across a great gulf, it seemed, but his words pricked my heart. He meant to pull me towards him. Like he was a drowning man who I could pluck from the river.

Jamie, I thought often of you, of that one afternoon we spent entwined, arms and legs and mouths and flesh, the warmth of your skin, the sheets, the light through the window, golden on your back. I dreamed of you. I felt a heat gathering, my breath quickening.

"I so wish that you would write your own book, Mrs. Timberlake. It's been so good to see you again."

"And you, sir, as well."

"Perhaps you will call upon us," Wolfe said. "We would enjoy your company when you are in town."

I would enjoy you. We couldn't say what we ached to speak.

"Yes, I would be delighted." Boswell's smile was as weak as mine was thin.

***

The light weakened at this late hour in England, in winter, the days giving out much quicker than I recall from the mountains back home. By Mr. Wolfe's time-piece, it was only half past the fourth hour. We hurried through the darkening streets, quickening our step toward the safety of our own hearth. At this changeling hour, all matter of spirits were in the air, along with the smoke and fogs and vapors that swirl around the lamps lit by the men with their poles.

The London I had loved was leaving me, bit by bit. I counted all the men I had known, befriended, loved and lost along this strange journey. Henry, of course, but also Walking Mountain and Truelove, dear Frank who fought for me, but who died in fighting for a king he'd rather not have served. The Overhills were gone too. The world I knew had changed in the long winters and summers I have been away in this distant land.

Boswell had asked what I missed of home in the new place named America. I'm not sure that there is a home on a river for me. Cat Walker lies beneath stone as does my father Ostenaco, Woyi and Cunne Shote, that sweet man, Stalking Turkey, the head warrior of Chota has fallen to the traitors. They buried him after the town was burned, with a great broadsword, a trophy from when the Spaniards marched through the mountains. The spectacles on his closed eyes, the rocks piled high. I can see that old man still in the flesh, long after I saw his painted likeness in Reynolds's studio.

I fear the towns have been burned. The mounds are overgrown. The Tsalagi are ghosts haunting the old fields.

Trapped here on this island, our shipping disrupted by the war, and passage unsafe for even the bravest woman, Wolfe keeps insisting. I can only wait and pray. I try the Christian God to whom I have been baptized. I also pray the way Cat Walker taught me, dousing my forehead with clean water from a porcelain bowl each morning when I rise from my bed. But my sleep is troubled, and I cannot wash away a mother's guilt.

All I pray is that you still live, dear Richard.

Chapter 34

St. James Park, London, 1785

They are of a very gentle and amicable disposition to those they think their friends, but as implacable in their enmity, their revenge being only completed in the entire destruction of their enemies. They were pretty hospitable to all white strangers until the Europeans encouraged them to scalp, but the great reward offered has led them often to since commit as great barbarities on us, as they formerly only treated their most inveterate enemies."

Timberlake, Memoirs

We walked in St. James, taking our time and our pleasure in our reduced circumstances. We were nearly paupers, but as Wolfe said, so long as we had our legs, we should walk to keep our hearts glad.

Squire Wolfe had pressed my petition for a widow's pension given Henry's brave service twenty years now. But there was an obstacle, some bureaucrat or unseen hand, making sure that my petition did not proceed.

"Col. Carrington is back in town now that the war is over. I would suspect he may have some pull with the War Office even when it comes to widows." Wolfe sighed. "Evidently he has a bone to pick."

"The man is a cannibal?"

"A figure of speech, Mrs. Timberlake, do not take it literally. It means to have a grudge to settle, an argument to make."

"He always blamed Henry for what happened to his cousin, Demere. He could not let that blood debt go."

Wolfe shook his head. "Blood spills more blood. At least, you are different."

"I should like to slice the man's throat for what he's done to my family."

"Revenge is not worthy of thee," my friend insisted. "Many men lose their souls to this temptation."

Wolfe had always preached that I should turn the other cheek, that vengeance was not mine but the Lord's, that in some afterlife my husband's nemesis would be rightly judged and get his just dessert, standing in a lake of hellfire for all eternity. Wolfe couldn't say what the rest of us would do sitting around heaven, singing to some Almighty in need of constant chorus.

If Tyndale's scripture weren't word enough, he liked to quote Dr. Johnson as well. "Many who could have conquered their anger are unable to combat pride, and pursue offenses to the extremity of vengeance, lest they should be insulted by the triumph of an enemy."

"You say I'm proud because I seek justice," I countered.

"Pride goes before the fall," he rejoined. "Besides, Christ preached turning the other cheek, let the Lord take vengeance."

Alas, Wolfe, I feared, was not wise to the ways of the world I had seen in both the Overhills and in Londontown. Men and women lived by vital juices, blood and sweat and spit and the juices of their sex. The angels he preached of seem dry and windy creatures, insubstantial as fog and mists, having no juices within them.

"Gangway," a shout came behind us and a thunder of hooves. A coach whooshed by, just as Wolfe and I hurried to the grass to avoid being trampled to death. St. James Park had graveled paths posted only for pedestrian travel. No salon chairs and shouting footmen permitted nor runaway hackneys with whipped horses on the hurley-burley of the city's muddier, more congested thoroughfares. Only the royals are allowed such conveyance within their property, but there went a carriage with wheels higher than a man, four frothing steeds tossing their heads under the lash of the whip and kicking gravel beneath their sharp hooves,

"Taking a walk in London is taking your own life into your hands, it seems these days." Wolfe brushed off the white dust that coated him like a ghost.

Only two times I had seen my friend Wolfe raise his voice, show his anger. Once when he and Frank rescued me from the clutches of that dwarf, John Coin, who would have pimped me out, and my story would have ended in a tragedy. Once when we had our audience with Laurens, how he railed against the injustice of war, the tyranny of slavedrivers.

But any affront to his own person he would simply brush away like so much dust.

He was still looking after me in his own way.

We passed by the sign at the gate, the park and its royal property clearly posted and closed to all horse traffic and sedan chairs, only personal perambulators and pedestrians permitted.

But in today's less civilized, less social city, some brazenly disregarded the rules.

At the gate, another coach flew through, the driver drunk and pulling back on the reins. The carriage on two wheels nearly tipped over in the turn. The passengers were drunk as lords and yelled their approval. The horses were mad with froth, their ears back, their eyes wild. We stepped back, barely avoiding a collision, but we were left sullied. Wolfe's stockings, with mud, my best skirt, with mire.

"The Quality has gotten into the quantity, it seems," Wolfe huffs. "They act like would-be Caesars racing chariots around the Coliseum. There is no respect for probity, let alone sobriety in these last days." Then he sighed and quieted his Quaker outrage with what Jesus would say. "Forgive them for they know not what they do."

I did not always agree with Wolfe's interpretation of his Scripture. It seemed to me that the stories and sermons he loved did not always agree.

"I thought in the last days, your Christ came bloody with a flaming sword, ready to smite his enemies?"

"Thou miss the point, Mrs. Timberlake," he said quietly. "Only the heathen in heart think of God as bloodthirsty. There is mercy as well as justice."

"Blood responsibility is justice," I countered. "No one, let alone my grandmother, rejoiced in such a duty."

In all our years together and talks, I still had not shared with Wolfe all I had seen in poor Demere's last dance. His mouth stuffed with grass, his terrible blue eyes drained of life, how his arms and legs lay severed from his body. Cat Walker and the women took no joy in the solemn blood responsibility. They sought only Justice to right the world put dangerously off-balance by one man's evil deed against the clan.

Would I be up to the same duty if the opportunity presented itself, and the man I had feared and hated fell in my grasp?

For an instant, in the park an ocean away from the Overhills of my childhood, the corner of my eye caught a glimpse of something large, slithering behind the hedges of the gravel path ahead. It was a trick of the eyes and perhaps the bright light of this suddenly chill afternoon. I shuddered again. For a moment, I believed it was baby Uk'tena that I had smuggled aboard the Raven years ago and unleashed upon this land. The monster had grown up and followed me through the years in London.

We continued on our walk, on our contentious argument, which Wolfe would not let go.

"Consider this: if thou were to find this Carrington fellow, who sent Timberlake into debtor's prison — "

"And to his death," I added.

"Wouldst thou kill him with that knife I know thou carry?"

"If you were to find the men who took Frank, what would you do?"

"I have been commanded by my Lord to forgive them."

"But what would your heart say?"

Wolfe looked at me, his mournful eyes behind the flash of his spectacles that made him see his world clearly.

"Thou have forgiven me, have you not, for keeping you here by my side, when your heart wanted to return home to your son?"

"I have not forgotten that deception."

"I know thy heart, Mrs. Timberlake, and it is good," Wolfe said. "Thou have not cut me with that knife."

"Not yet." I smiled.

"What would Richard say if thou returned with bloody hands?" Wolfe asked.

And I had no easy answer.

"All children, even the saddest orphan, carries some imprint of their mam, the breast that suckled them," Squire Wolfe was kind enough to inform me. "Surely,

Richard will remember. He will have grown up, hearing stories of your bravery, Helena Timberlake."

Children are like quivers in the arrows, Wolfe liked to read in the papers of his scripture, taking comfort in the words of shepherds and a caring Creator when all evidence in this world pointed to sorrow, evils, and weeping. His Jesus said suffer the little children to come unto me.

Suffer seemed the proper word.

Revenge remains the law of the clans. I could see Cat Walker pulling at her long gray hair, trilling her tongue at such nonsense as Wolfe spouted. Eye for eye, hand for hand, life for life, that is the balance of this ever-shifting world.

But Wolfe was right. I was not sure I had the heart to slay a man. I was not the Tsalagi woman that Cat Walker had proved herself. Something inside me wanted to look away from the blood on her hands.

Gouge enough eyes, and we are blind, Wolfe kept arguing. Sever enough hands, and we are all maimed. Take all the lives and leave nothing but bones.

"Helena!"

The drunken chariot suddenly, swiftly arrived at our backs, catching us unawares. Wolfe pushed me aside, sidestepping the horses, but the wheel caught his out-thrown hand, and he was hurled like a rag doll into the air. I was face down in the English earth, with tufts of grass in my mouth, and the coach had fled, and the dust was settling. Wolfe was lying close by.

His bare stocking foot twitched slightly, his buckled shoe lying empty on the gravel path. His head at an odd angle, turned too far on his thin neck. The spectacles hanging askew from one ear, but his blue eyes stared sightless upwards, the Light that he had so loved within his and every human soul already draining into the sky-vault, the day-blind stars on the wrong side of night.

I was on my knees, over him, shaking him, then throwing back my head, to keen a long Tsalagi scream never heard before in the thin English air.

Chapter 35

Grosvenor's Square, London, 1785

When Ostenaco landed in Portsmouth, the white sails billowing in the brilliant blue sky, he sang his war song cheerfully, the sacred formula to destroy life. Perhaps he was warning the English that he meant business, or perhaps my father was singing his prayer to Death itself. I knew the words. I had heard them sung by warriors filing out of the Council House with their shrieking cries, off to war against our enemies, be their skins red or white, but always their hearts black.

Listen, I have come to step over your soul. Your soul I have put at rest under the earth. I have come to cover you with the black rock. I have come to cover you with the black cloth. I have come to cover you with the black slabs, never to reappear. Toward the black coffin in the Darkening Land your paths shall stretch out. So shall it be for you. Now your soul has faded away. When darkness comes, your spirit shall grow less and dwindle away never to appear. Listen.

If he'd bothered to listen, Carrington might have heard my song. Or so I trembled at the thought. I was whispering the words to myself, worrying Cat Walker's stone knife in the palm of my hand. I walked on the cobblestones in the dawn, looking up at the darkened windows of Carrington's leased townhouse a stone's throw from Grosvenor's Square.

I wore the last red dress I had saved. I looked every bit the lady, Helena, and I had covered my redskin with the white of ceruse paint. In this morning's glass, I looked like a ghost of Mrs. Rolfe, but I could pass for English. More Timberlake than Ostenaco. Appearances deceive. Inside my muff of green parrot feathers on my wrist, I concealed my trusty knife.

Given my station as a successful woman in the import business, a widow of a war hero, a baptized Christian, the daughter of a chief of the Tsalagi Nation, I would have been in my rights to climb those white marbled stairs and raise the brass knocker at the door, to announce my visit.

I would perhaps have been ushered into another anteroom, perhaps seated at a meager fire on an uncomfortable chair to wait, admiring another rich man's collection of rusty armor suits, perhaps a bear shot in the Caucasus and stuffed in a grimacing pose. The clock on the mantel would tick away Greenwich mean time.

But I was a woman tired of waiting.

Instead, I walked past the house and ducked into the side alley, past a parade of working class, men delivering buckets of coal, scullery maids bringing in victuals for the day's cooking, to the back gate of the enclosed garden, left unlatched at this hour by the night soil men, who emptied the night's chamber pots and piss buckets for better sanitation to dispose of discretely.

I slipped into the back garden and found a seat on a stone bench by a fountain. A stone lion roared out a steady soothing stream of water plashing into the pool of floating lilies. I put my portmanteau on my lap and waited.

With me I carried Wolfe's long opus and the stray notes I had made of my own story, as well as my dog-eared copy of Henry's journal, recounting his adventures among my Tribe, and his downfall. Hopefully, these would be bait enough for an audience with my adversary.

Rumors of Carrington's large collection of Indian artifacts was whispered among the dealers and sharps of London's shops where all was for sale and could be dealt for at precious prices. I had frequented more than a few pawnshops and dealers of antiquities after what little Wolfe had left me in his reduced estate had been exhausted.

A butler passing by the long-glassed doors at the parlor spotted me in the garden and stopped. Through the very clean glass, I could see the staff conferring, the butler asking a footman in livery if he had admitted a visitor through the front door.

The footman came out and down the pea gravel path.

"Can I help you, madam?"

"Yes, would you please tell Col. Carrington that he shouldn't keep a lady waiting even in as pretty as garden as this?" I set my two hands back on the bench and kicked my french heel playfully over my crossed knee.

"Excuse me, madam. Exactly whom shall I say is waiting?"

"Mrs. Helena Ostenaco Timberlake. He may remember making my acquaint-ance some time ago. Tell him that I have some items that would be of interest to the Colonel's collection."

It was all quite the lie and very forward of me, but I knew Carrington would be intrigued.

I desired a face-to-face conversion with the man who Henry had disguised as Kaxoanthropis in his book. I wanted to know the nature of Carrington's quarrel with my late husband, as if knowing, I could put it all right.

A bird sang in the hawthorn. Clouds sailed across the blue sky. Bound by high brick walls that shut out the sounds of the suffering city beyond, I could have stayed there forever. I did not have the habit of carrying any time piece with me, so I knew not how much of the hour had passed.

At last, the footman returned. "Follow me. The Colonel is waiting."

We went into house, down a hall to the study where a man sat at his table in silk dressing gown, fine flowing paisley pajamas, and embroidered slippers with points upturned like a great Pasha. He thought it respectable to put on his wig to receive me. He wore a length of cheesecloth wrapped around his nose and mouth, as if to ward off plague like undertakers wrap over their faces when digging up the dead, or perhaps a highwayman hiding his features as he holds up a gentleman's couch at gunpoint.

"What a pleasant surprise. A nymph in my garden. What do I owe the pleasure of your company, madam?"

"Mrs. Ostenaco Timberlake, if you please."

"Do I know you?"

"You knew my husband. Lieut. Henry Timberlake."

His icy blue eyes glittered behind the mask. His hand was wrinkled and shook with a palsy. "Timberlake?"

"You remember my brave husband. He led an expedition to my town, then took my father and other headmen to London for an audience with the king. I returned with him two years later as his lawful wife, in yet another delegation to protect my people."

"This is all very fascinating, Mrs. Timberlake, but I'm not sure what this has to do with me at this late date."

"Mrs. Ostenaco Timberlake," I take trouble to correct him. "You may remember my father, Ostenaco."

"I was fighting in America at the time when Timberlake was escorting our enemies around town, but yes, I have seen the engravings of Reynolds portraits of the Chiefs. Oh, thank you, Noakes. That will be all."

The butler entered with a tray of tea things and a dish of scones and placed it on the side table. The butler whispered in his ear.

"Goddam no," Carrington erupted in a scream. "Begone with you."

The man had a temper beneath his makeshift veil. He closed his blue eyes, and I could see the cheesecloth billowing and collapsing over his hidden mouth as he breathed slowly to collect himself.

"Let me ask you a question," Carrington said quietly. "How do I really know you are who you claim to be? I see no papers or documentations that you are, as you say, the daughter of Ostenaco nor the widow of Timberlake."

"I am my father's daughter. I do not lie."

"Given the Chief's celebrated tour of our town back in '62, I would hazard a guess that he entertained more than a few willing women. I would wager that the parish records might have a whole list of babies and bastards who could claim the red bloodline, if not his swarthy looks."

He sought to fluster me. "I need no records to prove myself, only my word. I do have these books you may be interested in. The man at the Drury Lane pawnshop said you are quite the collector."

"Books," he said. "You think I read books?"

He opened the drawers of his desk and brought out small boxes and wooden compartmented trays, numbered and filled with what looked, at first, like rotten and dried fruits and tufts of fur and hair. Then I saw that the hair was rooted in patches of dried skin, torn from ancient heads. I touched the hair, the dried skin, rubbed those dead locks between my fingers.

"There are scalp dealers I've seen, bloody men, who could hold a fresh hide and take a good whiff and tell the tribe."

He lifted the lower veil of cheesecloth from his face and seemed to breathe in the scent. "Cherokee, perhaps, more likely Tuscarora or Creek, I've been told. Depends on the flavors of woodsmoke and animal grease. But then some men pretend they can smell subtle differences in the wine they drink."

He opened another box, and inside were what looked like dried fruits.

I looked closer and could see the whorls, the earrings hung on the lobes of human ears. His eyes glittered above his cheesecloth mask, watching my face, how I would react. He lifted the lid of one box, and within, I could see white pieces of finger bones and cracked knuckles. He had necklaces of human teeth, and these were not the milk teeth that fell from babes' mouths.

Some men collect butterflies and insects, others, the skeletons of small birds and rodents. Carrington was fascinated by bigger game, the most dangerous of animals.

Wolfe once told me the back rooms of the Royal Society hold dusty shelves of indigenous skulls, souvenirs to be measured by rulers and compass, as if men's minds and souls could be weighed or ruled or circumscribed. If the British beat the French to Heaven, some would want to shoot and stuff a cherub for the trophy room of their country house.

"I generally do not share these items with the weaker sex, but I know that the women of your race are not squeamish in that regard," Carrington cooed.

Next, a small velvet pouch. He tugged open the drawstrings, and out fell a dried thing, a former manhood, shriveled sacs with their firm rounded balls and a sad shriveled penis. "A rather fine specimen from an African eunuch. They are quite long when they are alive, I've been told," Carrington said with a grin.

Lastly, proud as a boy, from the bottom of a deep drawer, he produced his collection's prize treasure, an Old Testament Bible, of the King James version, bound with the softest, most supple and strange of covers.

"Go ahead, touch it, have you ever felt the like?"

"What animal's hide is this?" But I already knew, flinching at the terrible feel between my fingers.

"Such a book comes with a story." Carrington chuckled.

Carrington's supplier had said this volume was the handiwork of a missionary, a man of God, an evangelical who saw the need to spread the Gospel into the wilderness. Bad enough he believed such fancies, but he took his young wife and his babies into those dark woods, sprinkling holy water and wafers and good intentions along the way. He even went into the towns of the savages, chided them for worshipping fire and winds and demons in the wild, offered them enlightenment.

"Some men are such fools," Carrington said.

But while he was out making his missionary pleas, the Yemassee came for his family. He returned to find his new cabin on fire, his babies burning on the fence, and what remained of his wife in the pigsty, her beautiful hair taken from her, his youngest child floating in the cistern, poisoning the water. He became a man no longer of God, but of Yahweh. He put down his incense sprinklers and crozier and took up the sword. Vengeance belongs to God, but he aimed to be the Almighty's agent. He returned to the town, the capital where he had preached forgiveness and love, and brought war and pillage. They say he picked out the youngest child himself, plucked it from a screaming woman's arms.

He was a bookbinder by trade and knew his craft. He bound the Old Testament in a Redskin and prayed daily until he died that the Lord would judge the wicked. He returned to London with his book, and some say he gave up church all together, but stood on a crate in Hyde's Square, preaching the end, waving his last testament.

"Or so I was told." Carrington chuckled.

The color was that of dried blood and almost transparent skin. Who would have thought it would be so soft. Its only blemish an oily shadow across the spine where a man's fervid grip had discolored the supple hide.

"You don't look well." Carrington peered at me across the long desk, all the atrocities laid out, remnants of what were once breathing bodies, human flesh.

Inside my muff, without thinking, I had been trying Cat Walker's knife, worrying my thumb along the flaked edge and facets of the ancient flint. A sudden cut. I pulled my hand free, the red stream running through my palm and down my wrist.

"I was careless carving an apple for my breakfast this morning. You know how silly women can get when they start to think and do at the same time. It's nothing."

But it is something. I see the bloodlust in the old soldier's eye, the lust that comes over warriors when they see the red of life and death.

I licked the ball of my thumb, the heavy taste against my tongue. I had to speak or forever hold my peace.

"In his book, my late husband wrote of a Kaxoanthropos, who slandered his good name while taking money himself from my father's tour. You are Mr. Kaxoanthropos."

"Ah, Greek. You surprise me. You ask me, am I the Bad Man in your husband's narrative?" I could not see his smile beneath the cloth, only his glinting eyes.

"Sir, I must know the answer. Why did you hound my husband? He was serving as an envoy, an escort to ambassadors from my country at his own expense. Why would you stand in the way of any official compensation for his sacrifice?"

"Savages," Carrington said. "Howling wastes of wilderness. Demons, vermin. Let them be exterminated, as far as I'm concerned."

"But Henry was white like you."

"I'm sure he would have been a damned rebel if he'd lived longer." Carrington waved his palsied hand, then he shifted in his chair, which groaned under this weight.

"But you ask me am I a bad man. Are you a bad woman?" His cold, blue eyes looked hard over his bandaged face. "Look at what your kind-hearted sex did to poor Demore at Fort Loudon. He was my cousin, you know. We had played together as boys before we went to war. Our troops found him with grass stuffed in his mouth, his eyes bulging in a final fright.

"The grass was a message," I said.

I was there. I had been a young skinny girl, hungry and tired. All the women were tired. Here was the man who had turned away the starving town. "Let them eat grass," he had said.

I had stood by when the women fell upon Demere, Cat Walker first with her flaying blade. I had shut my eyes, but I could not stop my ears from his screams.

Carrington began to cough, a muffled sound behind his gauzed mouth, and I could see a black stain begin to seep through the cloth.

"I do not get much company these days. I'm positively hideous to look at for someone who is unused to my wounds."

"A war wound?" I ventured. "I have seen many. I am not squeamish."

He laughed. And he unwound the cloth that masked his face.

There was an open running sore where his nose had been, and his cheeks were terribly scared, a trickle of black saliva dripped from his mouth. Though from what I had seen and learned during my years in London, men were more disfigured by the symptoms of the French Pox, and from the mercury they were administered as a treatment, but more as a poison. A pity I had not been able to bring him sassafras as a salve for his disease.

"My face doesn't not frighten you, Mrs. Timberlake?"

"I have seen worse, sir." I stared at him and did not flinch. I could feel the gorge rising within me; I swallowed hard. I was only looking at a dead man.

"You are too kind, madam."

He wrapped the cheesecloth over his ruined features once more. He seemed in his right mind. Wolfe had once pitied such sufferers. Many of them would wind up in a madhouse as their reason disintegrated along with the soft flesh of their face, all for sleeping with the wrong woman.

"Should I be scared of you, madam, with your bloody hand?" he asked, as if he could read my red heart and knew why I had come.

The moment was at hand. Now I must choose my path.

"You don't care for books, but I may have something for your collection."

Slipping it from my feathered muff, I laid Cat Walker's stone knife upon the top of his mahogany desk.

"This is the blade my grandmother used upon your cousin," I said coolly, even as the blood was rising, burning in my face.

"Really?" His chair squeaked forward; his hand outstretched "May I?"

He drew it across the back of his hand gently. "Aho," he said. Then he raised his head, showing his long neck, and traced the blade across his windpipe just under the bob of his Adam's apple. "Quite a close shave," he japed.

He lay the knife carefully on the desk.

"What makes you think I would pay for such an item?"

"This only completes your collection, sir. Your cousin's blood was shed by this stone, wielded by my grandmother's hand."

His icy blue eyes widened. He touched the napped blade again with his fingertip and spun the balanced blade on his desk.

"And you are willing to sell?"

"Just as you are willing to purchase."

He laughed. "Oh, you are quite the trader, madam, I can see."

If I had leapt across the desk and slit his throat, how far could I have run? I would have to have kicked off those french heels and gone barefoot down the stairs, along the cobblestones, raising my skirts in two hands. They would have caught me, taken me to Newgate. I would be that woman, hung on the gallows, dangling with a knotted rope around my own neck, never to see the Overhills in this life again.

But then something flashing through the windows stopped me. Looking past my hated adversary, I swear the Uk'tena was slithering through the garden, stretching its bright scales. That crystal glaring between the horns on the great snake's head, blinding me.

"The knife is yours for the right price," I said.

In the crystal's light, I had a glimpse of Carrington's path. A sick old man living in the remorse, vengeful, full of bile and poison. Fascinated by blood. He was dying, I could tell by the strange wheeze of breath whistling in his nose, the shallow rise of his thin chest. Gray whiskers sprouted under his chin where his barber's razor had neglected to reach. And the smell of him, beneath the cologne, the stench of the breath between his yellowed teeth. He was an old man.

"For a moment, I thought you might cut my throat." He laughed a garbled sound behind his terrible veil. I couldn't see it, but I supposed he was smiling.

***

I walked out of Grosvenor Square, leaving my old enemy in his study with his Bible bound in human flesh and Cat Walker's knife. I was glad to be rid of that stone I had carried so long, the cuts on my thigh. His new plaything, let it kill him soon enough. I left with a purse of gold sovereigns he had slid across his desk at me.

Carrington had me confused with Cat Walker, a woman after his own bloody heart. But I could not bring myself to a man's blood, no matter how vile. Perhaps I am not as Tsalagi, true born of my people. After all, I had deserted my home and my son, and for what?

I couldn't hear Ostenaco's war song any longer, only Wolfe's words in my ear now. In the next breath, I found myself reciting a scripture that Wolfe had often read to me, the words that Christ himself had spoken to his apostles.

Judge not, and ye shall not be judged. Condemn not, and ye shall not be condemned. Forgive, and ye shall be forgiven.

Wherefore I say unto thee, her sins, which are many, are forgiven, for she loved much. But to whom little is forgiven, the same loveth little.

Richard, would you have thought less of your mother if she had returned to you with blood on her hands, a murderer? Or would you have wanted your father avenged, the man who caused his downfall and death losing his own life?

I am not a woman with blood on her hands.

It has been years since I have been Cat Walker's granddaughter, Skitty, who could skin a rabbit or pick corn from the field. For too long now, I have been Helena, bound in my corsets and by the Golden Rules that Wolfe kept preaching in my ear, perhaps only to keep me by his side for his own selfish reasons.

Cat Walker had predicted that I would meet seven men on my journey. What she didn't foresee is the strange woman I would meet on my path no one could have predicted, the woman who was my true self.

Chapter 36

London, 1786

I'd been shivering most of the morning by the paltry fire.

Prithee, I should ask Amherst, why must his antechamber in England be so cold as to pimple your flesh and chatter your teeth?

Prithee, such a fussy word I had learned from the meek Squire Wolfe. How I missed that gentleman.

Still, not a word that Cat Walker would have used. Ehlawe, my grandmother always said to hush my girlish chatter. Silence, listen is what she meant, neither prayer nor plea, but command.

I close my eyes and listen. I can still hear Tomotley, the old life. The river runs through the sycamores, flashes behind the mottled trunks. A flute trills, soft as birdsong, a young man tempting a maiden with its sweet sound. A baby cries. A new mother rubs beans on it, slips to make it happy and strong. The men stretch and talk softly. Children run across the plaza. The breeze ripples the sea of tassels in the corn like a mother's hand traveling across her child's sleeping brow. A hawk screes across the sky vault. The drums will beat tonight, and the fire will blaze higher. The women are already rubbing their buckskin boots, dreaming of men, fathers for their children. Listen.

Raindrops pattered on the glazed windows. Rain dripped down the flue, hissed against red embers of North Country coal hauled to Londontown. I never was warm in England, nor warmed to the English.

No wonder Lord Amherst declined to smile in his portrait hung above the blackened hearth.

It was the same painting we had sat beneath twenty years before, Henry and Chutatah and myself, waiting for our audience with this general, the Conqueror of Canada. No show of tooth, but a wistful twist of his thin lips, Lord Jeffery Amherst gazed into the distance beyond the gilt frame, through the window into the London rain. He was dressed in armor like a knight of old, thin shoulders bulked with hammered steel, greaves likely on his shins, his helmet a useful prop for his elbow and his hand to thoughtfully stroke his chin. Storm clouds gathered at his head. A map of Montreal curls from under the helmet, the city and territory he wrested from France's fist.

My father was bewitched by a similar portrait of the king, a slender man who bore the namesake of a saint who had slain a terrible dragon, an Uk'tena here in England.

I have seen the dragon for myself, though I would never slay it myself.

The English are good at portraying themselves as heroes. And we are driven by painted dreams.

***

"Yes, you." A steward poked his white-powdered periwig from behind the door. A practiced superior look, a majordomo who has mastered the social art of raising his several chins and squinting his eyes down an upturned nose. "Mrs. Timber-lake?"

"Mrs. Ostenaco Timberlake." I rose from my uncomfortable chair.

The steward grumbled, "As you wish."

He swung wide the door, not for any grand entrance on my part. I was expected to be awed by admission to the inner chamber, humbled by the grandeur of the man I came to meet, a peer of the realm, who had deigned to see the classless likes of me.

"Milord, Mrs. Ostenaco Timberlake is arrived."

My host, my would-be benefactor, rose from behind his desk, without armor or uniform, dressed in a drab jacket and brocade waistcoat. A ghost of his former self. More color in his painting than in his real face. His joints cracked as he tested his old soldier's balky knees.

"Lord Jeffrey." I performed my best curtsey, which Squire Wolfe taught me along with all the fine words and manners that the English use to wound their enemies in parlors and in treaties, so polite, how proper, yet poisonous.

"Sorry to keep putting you off." He waved me to another uncomfortable chair before his massive desk. "Your late husband was a brave man, I've been given to understand. Deepest of sympathies for his situation, for yours, but I must confess I haven't had much time to sort through your petition. Timberlake, Timberlake, where is that file?"

His desk was a bureaucrat's battlefield with regiments of parchment, plumed quills, penknives, letter openers, candles, wax, and seals. See the maker and breaker of lives and lands with a sign of his pen. Wax dripping like red blood to be stamped under his seal.

"Beg pardon, milord." The lackey harrumphed, clearing his froggy windpipe, like he had swallowed a fat fly. He transferred a sheaf of papers from the credenza to the desk.

Amherst read, furrowing his shiny forehead beneath the curls of his wig, his lips slowly moving. He nibbled his lower lip. He set the lifted page aside, wet his fingertip to snag the next from the sheaf, then the third. He struck the pose from his portrait in the anteroom, his hand supporting his small chin, the forefinger alongside his smirking mouth. His head on a pedestal of his own importance. With a sigh, he put aside the papers and looked finally at me.

"I recollect your father's trip. Made quite the splash that season in London, Cherokee chiefs entertaining the masses. A pickpocket in the Vauxhall crowd took my best watch without my notice."

"My husband lost more than a timepiece. Timberlake risked his life to visit my people after the war. He risked his reputation in England to wage peace. He lost his life in a debtor's prison after serving his king and country and helping my People at his own expense. He wrote it all down."

I pushed Henry's book across the polished desk, but Amherst declined to handle it.

"Ah. I have far too much to read these days. Mr. Gibbons has yet another fat volume about the fall of the Roman Empire. Depressing theme, if you ask me, but apropos. We have seen our own Empire set back, with these treacherous colonists."

"They slaughtered my people, the king's own faithful friends after my father, Ostenaco, swore that no Cherokee would kill an Englishmen."

"Yes, pity that." He hesitated, then plunged ahead. "But still I wonder. Why did you linger in our land after your husband's death? Illegally, if I'm not mistaken."

Why so long? Amherst had all the questions that I had asked myself for ages. Why England? Did you not miss your home, your people, let alone the flesh and blood of your own firstborn child, the son of the man you loved and followed to a distant land?

Anyone would want to know that part of the story, but sometimes stories don't make sense, or come with reasons or excuses.

Sometimes the girl goes into the woods or picks up the snake or disobeys the gods. Oft times she falls in love with the wrong boy. Perhaps, she drinks the poison meant for her foe. She falls into a slumber, only to awaken in a different land, lost. But those are stories we tell children. It is rarer to tell oneself the truth.

"I fell in love," I told Amherst the truth.

"Aho, is that so?"

A Tsalagi maiden is raised to always to deflect her eyes, speak softly to elders and the powerful. And from what I've seen of English ladies, they are no more listened to by Englishmen. But I put on the mask that I have learned to show any yoneg. I looked my interlocker in the eye, and I smiled into his white face.

"I fell in love with England, with this city. I have made my life here. Learned so much. But it is time now. The world is changing."

"Well said, madam."

Oh, bless Wolfe. He had taught me the right words.

He checked the pocket watch from his vest. Was my audience at an end?

"I'm taking too much of your lordship's precious time."

"Nonsense, my good lady. I haven't heard such a tale in such a long time. Your husband was quite the hero in any estimation," Lord Jeffrey allowed in his patrician drawl. "He fought bravely against the king's foes, but unfortunately, he made some enemies. Col. Carrington was adamant against any recompense for your husband."

"I recently paid the colonel a visit. We made our peace."

"Pity, I heard the man slit his own wrists just the other week. God rest his soul. He was eaten up with pox and old hatreds."

"His war is over, milord, as far as I'm concerned, and so is mine."

"I've heard enough, then," said Amherst.

He unfolded his white hands, long and soft-looking, a man who has never farmed or sailed or dealt with dirty business. He took the quilled pen and dipped the proper ink and, with a flourish, scratched the nib against the paper drinking the oak gall stain. He signed his name, and then he poured the wax against the candle and poured the red dripping, like blood responsibility, what was owed Henry was owed me. The blood red wax hardened into a blot, and he pressed his signet seal with the face of his ring.

I fished into my pocket of my gown and found not the sharp edge of the bloody knife, but a pair of dusty glasses. I put them on my nose, hooked the wires tight behind my ears, Wolfe's old spectacles. The words swam up to me like fish from beneath the currents of the Tanasse.

"Your papers for due passage, Mrs. Ostenaco Timberlake. I know not why you would want to return to that wretched country. The Americans are worse savages than your own race."

"I can't help it, milord. It is still my home."

"As you wish. The British Crown and His Royal Majesty's government give their blessing."

***

Blood cries to blood and never ends. I can see that now. Names change with your deeds over the years. I once was the Mankiller's Daughter, once the wife to the intrepid Timberlake.

For too long, I had been Helena. I had forgotten my name from my homeland. Skitty was a different time, a different person. I was but a girl then, lovelorn and unlucky, not knowing much of how deceptive men could be, too trusting.

What I truly feared: I kept asking you, Richard, to listen to my tale. But I'm afraid of listening to what you may one day ask of me. Why I waited so long to make my return to my rightful place, to even request permission for voyage. A fair enough question that's haunted me by the fires of many a night, a widow tending her small hearth.

The first ten years in England, I was young and foolish, learning new ways, a new tongue. Where my father had once traded deerskins in Charleston, I made my fortune exporting white clay and sassafras dug from the rich earth of our Cherokee mountains and shipped to London. I banked the profits, hoping to share it with my people, saving for a proper passage, fit for a Chief's daughter, but then an ocean away the colonists revolted against their rightful rulers, and their backwoods armies began to swarm our mountains.

The next ten years, as I waited word amid reports of war and battles and carnage from across the ocean, cut off from all correspondence. I had heard of the destruction, the towns razed again in our homeland. I did not know if you were alive or dead. But I never forgot you.

Cat Walker was right in her prophecy of the Seven Strangers I would meet on my long arduous journey. Wolfe who saved me, and Frank who I saved before I lost him. Boswell, who I loved but lost. Griffin, the one who made me rich, but the trade was lost. Amherst, who stood in my way, and Carrington, whose life I spared, trusting him to slash his own wrists in the end.

At Gravesend, I boarded a fast frigate headed for Nova Scotia and beyond, Amherst's conquered domains. I stood at the bow of the ship, the papers of Lord Amherst signed inside my cloak, the spray of the sea obscuring the western horizon, but now I chose finally the One Stranger who I thought I had lost from the start.

My only memories of you, Richard, are as a baby. I want to meet the man I don't know, the man you've grown into in my absence.

Listen, I am the spider making her way back. The fire I carry is small and warm and doesn't not scare me or burn me. I glow inside.

Diguenvsvi gegv.

I am going home.

Chapter 37

New Tomotley, Overhills
1790

The Indians expressed the highest gratitude and grief for my misfortunes. All the recompense they could offer was an asylum in their country, which I declined, since their murmurs and some unguarded expressions convinced me they would not fail at their return to spirit up their countrymen, to vindicate their right by force of arms, which infallibly again have been laid to my charge, and I perhaps be reputed a traitor to my country. My circumstances, however, are not so much in the decline, that when I satisfy my creditors, I must retire to the Cherokee, or some hospitable country, where unobserved I and my wife may breathe upon the little that yet remains."

The Memoirs of Lieut. Henry Timberlake

Ah, Henry, my husband, your tale came too quickly to a close. Coughing even then over the final page, your spittle mixed with the ink of your final breaths. You were no traitor, but faithful to your oath as an officer, true to your king and true to both your wives, even Eleanor, and always to me to the end.

Books can burn, pages can crumble with heat, green mold can eat away at the deckle cut edges, spines broken, threads come undone with time. Words scratched in oak gall will run with water as Henry discovered to his chagrin when his canoe capsized in the frigid rapids of the Tanasse on his journey toward our town.

Stories survive only as long as there is breath to tell them and ears to hear them. Fleshy appendages sliced off and kept in Amherst's curio cabinet, souvenirs of Empire and savages brought to heel. Their stories dried up and died with their tribe.

Villages laid waste with pestilence, bodies stacked in the doorways, the corn-stalks withered and brown, the sacred fire snuffed out in the mound, weeds cover-ing the waste. Whole towns that disappeared as the few survivors faded away into the woods, the hills, never to look back home.

Mark, Helena, your own journey.

You are no more Skitty, the brown girl who went to water in Tomotley a fort-night of summers past. The girl who forgot her mother's tongue and all the sacred formulas Cat Walker made her recite.

Dear Henry, I have continued the book you started, my hand not as fine as yours. The quill and the oak gall I have fashioned for myself.

Listen, Richard, my tale is done.

***

"Granny, are you finished yet?"

"Hush, girl." I pretend to scowl at her, but she is not fooled. She knows what writing is, how important. But she stands at the side of my desk, nibbling at her knuckle bone with her milk teeth, lost in a still green world, and the river chatter-ing across the rocks.

I pull Wolfe's wire-spectacles from my face. I can see what his eyes saw in Eng-land, I can see what old Cat Walker saw deep into the future. But the present is here with me, young Cat Walker, Richard's daughter, is pulling at my sleeve of my paisley blouse.

My knees creak when I rise from my writing desk, scattered with the papers.

My son sits on the porch, the sleeves of his white broadcloth shirt rolled up his strong brown arms. He is going over his own books and accounts, a trader after his mother. Utwena'i is the image of his father, older now than Henry ever lived to be, with the furrowed brow and the proud nose of his grandfather. Beyond are the fields that he farms beside the river. Here he has built the homestead of felled timbers. Here he is making a new Tomotley. Home is never given, but always won. Home for now.

"I'm taking your daughter for a walk in the woods," I say as the girl tugs at my sleeve. "It's about time she learned how to tell feverfew from skullcap and where to find the best Kan'sta'tsi."

Richard looks up and laughs. "Who's leading who, agitsihi?"

***

Into the woods, I show her the manroot of ginseng, pick some horsebalm and fern. We have root and leaves for her persistent cough, to make her blood strong, her teeth sharp. Sassafras to sweeten her, and ginger to settle her tummy when she eats too fast. We give thanks for the bounty, the plants that offer themselves to us, the balance of the world.

She skips ahead, stops, and freezes on the trail at the sight of the racer slithering underfoot.

Galegi, the blacksnake who turned to the color of ash, trying to bring back the fire. One is climbing continuously. "She won't hurt you, girl. We have no feud with the Uk'tena's clan today." We watch the mother snake slide off into the leaves.

Coming down the hillside where I so often gathered herbs, roots, the berries from the thickets on top, down through the trees toward the river, stopping to dig for fragrant sassafras root, balancing a basketful on my head. The path falls into a clearing amid the trees. The morning sun slants through the leaves. The fog on the mountain drifts by, clean and white, not like the fouled spirits in the air I left behind in Londontown.

I halt the girl in her loud tracks with my upraised hand.

"What is it, Grandmother?" she whispers too loudly for the hushed woods.

"Listen, child. Heya."

I point and watch the little girl's eyes widen with wonder.

The sun catches the gleam in the tree branches overhead, the light of this world caught in a shimmering web. The patient spider makes her rounds, steadily round and round as if circling an invisible fire. She is offering her hand to mine in the friendship dance. She sings out in silken threads. She has snared the fire of the sun on her back. See my sister weaving my name in the morning sun.

Acknowledgements

Nov els are never the product of a single imagination, but have roots in reality, in other books and in other readers especially as a story grows on the page and into a book.

I was intrigued by a footnote in the exhibit "Emissaries of Peace" curated by the Museum of the Cherokee and based on the Memoirs of Lt. Henry Timberlake. A young Virginian soldier, Timberlake led a remarkable life, visiting the Cherokee people in 1762 and escorting the tribe's chiefs on two voyages to the court of King George III. In 1786, years after Timberlake's death in debtor's prison, a woman who called herself Helena Ostenaco Timberlake came forward, claiming both the names of the white soldier and the Cherokee chief. Who was this mystery woman? I had to write a novel to imagine her life in the cracks of history.

My friend and mentor Kevin McIlvoy wrote "The writer who 'trespasses' into cultures, historical moments, settings, etc. that he has not directly experienced should, by my reckoning, write not with the intent to speak for these cultures, historical moments, settings, etc., about human certainties but speak through them about human uncertainties."

I claim no certainties nor secrets of the tribe, and I have no native American ancestry, only a lifelong appreciation for the rich culture of our continent's original people. As a writer, I do not presume or pretend to speak for anyone other than myself.

I am grateful for suggestions and encouragement from Barbara Duncan of the Cherokee museum and Eastern Band of Cherokee members Gilliam Jackson and John "Bullet" Standing Deer, who taught me elementary lessons in speaking Cherokee. Sgi.

I drew heavily from the original text of "The Memoirs of Lt. Henry Timberlake," as edited by Duane H. King (2007), as well as James Mooney's seminal History, Myths and Sacred Formulas of the Cherokees dating to 1891 and 1900, and The Travels of William Bartram.

I also relied on these valuable texts:

Dr. Johnson's London by Liza Picard, St. Martin's Press, 2000.

Samuel Johnson, A Biography by W. Jackson Bate, Harcourt Brace Jovanovitch, 1975

The Cherokee People by Thomas Mails, Marlowe & Co., 1996

Living Stories of the Cherokee, edited by Barbara R. Duncan, UNC Press, 1998

Cherokee Heritage Trails Guidebook, Barbara R. Duncan and Brett H. Riggs, UNC Press, 2003

Cherokee Dance and Drama, Frank G. Speck and Leonard Bloom, University of Oklahoma Press, 1983.

Other readers offering valuable insights and encouragement are Nan Cuba, Marjorie Hudson, and "Mc" McIlvoy. I would also like to thank my friends among the alumni of the Warren Wilson College MFA Program for Writers. And a shout-out to my crack publicist Lauren Harr at Gold Leaf Literary. I am appreciative for fellowships at Hambidge Center in Rabun Gap, Ga., and Weymouth House in Southern Pines, NC.

And as always, special thanks to my wife, Cynthia, who has been the reader of my heart over all these years.